*F*FERAL *ascination*

T.J. MICHAELS   LAUREN DANE
RAVYN WILDE   TIELLE ST. CLARE
MICHELE BARDSLEY

ELLORA'S CAVE
ROMANTICA PUBLISHING

$\mathcal{W}$*hat the critics are saying...*

&

"WIZARD'S MOON is a beautiful romantic fantasy, a charming adult fairy tale complete with a handsome hero, a fair damsel and an evil magician. The world of Avalon contains fire breathing dragons and tiny fairies that seem so real readers will call travel agents to book passage to the island." ~ *ParaNormal Romance Reviews*

5 kisses "RELUCTANT is hot and intense. Sid and Layla are meant for each other and Sid does an amazing job of showing her how a modern alpha male werewolf can keep his "alphaness" while allowing her to be the strong alpha woman she is. Keep a watch out for more Cascadia Wolves, I am!"

~ *Two Lips Reviews*

"**TJ Michaels'** *Spirit of the Pryde* is a perfect mix of mystery and hot, steamy sex. Neesia and Jason have something between them that will not be denied. The two are intensely attracted to one another and unable to deny the temptation but are also able to connect on an emotional level. **Ms. Michaels** has created wonderful characters that will charm the reader." ~ *Fallen Angels Reviews*

"*First Moon Rise* is an extremely quick paced truly erotic short story that literally is sex in a small package. Any paranormal romance lover that appreciates an Alpha will not be able to help falling in love, or rather lust, with Fallon. Tate makes for a one strong and gutsy heroine, perfect for Fallon. […] If you like slow and tender, *First Moon Rise* is not the story for you. [...] If you like hard and fast, then by all means, grab this quickie [...] I am certain you'll devour it in one sitting."

~ *Just Erotic Romances*

"*Uncontrolled Magic* is the sequel to *Undying Magic* though it easily stands alone. Ms. Wilde provides a sexy, witty, paranormal romp with a bit of a twist." ~ *Just Erotic Romances*

An Ellora's Cave Romantica Publication

www.ellorascave.com

Feral Fascination

ISBN 9781419957130
ALL RIGHTS RESERVED.
Wizard's Moon Copyright © 2006 Michele Bardsley
Reluctant Copyright © 2006 Lauren Dane
Spirit of the Pryde Copyright © 2006 TJ Michaels
First Moon Rise Copyright © 2006 Tielle St. Clare
Uncontrolled Magic Copyright © 2006 Ravyn Wilde
Cover art by Syneca.

This book printed in the U.S.A. by Jasmine-Jade Enterprises, LLC.

Trade paperback Publication September 2007

FERAL FASCINATION

໊

WIZARD'S MOON
Michele Bardsley

RELUCTANT
Lauren Dane

SPIRIT OF THE PRYDE
TJ Michaels

FIRST MOON RISE
Tielle St. Clare

UNCONTROLLED MAGIC
Ravyn Wilde

WIZARD'S MOON
Michele Bardsley

&

Chapter One

ಐ

"You can't go out at night, Alissa. It's the first night of the wizard's moon."

Alissa Rogers put on her cloak and pulled up the hood. "The wizards only hunt pretty girls."

"You are pretty."

"No, I have a good personality." She smiled. "Besides, hardly any wizards bother with Mreben. Our town isn't worth their notice."

Alissa looked around her sister's tiny, cramped house. Janele collected everything—books, paintings, shiny objects, and ex-boyfriends. Two were living with her at the moment, both down on their luck, one a musician and the other a painter. Neither of them was good at their chosen crafts, but they were sincere and soulful—and cute.

"Lady Felicity told me that Wizard True Karn was spotted flying above the town. He's on the prowl for a new bed slave." Janele's eyes widened. "They say that when he's finished with his lovers, he eats their hearts."

"Tears of the Goddess!" Alissa laughed. "What nonsense."

"Hmph. Nonsense is you working at the Purple Palace," said Janele, grimacing. "I can give you some money. I have lots now."

"It's *your* rightful inheritance." Alissa picked her way through stacks of towering magazines and boxes filled with heaven-knew-what. "I don't mind working for a living."

Janele followed her to the door. "I can pay your tuition at the Academy of Healing Arts. You're very good with poultices and teas."

"I'm very good at counting other people's money." She turned and kissed her sister's cheek. In Janele's sapphire-blue eyes, the eyes of their mother, Alissa saw genuine concern. "I'm content. I have no complaints."

"You shouldn't settle for such a mundane life." Janele grabbed her hand and clung to it. "I know we didn't have the same father—and I'm sorry mine left me rich and yours left you nothing. I love you. I don't wish you to suffer."

"I know." Alissa gently pulled away from her younger sister. "Please don't worry. I'll visit you next week. Good Moon."

Janele sighed. "Good Moon."

Alissa slipped out the door and shut it behind her. She hurried down the steps and down the sidewalk. The wind whipped against her and she shivered. Wrapping her cape closer, she quickened her pace. If she could find a taxi, she would gladly spend her meager funds for its safety and warmth. But since only the bravest souls ventured out during the wizard's moon, she had little hope of finding transportation. She had to trudge all the way to the Purple Palace. The high-class brothel that catered to so-called gentlemen was a long walk from Janele's house.

Alissa didn't have the exotic looks required to work as a prostitute for Madame V, but she had the mind to keep track of the incoming and outgoing funds. Since the Palace opened its door in the evenings, she kept a prostitute's schedule—sleep during the day, work all night. Only her job was a lot less exciting and involved no pleasure.

She glanced up at the moon, which glittered like a colored jewel in black tapestry. During the final two days of its last lunar phase, it turned a brilliant teal—and wizards supposedly swooped into towns and procured slaves and lovers for their castles in the Barrens.

I don't have anything to fear. Wizards only like the pretty ones. Her mother, a strikingly beautiful woman, had called Alissa "sturdy" and "solid". It wasn't that Mom meant to insult her. No, she hadn't been capable of real malice. Yet she managed to raise her eldest daughter to feel like a rhinestone among diamonds. Sturdy. Solid. Plain. Alissa spent her life becoming those adjectives.

Alissa had two decent features — clear, pale skin and brown, almond-shaped eyes. But her cheeks were too round, her chin too small, her lips too full. Oh, she knew her flaws very well. Short and thin, cursed with small breasts and bony hips. Her mud-colored hair swung down her back in a long braid. Her simple gray dress went all the way to her ankles, touching her sensible black ankle boots. Her mother always said that to be pretty was a burden, not a boon. *Oh, what I wouldn't give to have that burden, if only for one night.*

"Well, well, well… What do we have here?"

Alissa nearly stumbled into the broad chest of a man blocking the sidewalk. She looked up — and up — into the unkind face of a guardsman. She gasped and stepped back. "E-Excuse me, sir."

"Rek, look what I found."

Another guardsman — just as tall and imposing — appeared next to his friend. He fingered the handle of the sword hanging off his hip. Both men wore the guardsman uniform — black pants and shirts embroidered with red, capes and hats solid red — Mreben's colors.

Alissa's heart nearly pounded right out of her chest. She might not have anything to fear from a wizard, but human males didn't need beauty to satisfy their baser lusts. Unease skittered up her spine. Still, she managed to square her shoulders. She nodded toward the gap between the two men. "I will be late for work. Please let me pass."

Rek chuckled. "Adorable, isn't she?"

Her mouth gaped. Was he kidding? She peered at them. They had been imbibing, obviously. How else to explain their interest in her? Her throat knotted as she clutched the edges of her cape.

"Sard, since you found her, you get first dibs." Rek's eager smile wasn't reassuring. He licked his lips. "Just you wait, sweet one. We'll show you a good time."

Sard grabbed her arm. Lust glittered in his black eyes. She'd seen that look in the gazes of men who frequented the Purple Palace. Fear chilled her in a way the blowing wind never could. Goddess above! They were going to hurt her. "No, please...*don't*!"

"There you are, darling." A big, male hand settled on her shoulder. She looked up and almost swallowed her tongue. The man wore black too—from his shoes all the way to his shirt. Only his cape held color.

It was as teal as his eyes.

Her heart skipped a beat. His long hair was blond, cut in jagged lengths that framed his handsome face. Each of his earlobes held three gold hoops, and his eyes—yes, they were *teal*. That color belonged to the sea, to precious jewels...and to wizards. She stared at him, wide-eyed. Oh no. Surely this man with his muscled arm around her shoulders wasn't True Karn.

"Move along," said Sard in a firm voice, though Alissa noted with some satisfaction that he let go of her and stepped back. "We're escorting this woman to her job."

"Yeah," said Rek. "It's not safe around here."

"You're so admirable," said her rescuer in a voice that suggested the guardsmen had been acting the very opposite. "Since I am here, there is no need for you to take the lovely lady anywhere. Leave us."

He flicked a finger at them. To Alissa's amused surprise, they yanked up straight, arms and legs smacking together. Then, kicking high, they turned around and marched away like puppets jerked along by their strings. The wizard looked at her, obviously pleased by his magical dispatch of the guardsman. "Impressed?"

"Would you like me to be?" she asked.

"Of course." His full lips hinted at a smile. "Where to?"

For a moment, she considered lying. She didn't think it wise to admit that she worked at a brothel. Damneth. Had she traded one bad situation for another far worse?

"Worry not, m'lady," he said in a deep voice edged with an accent she couldn't place. "I wish only to deliver you safely to your destination."

"How can I trust the promise of a wizard?" Alissa blurted, shifting out of his embrace. She immediately wished she could call back the words. What was wrong with her? Challenging a wizard like she had the right! With a single spell, he could bind her to his service. "I-I'm sorry."

"For speaking the truth?" The half-smile bloomed fully and her heart trilled. Wizard or not, he was the most gorgeous man she'd ever seen. He bowed from the waist. "I am Wizard True Karn."

Oh. My. Goddess. Swallowing the knot lodged in her throat, Alissa managed a curtsey. She whispered, "My name is Alissa Rogers."

"Alissa. A beautiful name for a beautiful woman."

Silky promise edged his words. Her stomach clenched. She pressed a palm against it, trying to still the vicious fluttering. "You need not flatter me. I'm already in your debt."

"Hmmm." His eyes gleamed in the colored moonlight. "How do you propose to repay your...*debt*?"

Slack-jawed, Alissa stared at the wizard. Having already insulted him once, she dared not offer another cheeky comment.

He met her gaze, eyes twinkling, and laughed. "Despite rumors to the contrary, I will not take what isn't offered." His blond brows rose as if to say, *Are you offering*?

How she wished she could be bold, impetuous. *I'll give myself to you*, she would say with a saucy tilt of her head, *if you think you can handle me*. She blushed furiously and dropped her gaze. What was wrong with her? Even if she had the looks and the willingness to take a man to her bed, she still wouldn't be brave enough to seduce a wizard.

"I work at the Purple Palace," she said, staring at his shiny black boots. Embarrassment burned through her. She didn't know what would be worse—True Karn believing she worked there as a prostitute...or believing she didn't. "I would be honored if you would escort me."

"The honor is mine, m'lady." He held out his arm and she placed her hand in the crook of his elbow. The streets were empty, silent. Only their shoes clicking on the sidewalk interrupted the unbearable quiet.

"Do you like working at the Purple Palace?" he asked.

"Not particularly."

"Then why do you?"

"Men own most of the town's businesses and none would leave their finances to the mind of a woman."

"You handle Madame V's money?"

"Don't sound so astonished." She bit her lip. She couldn't stop bristling around this man and he'd done nothing but help her. Why couldn't she hold her tongue? Goddess knew she'd had enough practice keeping her mouth shut during Madame V's rants.

"I'm not astonished that you handle financial matters, m'lady. What surprises me is that Madame V allows anyone at all near her books."

"Yes, she can be...prickly."

True laughed. "Prickly. That's a tame word to describe Vivian."

"You know her?"

He stopped and clasped her hand resting on his arm. "Should I lie to you, Alissa? Should I tell you that I have only heard of Madame V? Or should I tell you that once, long ago, I knew her very well?"

Lie to me. I don't want to know if you've bedded that cold-hearted woman. The unusual color of his eyes enraptured her. She stepped closer. "Is your first name only a word?" she asked. "Or does it have meaning for you?"

"All words have meaning for me," he said softly. "That's why Vivian is part of my past and not my future. She and I had different definitions of loyal."

"What was your definition?"

"Loyal means you are faithful to a person."

Alissa nodded. "She wasn't faithful?"

"Ah. Well, Vivian is faithful—to herself. She has always remained true to her own nature."

"Avarice?" asked Alissa boldly. "Nothing seduces Madame V more than money. It is her favorite lover."

"Such disrespect, *anonvie*." He laughed conspiratorially. "You know your employer well. Tell me, Alissa—if you could find a different job, would you take it?"

Alissa shrugged, unable to answer such an impractical question. She glanced down the street. A few blocks away, the lights of the Purple Palace flashed, beckoning well-heeled gentlemen for a night of gaming, drinking and sex. For a moment, Alissa wished she could live on Janele's generosity. How lovely it would be to pursue a career in the healing arts. No more all-nighters. No more juggling numbers. No more Purple Palace.

"Such longing," whispered True. "What are you thinking?"

17

Honestly, why was he bothering so much with her? She was plain girl from a small town—surely not worth his notice. She couldn't fathom why he wanted to know her thoughts. Instead of burdening this stranger with her silly musings, she said, "Just wondering what an *anonvie* is."

"It's very old Haldanian."

"Old Haldanian?" Humans had stopped using the old dialects hundreds of years ago. She wondered if wizards still taught their children the ancient languages. More likely, True was just a learned man. "When I was little, my grandfather told me that all words in Old Haldanian had two meanings. The pronunciation determined which meaning the speaker gave the word."

"That's true. When I use it with you, it means 'precious one'."

Why would he offer her such a tender endearment? *Either he is nice or he pities me.* Oh, posh! She didn't need a wizard's benevolence. "And the second meaning?"

"Perhaps I'll tell you another time."

Another time! Did he think he would see her again? Damneth. She had grown too comfortable in his presence. Flirting had never been her strength. She was too prone to speak her mind and well, she thought it silly to bat eyelashes and giggle like a twit. Hmph. The few chaperoned outings she had with potential suitors made her feel awkward and lacking. Yet, here she was walking and chatting with a wizard as if she did it every day. Had he somehow used magic on her? The very idea frightened her out of her wits.

"Thank you for escorting me, Wizard Karn. I'll be okay from here."

"What kind of rescuer would I be if I didn't deliver you as promised? No, m'lady. I will drop you off at the door." True started walking and since he had her hand trapped within his, she could do nothing else but hurry along too.

The closer they got to the Palace, the harder Alissa's heart thudded. What if someone saw her with the wizard? Her safety was of no concern—not even the scullery maids would believe such an imposing, attractive man would claim someone like Alissa. No, her fear was for True.

"Please," she said, yanking on his arm and bracing her boots on the cracked concrete. "You must be careful!"

Halting, he looked down at her and frowned. "Why?"

"Madame V pretends to cater to the well-heeled, but some of her customers would trade their children for a chance at a wizard's blood." She gulped. "Or a wizard's heart."

"Oh, that." He rolled his eyes. "Despite what some idiots believe, my internal organs don't hold the key to immortality."

"It doesn't matter what people believe," said Alissa. "It matters how they act."

"Such wise words." He studied her, his eyes blazing with an emotion Alissa dared not name. "You are a fascinating woman."

"Oh yes," she said drolly. "I'm so fascinating and so beautiful I turn away wizards and their charming lies day and night."

"I do not lie, Alissa." True lifted a finger to her face. "I am glad you have not turned me away." She gasped as fear and longing jumbled together in the pit of her stomach. He traced her mouth, allowing his finger to rest in the middle of her lower lip. "I am in no danger, m'lady. You, however..." He slipped his finger between her lips and of its own accord, her tongue flicked against the tip. His eyes went dark, he inhaled sharply.

Yanking away his hand, he stepped back. "Perhaps...yes, I'll wait here until you get inside the Palace."

"I didn't mean—" She covered her mouth. Oh, heavens! Her whole body trembled. Sensation skittered, and heat rushed to her core. She realized then that she wanted True.

"Hey, wizard!"

Alissa and True turned. Sard and Rek hurried toward them, followed by several other guardsmen.

"Bet you can't fight all of us," yelled Rek.

True looked at Alissa, his eyes glittering like polished gems. While fear scraped up her spine, he winked conspiratorially at her. He wasn't afraid of the guardsmen. He was amused by their actions. What would it be like to not fear? To laugh at those who threatened with fists and with words? Oh, to know that kind of bravery!

"Shall we go?" asked True. To Alissa's thrilled shock, he scooped her into his arms and took a running jump. They lifted high into the air.

She threw her arms around his neck and held on for dear life. He chuckled, his warm breath skittered across her throat. "True!"

"Ssshhh. You are safe." He nuzzled her cheek, his lips warm against her skin. She shivered as heat undulated from breasts to pelvis. Such a strange reaction—was it magic? Or desire? She had never felt this way with anyone. Hah. Not that she had many opportunities to experience the throes of passion.

"I'll circle around. Then I'll drop you at the Purple Place."

"*Drop* me?"

"A figure of speech," he said, lifting his head and grinning at her. "I like holding you. Perhaps I'll spirit you away to my castle in the Barrens."

"Would you?"

"Is that a question or a request?"

A request. Spirit me away, please. Her cheeks heated with humiliation and she dropped her gaze. "Why would you want me?"

"Why wouldn't I?"

She couldn't answer. No, she wouldn't answer. If he was ignoring her lack of beauty, for what reasons she did not know, then she gladly accepted his compliments.

"The guardsmen have dispersed," said True. "Don't you want to look down?"

Her heart jolted to her throat and lodged there. She buried her face into his shoulder and tightened her grip. The wind whirled around them and brought with it the scent of wood-smoke. Alissa felt a slight jerk and heard the scrape of shoes against concrete. The breeze dissipated and the autumn scents faded into the too sweet smell of roses.

She ventured a peek. True had landed on the roof of the Purple Place. More precisely, he had landed in the middle of Madame V's rooftop garden where she only grew fragrant red roses. Any bloom daring to grow malformed or in another color was ruthlessly cut and destroyed.

"Do you want me to let you go?" asked True. Sensual innuendo seemed to cling to his otherwise tame words.

"I feel as though you're asking me something else." Her whole body tensed as excitement and apprehension wound through her. She looked into his eyes. "Are you?"

"Yes." True put her down. Then he removed the ring from his left hand. "If you wish to see me again, wear this. I cannot visit you during the day, and after the wizard's moon passes, I cannot return to Mreben until the next one. But I can always share your dreams." His palm ghosted under her chin, his long fingers trailing over her jaw. "Dream with me. I'll give you great pleasure."

"Pleasure? That's what you offer?" she whispered.

"I'm sorry, *anonvie*. It is all I can promise you."

Though his words cut through her like jagged blades, Alissa took the ring and examined it. Thanks to her mother's keen eye, honed by judging the worth of suitor gifts, Alissa had learned the value of jewelry. This ring was obviously an antique—a valuable one. The band was silver, about a half-inch wide. In the center rested a round stone—teal, the color of True's eyes. Only wizards could make such jewels. They were highly prized, not even wealthy humans could afford such gems.

"It's beautiful. But it's...too much."

"You refuse a wizard's gift?"

"I refuse a kind man's gesture."

"You give me too much credit." His fingers drifted over the lace collar of her dress. "I want you."

"You want to—" She sucked in a nervous breath. "Is this the way—"

"Wizards claim those they want?" His lips tilted, but pain shadowed his expression. Once again, she found herself snared by his eyes. He had such a strange, mesmerizing gaze.

"Despite what you believe, Alissa, wizards rarely mark humans. We already have servants—people who are *paid* to care for us and do not fear us. And we don't have to compel women into our beds."

"Hmph. I'm quite sure they leap in of their own accord."

"Ah, but not all of them. You, for example, are doing the exact opposite of leaping into my bed." Chuckling, he took her hand and bent low over it. He brushed his mouth across her knuckles, his gaze lifting to meet hers. In that moment, she saw his regret, his pride, and his...desire? Need seared her. What kind of fool was she to resist such a man?

"A wizard's mark changes you. Wizards will know you are bound to me and humans will avoid you, but not really know why. You will never be able to look at—or serve—another man. You will never have another lover." The low throb of his voice made those odd sensations wiggle through her again. Heat jolted her pussy and she let out a startled breath. Lust flared in his eyes and she realized he was aware of how she reacted to his words, to his voice. "You tempt me, *anonvie*. But if I marked you, you would be mine forever. I would never take away your choice."

So, he wanted her, but he would not burden her with such a terrible fate. Truthfully, she couldn't find much wrong with belonging to True Karn forever. He was the first, and could well be the last, man to ever want her. He looked at her as though she were a worthy woman—worthy of his time, of his attention.

The ring bit into her palm. What did it mean that she refused his gift with words, but had not returned it to him? *It means you want him. So take him.* "I invite you to share my dreams."

"Thank you, Alissa." He took the silver band from her and placed it on the first finger of her right hand. Then he pulled her close, his hands enfolding hers. "The ring is charmed. No one will be able to take it from you. If you should ever need me, kiss the stone."

She nodded.

"That's my girl." He brushed his lips across her knuckles then stepped back, his cape fluttering. "Good Moon, Alissa."

"Good Moon, True."

He executed a bow and then he rose into the air. Higher and higher he flew until he disappeared completely into the night sky. For a long moment, she stared at the teal moon and wondered if True Karn had been a delusion.

* * * * *

"You're late."

Alissa jumped, startled by the ominous tone of Madame V's voice. She attempted a smile. "Some guardsmen stopped me. I b-barely escaped."

"Oh, you poor darling." The words dripped sarcasm. Madame V was tall, redheaded and voluptuous. She paid for the best spells to keep herself young and beautiful. As she unfolded herself from the chaise, she made sure her thin robe opened so that Alissa got a good view of her big breasts and shaved pussy. Embarrassed, Alissa looked away.

As usual, a glass of champagne graced one hand. In the other, Madame V clutched a mint cigarette. "You work in a whorehouse. You've seen more naked women in your two years as my accountant than most men see in their lifetimes."

Madame V sauntered across the lavishly decorated room. Everything was red and gold—from the wallpaper and furnishings to the statues and trinkets glittering on the shelves. The woman had a fondness for brash colors—herself among her favorite *objets d'art*. Unfortunately, she harbored the illusion that her taste in jewelry, furniture and men was bold and elegant.

"Just say the word, Alissa dear, and you can be relieved of your virginity." Madame V's wide green eyes assessed her. "If you got some good sex, you might be a tad less boring. Goddess knows you're as interesting as dirt."

Alissa kept her gaze on the floor, but she gritted her teeth. Her employer was in a particularly vicious mood tonight. "I will keep my virginity."

"A shame. We could make a bundle. I'd split half the profits with you."

"No, thank you."

"Prude." Madame V stopped less than a foot away from her. "What are you waiting for, you silly girl? Get to work! I'm expecting customers any moment and if they see your face, they'll wonder about the quality of my prostitutes."

Alissa swallowed the stinging retort that hovered on her lips. How she wished she could slap the gloating expression off her employer's lovely face.

Madame V waved her champagne glass toward the small office Alissa used to do her work. "Go on! You might count the money, dearest. But I'm the one who earns it."

Curtseying, Alissa hurried to the office and shut the door behind her. She tucked her hand into her dress pocket and touched True's ring. She hadn't dared to wear it front of

Madame V. Somehow, having that small piece of jewelry reassured her more than kind words or thoughtful deeds.

"Go to Hades, Madame V," she muttered darkly. "I hope one day your beauty no longer hides your poisonous nature."

Chapter Two

ଚ୍ଚ

The sounds of lovemaking filtered into Alissa's office. Even as her face heated with mortification, peculiar tension wound through her, tightening as Madame V and her two male lovers grew more boisterous.

Soon, her curiosity outweighed her discomfiture. Her pussy was so wet and swollen from hearing the lovers interact she simply had to see what they were doing. She crept to the door, cracked it open, and peered into the sitting room.

An older man—naked, his skin glistening with sweat—sat on the oversized red couch. Madame V climbed on top of him, her moans deep and purring as she took his cock into her pussy inch by inch.

Behind her, another man, this one youthful and muscled, kneeled on two stacked pillows. He grabbed Madame V by her long red hair and swatted her ass.

Alissa's pussy reacted to that slap. He gave Madame V a hard spanking while she fucked the other man. With each smack, the woman's buttocks reddened, which excited the younger male. Her own ass tingled as if she was the one to receive the blows.

Breathless, her body trembling, Alissa watched him lube his cock. He parted Madame's V sore, pink buttocks and inserted a finger into her anus.

The daring act caused a hot thrust to her pussy. Heat crackled from her core to her tight nipples and she pressed her palm against her sex, daring to add pressure to her sensitive clitoris.

The young man worked his cock into Madame V's primed ass and groaned. After a few experimental plunges, he found a rhythm that forced Madame V to quicken her own pace.

They fucked each other, sweating, panting, moaning, until one after another they came, their harsh cries intermingling. As they collapsed against each other, Alissa quietly closed the door and returned to the boring columns of numbers. But her body felt scorched. Her mind whirled with images of True and how he planned to pleasure her.

Unable to bear the sweet tension between her legs, she reached under her dress and peeled her underwear down just enough to reach the slick folds of her cunt. She rubbed hard and fast, thinking about True...of his mouth suckling her nipples...of his cock penetrating her...of him fucking her wildly until she—

"Oh!" The orgasm exploded, leaving her breathless and shamed. She pressed trembling fingers against her swollen sex, her hand drenched with come.

She ached for a real lover. She ached...for True.

* * * * *

The hour before dawn, customers ordered their last drinks and made their last wagers. The prostitutes retired for a day's worth of sleep. And Alissa hurried out the Palace's front doors, stopping at the sidewalk's edge to hail a taxi. She didn't care that it would cost almost all her pocket money. She wanted to escape the Purple Palace and Madame V's barbed tongue. Her employer's unsettling scrutiny plagued Alissa the rest of the night. *Something's different about you, darling. Hmmm. I can't quite put my finger on it...*

A carriage stopped, the driver opening the door from his seat atop the small vehicle. He tipped his hat, smiling affably. Alissa gave him the address of her flat and climbed inside, grateful for the plush seats and quick pace of the horses.

If Madame V ever found out Alissa had met True Karn— she batted away the concern. Her boss would scarcely bother with a woman she felt beneath her notice. Though Alissa knew the ins and outs of the Purple Palace's business transactions, including the "other" books that Madame V kept herself, she was still considered the equivalent of a troll's leftovers.

Alissa mentally shrugged off her worries. She felt exhausted, but also strangely restless. *I need a good meal and decent rest, that's all.* She closed her eyes and leaned against the pillowed headrest. If she had the prospect of another job, she would quit working for Madame V. Her other option was to live on her sister's charity, a thought that appalled her. Janele was kind-hearted, though sometimes petulant and shallow. All the same, she would never begrudge Alissa the money. *Perhaps I am spineless, but at least I have a scrap of pride left.* No, she wouldn't take a penny of her sister's inheritance.

"We're here, miss."

Alissa jerked out of her reverie. She stepped out of the taxi and handed the driver his fare and a generous tip. He nodded to her and then he snapped the whip at the two sturdy horses.

As the equines clopped down the street at a sedate pace, she hurried into her flat. The minute the door was closed and locked, Alissa removed the ring from the pocket of her dress and placed it on her finger. Relief washed through her. For some reason, wearing True's ring made her feel both peaceful and anticipatory.

After a sandwich and glass of wine, she took a quick bath and climbed under the cotton covers of her twin bed. Her naked skin rubbed sensuously against the clean, worn sheets. She had not put on a nightgown. No, she hoped that True would keep his promise and visit her dreams. She wanted to be prepared if...well, she wasn't quite sure what to expect.

Though she worked in a whorehouse and understood the nature and substance of sexual acts, she had rarely indulged in the idea that she might become someone's lover. Vaguely, she thought she might one day marry and have children. Such contemplations were sketchy—as if she were unable to fully picture her future.

"True," she whispered into the darkness. Her tiny bedroom had no windows, which made it much easier to sleep during the day. Unfortunately, she could still hear neighbors moving about and the muffled noises from street vendors and conveyances.

Alissa punched her pillow, settled onto her side, and within moments, fell asleep.

* * * * *

Alissa blinked awake. Was it already time to prepare for work? Yawning, she sat up and stretched her arms. Hmmm. The apartment had cooled considerably. Her nipples tightened as the sheets fell to her waist, exposing her skin to the chilled air.

Wait a minute. She glanced around, nerves jumping. She occupied a huge, black wrought iron, four-poster bed. A fat, white candle sat on a nearby table, but its tiny flame did little to combat the shadows. Startled by a soft noise, her gaze flew to the dark figure that appeared at the foot of the bed. Her throat knotted. "True?"

He stepped into the flickering yellow light. His broad, muscled chest was tanned and hairless. He wore tight, black breeches and black leather riding boots. His blond hair had been tied back, allowing her a mouthwatering view of his visage. She had thought him handsome, but...oh, Goddess. Her heart tripled its beat. Ardor needled her skin, crinkled her nipples, and swelled her pussy with heat and moisture.

"This is a dream?" she asked.

He nodded. His hungry gaze danced along her nude body. He looked as if he wanted to feast on her and couldn't quite decide where to begin nibbling. She responded to that intensity, yearning for his touch, for his words.

"You are so lovely, Alissa."

"So are you." She blushed. "I mean...you're handsome."

He grinned as he sat at the end of the bed. "Are you sure this is what you want, *anonvie*?"

"Do you ask because you doubt my choice? Or because you regret the invitation?"

"I ask because I want you desperately," he said. "I want to kiss you. Over and over again. You have such a delectable mouth. I want to conquer it. I want those juicy lips swollen and wet. And I want to suck on those beautiful nipples." His gaze dipped to her chest. The buds puckered under his lustful inspection. "I want to stroke every inch of your flesh until you're on fire for me. I want to taste your sweet cunt and lick you to orgasm and then...and *then* I want to fuck you." His eyes burned with passion. "I want your lips on my cock. I want you to suck me until I fill your mouth with my come. And when we are sweaty and tired and well-pleasured...I want to do it all over again."

Alissa stared at him. His words stroked her just as well as his fingers, his tongue. She nearly lost her breath and her heart...oh, her heart tried to beat right out of her chest.

"So, I give you one last chance to change your mind," said True softly. "Because if you say yes, Alissa, you are mine."

"And if I don't?"

"You will wake up immediately...and you will never see me again."

True watched the lovely Alissa impassively, though tension held him hostage. *What if she doesn't want me?* If she knew the truth about him, she wouldn't wear his ring or share her dreams with him.

In time, he *would* tell her...and she would choose. Yes, she would choose as all the others had before her. When she did, he would once again be alone. *That's the real pain of my curse...*

"Yes, True." She nodded as if her words weren't enough affirmation. "I want you."

"Thank the Goddess." He crooked at finger at her. "C'mere."

Immediately, she scooted across the bed until her knees were inches away from his thighs. Damneth, she was sweet. And she was strong. He was well aware that Alissa did not know her own beauty, but he was sure that she knew her own strength.

"You've never had a lover?"

"No." She blushed and glanced up at him through her long, dark lashes. "If we...*when* we make love, does that mean I'm no longer a virgin?"

"Only in your mind. We are in a dream world with our dream selves. Your actual body will remain pure, *anonvie*." He trailed one finger over her naked shoulder. She felt like silk. "And there will be no pain."

"That's good."

He captured her wrist and brought her fingers to his lips. He kissed each knuckle, enjoying her little sighs of pleasure. "You are so lovely. Do you believe me?"

"I believe in truth. I'm not unpleasant to look at," she said in a practical way that made his heart ache. "But I will never be the type of woman who entertains a roomful of eager suitors."

"Less men for me to kill," he said.

"You are too kind."

If she only knew that he even now he could not tolerate the thought of another man looking at her, much less touching her. What villainous creature convinced Alissa she was merely plain? He knew Madame V had likely seen what Alissa hid with simple hairstyles and unflattering clothes. No doubt his former lover hoped that her accountant might one day fetch a good price with customers.

She watched him, her eager gaze on his chest. He knew that she wanted to touch him, but was too shy. His hand

31

snaked around her waist and drew her into his embrace. She slid onto his lap, naked and soft and pliant.

He plucked a curl from her shoulder and used it to trace her collarbone. He saw her slight shudder and the unwittingly sexy way she wet her lips. Her lush mouth begged for a kiss, and though she probably didn't know it, her eyes telegraphed potent desire. His cock hardened as he imagined that little pink tongue flicking across his skin.

True played with the silky tendril of hair, wrapping it around his finger and tugging on it. He dropped the strand in favor of caressing her neck...until he reached the fluttering pulse at the base of her throat. Her breath hitched, her lips parted, and no longer able to resist, he leaned close.

"*Anonvie.*" He cupped the back of her neck and gave her a fraction of a second to prepare before ensnaring her lips. He traced the tender seam with his tongue, and like a blooming flower, she opened under his onslaught.

True drank her sweetness, tasting the corners, nibbling her lower lip. He swallowed her moan, and then slid his tongue inside, drawing her into an intimate dance as he deepened his possession of her mouth. Fire raced through his veins as she responded, uncertain but ardent, tentatively mating her mouth to his.

"Touch me," True murmured.

Alissa pulled away, her gaze swirling with desire. "Where?"

"Wherever you want."

Doubt seeped into her gaze, and he wanted to wipe that look from her eyes. He lowered his head and took Alissa's mouth again. He plundered her velvety lips until she melted against him, panting and squirming.

"Touch me," he said again.

Her soft, small hands coasting over his chest—fiery need erupted everywhere she caressed him. He pulled away, just a little, and captured her gaze. Goddess, she was beautiful, right down to her soul, which shone like imprisoned sunlight in her eyes. He grasped one of her wandering hands and placed it on his cock, which stretched against the black breeches with painful urgency. Gaze wide and disconcerted, Alissa's quivering fingers traced his erection.

True groaned as heat speared him. His balls clenched and his cock pulsed. "Alissa," he said in a strained voice. "That feels very, very good."

He saw her delighted expression. Ah. She had realized her own feminine power — and it was both boon and bane. Now, she would persecute him. And he welcomed her every torment.

"Would it feel better," she asked in a silken voice, "if clothing didn't inhibit my touch?"

"Oh, yes."

He lifted her off his lap and onto the bed. Then he stood and shucked off his boots, socks and breeches. For a long moment, he allowed her to look at him. Slowly, she reached out and stroked his cock. Then she boldly gripped him, her other hand cupping his balls. True sucked in an unsteady breath.

"It won't fit," she said. "It's huge."

Laughing, he gently pushed away her hands and kneeled at the edge of the bed. "It will fit, *anonvie*. And you will like it, I promise. But first…scoot closer."

She immediately complied. He watched passion flare in her eyes, and his heart skipped a beat.

"Do you trust me, Alissa?"

"Yes."

He pushed his palms flat, murmured a spell, and opened his hands. He presented Alissa with the silver chain. She took it from him, peering at the two silver cuffs. Then she picked up the small silver ball. "I've seen these before — at the Purple Palace. Some of the girls wear them."

"Nipple cuffs," he confirmed. "They will increase sensation and this—" he pointed to the silver orb, "is placed in the middle. It will create even more pleasure. May I put them on?"

She nodded.

True put the chain on the bed. "Let me prepare you. Bring those gorgeous breasts to me."

She leaned forward. Eagerly, he peppered kisses on the tops and sides of her breasts. His actions were tame. At least until his mouth trapped one nipple. He alternately flicked and sucked on the distended bud.

"Oh!" Alissa arched, her hands fisted in the covers. He switched his attention to the other taut peak. She moaned deeply.

After her nipples were hard and glistening from his wet mouth, he carefully cuffed each one. "How does it feel?"

"I-I don't know. Tight. Sorta painful."

He picked up the middle part of the chain, hooked the ball to it, and then let go.

"Oh! It hurts." She sucked in a steadying breath, her eyes glazing. "It feels good too. How is that possible?"

"Why don't you ponder that while I do this?" He grabbed her thighs, looping her legs over his shoulders. Before she could protest, he pressed his mouth against her mound. She writhed and panted, her fingers digging through his hair and clutching his skull, as he slowly licked the outer labia, down one side, up the other—doing it twice more to extend the exquisite torture.

"True...oh, True!"

Her breathy sighs and warbling entreaties embedded lust deep into his balls. He didn't think it possible, but his cock hardened even more, its thick length swollen with the need to feel Alissa's pussy clenching around it. He could hardly wait to plunge into her tender cunt, and bring them both mind-blowing orgasms.

But first…

True moved to the inner folds, nibbling gently, swiping his tongue around her tight opening, dipping inside for a taste before kissing his way to her clitoris. He flicked the hard nub, and was rewarded by her sharp intake of breath. She tasted like rare fruit, juicy and sweet. Everything about Alissa turned him on. He wanted her forever. To do this forever…

He licked her, plunging his tongue into her pussy. She yelped, but pressed closer, widening her legs just enough to give him better access. He trailed his fingers over her labia then drove two fingers into her soaked pussy.

He pumped his fingers inside her, and then pushed up, searching for the bundle of sensitive flesh. Ah, *there*. "Pull the chain," he begged. "Please, Alissa."

She grabbed the silver ball and yanked. He rubbed the knot of flesh at the same time he leaned down and nipped her clit.

Alissa screamed.

She pushed her pussy into his face as she came. True felt the quaking bliss as the orgasm overwhelmed her. He soothed her clit with his tongue, drinking her juices, and finally, when she released his hair and let her legs collapse, he looked up at her. "Are you ready for my cock, m'lady?"

"Yes," Alissa murmured. "Please, True."

She watched as the gorgeous wizard rose to his full height and grasped his big cock. She felt so wonderful, so pleasured and so needy. For him. She looked at his impressive erection. Though True seemed sure he would fit inside her, she wondered if he was being too optimistic. All the same, she wanted to feel her lover's cock slipping inside her, filling her, stretching her…

He stepped forward, obviously intending to lie with her on the bed. "Alissa —"

Thud. Thud. Thud. True paused, frowning as he looked over his shoulder. Alissa's gaze followed his, but she couldn't see into the darkness. *Thud. Thud.* BAM!

"Damneth. Not now!" He grimaced. "I'm sorry, *anonvie.* You must go."

"What's wrong?"

"Nothing. It's the fickle nature of my ... er, house."

Her brows rose in surprise. His house caused those noises? Or was he trying to protect her from something else? "Can I help?" she asked, though she had no idea what she could possibly do to help a powerful wizard.

"What I need, you cannot give me. No one can."

"You don't have to be alone anymore. You cannot offer me love, but I can—"

"No! Go, Alissa. We will dream again another night."

Within a single beat of her heart, True disappeared. Then Alissa opened her eyes and found herself in her own bedroom.

Damneth!

Stubborn men! Silly wizards!

She flung off the covers, allowing the cool air to soothe both her body and her temper. She could help True. She knew that whatever his troubles, she *could* help him. If only he would let her. Glancing at her clock, she saw that she had several hours left before she had to ready herself for work. She needed the sleep, but she felt too restless to lie down and close her eyes. All she would do was think about True...and about what had caused him such concern.

Oh, to Hades with sleep. For once, she wanted to enjoy the day. Rarely did she wake early enough to enjoy the sunlight. Her one day off a week was spent doing errands and housework.

She took a quick shower and wrapped herself in a thick, soft robe. She searched her closet for a suitable dress and found herself dissatisfied with the grays, browns and blues that inhabited her small wardrobe. For the first time since she was a little girl, she longed for a gown that was pink or violet or sage.

She chose a blue dress and spread it out on the bed. Maybe she could update its style, take up the length, get rid of the atrocious lace on the high-neck collar... Alissa frowned, considering the garment.

Knock. Knock. Knock. Who in the world? Alissa had no friends and Janele rarely visited. Trepidation crept through her as she approached the door. After checking the peephole, she opened the door to a red-haired boy, about ten years old, dressed in a yellow shirt, green overalls, and brown boots. He held a large box.

"Hello, mistress," he said. "This here's for you. It's from Master True."

"True?" She accepted the box. "Is he okay? Where is he?"

"I can't be tellin' you where my master lives," said the boy.

"Everyone knows wizards live in the Barrens."

"But no one knows exactly where now, do they?" The boy grinned proudly. "'Cept for me. And I ain't tellin'."

"What's your name?" asked Alissa, charmed by his ruffian manner.

"Marlik."

"I'm Alissa."

"I knows who you is. Master True likes you." He executed a perfect bow and turned to go.

"Wait, Marlik. Is True okay?"

Marlik considered her. His brown eyes measured her worth then he nodded, as if he felt she merited his confidence. "Master True be cursed. All wizards be cursed. I can't be tellin' the reason, o'course. But I tell you this, mistress—you be the first who gives him hope."

"I knew he was in trouble," she said softly. "How can I help him?"

"You take his mark, that's what. But no woman's brave enough for that." He tilted his head as he looked her over again. "Not even you."

Before she could dispute his words, he nodded goodbye, and took off. She watched him dodge people and carts, and soon, he had disappeared. Her gaze went to the east. All she could see was the buildings that lined the cobblestone street. But a few miles past Mreben was the road no one ever took. It led to the forbidding mountains and dark lands of the Barrens.

There, True was alone in his misery.

Alissa shut and locked the door. Then she took the package to her bedroom. She opened it eagerly. She hadn't gotten a present in a very long time. She saw a long, thin box and underneath it, a sheet of folded paper. Layers of pink paper covered the other contents. She opened the box and plucked out the finest silver chain she'd ever seen. Then she picked up the note and read it.

Dearest Alissa,

The chain is for your ring, so that you can wear it at the Purple Palace. I know you are wise enough to protect it from Madame V, but this way, my charm will be close to your heart.

The other gift is a selfish creation — I only hope that one day I may see you in it…and of course, remove it from your luscious body. You are beautiful, anonvie. *I cannot wait to dream with you again.*

Your one and only,

True

Alissa dug into the box and pulled out a simple gown made from the finest pink silk. Ankle-length, three-quarter sleeves, and V-necked, it was the most beautiful dress she'd ever owned. It was perfect. She hugged the frock and danced around. "Thank you, True!"

* * * * *

"My, my, my. Where in the world did you get that lovely dress?" asked Madame V as Alissa hurried into the brash room. She had hoped to get to her office before her boss could see her. Damneth.

"It was a gift."

"Hmmm. Some gift. That's Drellian silk. Very expensive." Dressed in a sheer red robe, Madame V sauntered across the room until she stood in front of Alissa. She blew minty smoke into Alissa's face. "And what's this?"

"Just a necklace."

"Another gift." Madame V looped one finger under the chain and tugged it. Alissa's heart leapt as the ring popped out from her dress and slid along the silver links. She looked up and saw Madame V's greedy gaze assessing the worth of the bauble.

"If there's nothing else, I should go," said Alissa. "I have several accounts to get up to date."

"Oh, pish-tosh. I want to hear all about your new acquisitions. Gifts, you say? From whom?"

Alissa said nothing. She had no intention of telling Madame V the truth. Though had she the nerve, she might've cattily replied, *Your ex-lover bestowed this ring upon me.* Then again, Madame V was no fool.

The woman's eyebrows winged upward. Her smile widened. "Do you have a suitor, Alissa? Am I going to lose you to some charming, wealthy gentleman?"

"No. These were just...um, from a friend."

"A friend." Madame V laughed gaily. Then she gestured toward the big, red couch on the opposite side of the room. "I want every juicy detail. Sit down, darling. We'll chat."

As Madame V sashayed to the couch, obviously expecting her to follow without protest, Alissa unclasped the necklace and put on the ring. The chain she slipped into her dress pocket. True had told her no one could take the ring from her while she wore it. No way in Hades would she allow Madame V to have it.

After one practically forced glass of champagne and two chocolate truffles, Alissa refused any more offerings from the suddenly generous Madame V. Her stomach cramped and her sight blurred. "I don't feel well."

"It's your palate, dear. You're not used to good bubbly and gourmet treats." Madame V leaned forward. "You don't really like that ring, do you?"

"Yes, I do."

Madame V's cherry lips brushed Alissa's cheek. For some reason, she couldn't move away from the unwanted contact. She felt the woman's teeth tug her earlobe. "Give me the ring, darling."

Unwillingly, Alissa complied. She raised her hand and offered it to Madame V, who grabbed the ring and tried to pull it off.

"Damneth!" she cried, jerking away. Smoke rose from her singed flesh. "It is charmed." She sucked on her burned fingers. "Who gave you the ring?"

Vaguely, Alissa realized the clever Madame V had put something in the drink or the chocolates. *Bespelled.* Fear beat a faint tempo in her head. She was helpless. Her employer would force the truth from her, no matter how much she wished to conceal it.

"Goddess above! I had no idea you could be this stubborn!" Madame V grabbed Alissa's chin, red nails digging in her face. "No one in Haldania has a teal stone ring. True Karn doesn't make gems anymore. So, you must've gotten it from a rotten thief or your stupid sister. Tell me, Alissa. Tell me now!"

"True Karn."

"Yes, idiot. True Karn makes the—" She hissed. Jerking Alissa's head to one side, she peered at her neck. "You are not marked."

"True Karn."

"He gave you the ring?"

Alissa looked at Madame V. She smiled beatifically. "Yes." She ripped her hand from Madame V's grasp and kissed the stone.

The woman's scream of outrage caused Alissa to giggle. Oh, she was upset, wasn't she? Goodie. Goodie. *Goodie.* She watched as Madame V's hand swung down. The blow snapped her head back, but she barely felt the throbbing pain. She was falling...falling...into the deep, soft darkness.

Chapter Three

80

Alissa blinked awake, feeling groggy and a little nauseous. Beside her, a naked Madame V sat primly, smiling. Her lips were so red. Like blood.

"What's going on?" Alissa tried to move, but found her wrists and ankles had been chained. She lay in a huge, luxurious bed. Looking down, she gasped.

"I should explain a few things. I'll start with what you're wearing. On your legs, are the finest silk stockings. These?" She snapped the white ribbons. "Garters attached to the cupless cami. The panties are called thongs. Men like to see a woman's ass and yours is cute. In fact, you have a nice little body. Not much for tits, but still not too bad. You'll notice that you're in all white—because you're a virgin. The men bidding on you right now want the whole fantasy."

"Bidding on me? No!"

"Sssshhh." Madame V tapped Alissa's lips. "You don't want to mess up your makeup. I had to use some of my best spells, which cost a pretty penny, to fix up that face of yours. Your hair isn't that bad, though."

Horror clawed through Alissa. No. No! This wasn't happening. Madame V had bespelled her, imprisoned her, and was *selling* her. She fought through the murkiness of her memories. She had kissed the ring. She remembered that much. Where was True? Her wizard hadn't come. Panic wormed through her. She fought against the chains, but it was useless. Hopeless.

"Please, Madame V. *Vivian.* Don't do this."

"Bad news, sweets, True probably wants your virginity. He uses virgin blood for his black magic." Madame V shook her head and tsked. "You may have the ring, but I have you. I'm helping you, Alissa. Once you're bedded, the wizard will have no use for you. You'll be safe."

Hah. As if Madame V cared for anyone else's safety and comfort. Alissa trusted nothing the woman said, but couldn't allay the doubts creeping into her mind. If True wanted her virginity, that would it explain his unusual interest in her.

Madame V rang a gold bell. Somewhere, a door opened and closed. Heavy footsteps treaded the red-marble floor. "I'm giving you a gift, Alissa. I'm going to show you what to expect. Mekal?"

The tall, dark-skinned man dropped the red towel draping his hips. The muscles in Alissa's stomach quivered. She wanted to shut her eyes, but she seemed oddly compelled to look at Mekal's genitals. His balls looked like oversized chocolate truffles and his thick cock hardened into a frightening length.

Then Madame V stepped in front him, rubbing her breasts on his chest. She took his mouth in a deep, hungry kiss. When she pulled away, Mekal cupped his mistress's big breasts, pinching the nipples. Madame V moaned. She cupped his ass and ground against his cock.

Alissa gasped when Mekal lifted Madame V. The woman wrapped her legs around his waist and pushed down, taking his cock in one harsh move.

"Yes, darling!" she yelled. "Fuck me!"

With a growl-groan, Mekal slammed her against the wall and plunged inside her, his buttocks clenching with every stroke. Madame V scratched her nails down his back, drawing blood. She clawed at him, demanding him to fuck her harder, faster.

Wetness pooled between Alissa's thighs. She was ashamed that Madame V's uncouth act made her ache, made her want. Tears filled her eyes and she shut them tightly. She might block the image, but she couldn't block the sounds of their pleasure.

No escape. Her only hope was that the man who bought her virginity treated her gently.

After her body was defiled, no one would want her.

Especially not True Karn.

She closed her eyes, tears falling. She tried to ignore Madame V and her lover's harsh coupling. Thankfully, they both climaxed and the awful noises stopped.

"You've ruined your makeup."

Alissa kept her eyes closed while Madame V's hand flitted around her face. She flinched when the awful woman placed a hand against Alissa's sex. "Ooooh. You liked what Mekal did to me. If you're a good enough fuck, I might give you a new job."

"Leave me alone."

"Hmph. You're so ungrateful, Alissa."

Her eyes popped open. "You're cruel and greedy. I owe you nothing! All you deserve is my pity."

"You little bitch!" Madame V grabbed Alissa's hair and pulled it hard. She yelped as pain shot down her scalp. "I don't need your pity, but I swear to the Goddess after your virginity is taken, you'll beg for mine."

She stomped out, dragging Mekal out with her.

An eternity seemed to pass as Alissa waited. Everything in the windowless room was white. A curtain hung to her left, hiding the hallway and the door, which was the only way to enter and to leave the room. A white dresser sat next to the bed, its lone lamp giving out a soft glow.

Straining against her bonds, she prayed for a way out of this horrible situation. If only True had answered her call for help. He'd given her the ring and his promise of protection—and she had believed him. *Trusting the word of a wizard. You are naïve.*

"Hello?"

Alissa jolted, her heart hammering against her chest. She looked toward the white curtain as footsteps approached. Oh, Goddess! She swallowed the scream vibrating in her throat.

The curtain parted. For the briefest of moments, she believed True would walk into the room and rescue her.

Instead, a man she didn't recognize entered. He was nondescript. Not too tall, not too short. Short brown hair, brown eyes, and a friendly, if not handsome face—he seemed the sort anyone would forget almost immediately. Dressed in a simple white jumpsuit, only the gold rings on his fingers gave away his status as a wealthy man.

"You're the virgin?"

"Please, sir. I am being held against my will. Would you take the virginity of an unwilling woman?"

He grinned, shaking his head. "You sure get into it. Madame V said you're a fine actress." He squinted at her. "But you're a virgin, right? I paid a lot of credits so I could be your first man."

Alissa closed her eyes. Damneth. "This isn't what I want."

"Oh, I know," he said confidently. "But we got all night, sweetling. We'll try what you want later on."

Alissa's eyes flew open. "All night?"

"Yep." He walked to the bed and looked down at her. "Is there someone else you'd want to...er, pluck your flower?"

Why should she tell this man anything? He had paid to take something from her that she wanted to give willingly to True. Given the choice, she wanted True Karn as her first—and only—lover. Oh, what did it matter now? She looked at the man, tears in her eyes. "No offense, kind sir. But there is someone else I would choose."

He nodded. "Guess you needed the money or something, right? Does your man not take care of you?"

"Yes," she whispered. "He takes very good care of me. I love him."

For a brief moment, the man looked flummoxed. Then his expression cleared and he shrugged. "Guess he doesn't love you. Because if you were mine, I sure wouldn't let you sell your virginity to the highest bidder."

"He believes in choice," she said. "He would never take away someone's choice. And that is what you're doing. I do not choose this. I will find a way to repay you, if you will let me go."

"Sorry, sweetling. I paid for you." He sat on the bed and trailed his fingers along her thigh. "And I'm going to have you."

Forgive me, True. Alissa looked at the man. He would not let her go, so she would have to endure his touches, his kisses...and his penetration. A sob caught in her throat. True would not want her, but she knew she would always want him. After she was free, she would leave Mreben. No one would ever take away her choices again.

"I hope...is it too much to ask for..." She couldn't get out the words.

The man lay on the bed next to her. She stiffened, biting on her lower lip. *You'll get through this. At least he seems nice.* His lips grazed her earlobe and she tried not to flinch.

"You were saying something?" he asked.

She shook her head. His tongue traced the shell of her ear. Then he whispered, "You would ask for gentleness, *anonvie*?"

Her eyes widened and she turned to stare at him. He put a finger to her opened mouth. "Ssshhh. Madame V has eyes and ears in this room."

Tears of the Goddess! True had come to her rescue. Joy rushed through her. He had disguised himself and spent a fortune to save her. Plain, sturdy, solid Alissa—a damsel rescued by a wizard.

The tears unleashed.

He wiped away each drop until no more fell. He nuzzled her temple. "The chains are bespelled, Alissa. I'm sorry, but I can't undo the magic. The only way to break the spell is to take your virginity."

Oh, no. Her breath shallowed. Yes, she was scared and nervous. But pleasure awaited her too. There were worse fates than giving her virginity to True.

"Okay." Alissa turned her face to his. In the depths of his brown eyes, she saw a glimmer of teal. "Will you mark me?" she uttered very, very softly.

"No."

"Why not?"

His eyes widened. "You offer yourself to me, *anonvie*?"

"I wish that I might have you as you really are," she murmured. "And that you did not have to take me as I look now—as a whore. I am not pretty, but—"

"You will not disparage yourself again—not in word, not in thought. Do you understand me?" The rough edge of his voice startled her. "You are beautiful."

"When you look at me," she admitted, "I feel beautiful."

"Good." He pressed his lips to her cheek. "As soon as the chains release, I will take you out of here—and you will never have to step foot in the Purple Palace again."

She nodded.

"You sure smell good," he said loudly as he sat up. He stood and unzipped his jumpsuit. "Okay, sweetling. Let's get started."

As he peeled the outfit from his shoulders, he winked at her. A luminous teal fog filled the room. Before she could take her next breath, the magical mist disappeared. When she looked at the wizard, he was in his true form—and still half-clothed. Anticipation plucked at her, warring with nerves.

"W-What happened?" she asked.

"Magic spell," he said. "I can't break the chains, *anonvie*, but I can bespell those bastards. I will not allow Madame V and her cronies to watch *us* make love."

"What will they see?"

"Anyone watching or listening will hear and see whatever they think is supposed to unfold. By the time the spell breaks, we will be long gone." He finished undressing and lay next to her. "I'm sorry it must be this way. This is not how I envisioned our first real time together."

"As long as I am with you, I don't care where we are." She looked at him. "Marlik said that you're cursed. Does it have to do with the wizard's moon?"

"Marlik has a big mouth." He sighed. "Yes, I'm cursed. I'm only allowed to take human form during the wizard's moon."

"What do you look like when you're not human?"

"I cannot tell you anything else, *anonvie*. I do not want to rush, but time is short. I must free you before dawn."

"Can I save *you*?"

"No." He kissed her, to distract her no doubt. Alissa decided to concentrate on freeing herself from Madame V and her house of ill repute. Then she would figure out how to save True from his curse.

Her wizard rolled on top of her, fitting his half-hard cock against her sex. One finger traced her cheekbone. He said nothing, but a smile curved his sensual lips.

She felt the steel warmth of his body as he pressed against her, his penis rubbing between her slick folds. He continued the light movements as he feathered kisses on her neck. True's hands drifted down to her thighs, trailing up her ribs oh-so slowly until his big hands cupped her tits. A moan escaped as he kneaded the firm flesh. Her breasts felt heavy, her nipples taut and deliciously achy.

Her pussy throbbed, swollen and needy. True's fingers drifted down her leg, stroking her thigh, before wriggling between them. He inserted a finger then two…then three into her pussy, pumping slowly, stretching it. One hand cupped her breast, tugging on the puckered nipple.

She felt the tip of his penis slip to her entrance. Despite knowing that True would never hurt her, that she wanted to feel him inside her, she was scared. She stiffened as his large cock breached her opening. The triangle of material covering her sex offered little resistance.

"Ssshhh." He licked her nipple, pinching the other one hard. Sensations zinged as he continued his sensual assault. She focused on the pleasure even as he inched his cock inside her, his breath harsh in her ear.

"Fast or slow?" he asked. "It will hurt either way, my sweet one. But I promise to give you pleasure."

"Fast," she said. "Fast and *hard*."

"Goddess," he muttered. He rose to his knees, ripped off her wisp of panties, and tilted her hips.

He plunged inside—his large cock surging right through her virginal barrier.

Pain broke the hold pleasure had on her. She cried out, tensing, and yanked at the chains holding her arms. "Why haven't they broken?"

"I must spill my seed," admitted True.

"Then get it over with it. You are too big!"

"You can take me. You can take all of me, can't you, my love?"

"Yes," she promised. "Oh, yes."

He lay on top of her, gathering her into his arms, and kissed her. He kissed her until she relaxed, until she accepted the strange fullness of his cock in her pussy. He bent to her breasts, laving the nipples, nipping at her flesh. His thumb stroked her tingling clit.

Endlessly, he touched her and kissed her. He created within her an aching need, a fierce lust. "Please, True!"

He ever-so slowly withdrew from her wet, tight pussy then pushed inside. Stroke after stroke, he built the fires for both of them. She wanted to wrap her legs around him, but they were chained.

Frustration roared through her. Her nipples tingled and her pussy clenched. "True," she demanded. "Please! Damneth!"

Once again, he rose to his knees. Then he grabbed her thighs for leverage, and fucked her. His breathing labored, his muscles strained, and sweat rolled down his chest. "I love watching our connection," he said. "My penetration, your acceptance. Come with me."

His words made her heart stutter—and already it pounded furiously. He slid one finger along the crease of her pussy, stabbing it under the clitoral hood and flicking it rapidly. She bucked and moaned, easily matching True's pace.

"Come on my cock, Alissa," demanded True. "And I'll fill up your sweet, tight pussy with my cum."

His words tipped her over the edge. Bliss exploded and her hips lifted off the bed, his hand pressed against her agitated clit.

"Alissa!" True tensed, and as her own orgasm ripped through her, she felt his cock jerk violently. He pushed deeply inside her as he came, his groan low, his balls pressing against her ass.

She heard four metallic snicks. The chains released and her tingling arms and legs flopped to the bed. Breathing hard, she looked up at True. His gaze was shadowed, but his lips formed a half-smile. "You are free, Alissa."

* * * * *

"I don't understand." Alissa stood on her sister's small concrete porch and looked at the black velvet bag True offered her. She didn't take it. "You whisk me out of Madame V's, refuse to let me go home—"

"Vivian will not like that you escaped. She will post guards at your house," said True. "You cannot stay long at Janele's, either. You must get away until Madame V loses interest in finding you."

"You paid her a fortune for me," said Alissa. "She should be satisfied."

"Money does not assuage the need for vengeance." He pressed the heavy bag into her hands. "Take this, *anonvie*. You can go anywhere. You are rich."

"She said you needed my virgin blood for your black magic." Alissa stepped back, still refusing the sack of gold coins. "I didn't believe her. But you are paying me, True, as if I was a whore. I would've given you my virginity freely."

"This is not a transaction for services rendered." Anger flared in his teal eyes. "Damneth, woman, I'm trying to help you."

"Why should I accept your help when you refuse mine?" Her heart trilled like a bird trapped in its gilded cage. "I could lift your curse. I *know* it."

"I will not let you!" He tossed the bag at her feet and clenched his fists. Teal magic sparked from his fists. "Do you think I would ask you for your life? Leave Mreben, Alissa. If nothing else, I can assure your safety."

Tears crowded her eyes. "I don't want your money or your promises of safety." She reached out, beseeching. "I want you." She looked at him, letting him see the depth of her feelings. "True, I love—"

"No." He looked away, his jaw tense. "Go away, Alissa. Far away. I do not want you. I do not love you."

Without meeting her gaze, he lifted his arms and rose into the air, his teal cape fluttering as he escaped into the night.

Janele opened the front door and stared at Alissa with sleepy eyes. "What happened? Are you okay?"

Fury erupted. Fury and pain. "Everything will be fine," she reassured her sister. She kicked at the black bag. "Pay me, will he? Hmph." She reconsidered the bag, thoughts windmilling—and smiled.

* * * * *

"Mistress!" Marlik looked at her, dumbfounded. "How the Hades did you find the castle?"

"With this." Alissa tapped the teal-stone ring. "I asked it to show me where True was and it lit the whole way here."

"He ain't gonna be pleased," muttered Marlik. "'Tis almost dawn. You should go, mistress."

"No." The castle was not a castle at all, but a huge jumble of metal and stone. To Alissa's shock, the crazy mess flickered, and as it did, it shuddered and creaked. Holy Goddess! She shouldered past an irritated Marlik and got inside just as a *thud, thud,* BAM ricocheted through the whole place.

"It makes that noise every time we move," said Marlik. "Master True says he can fix it, but he never has."

"The castle *moves*?" *So that's what happened during their dream time—the house had moved and interrupted True's mental connection to her.*

Marlik nodded, probably figuring that since Alissa was in True's domain, it wasn't necessary to keep secrets. "He ain't in a good mood."

"Neither am I," said Alissa. She had paid a huge sum to a daring driver to get her through the Barrens. She hung out the window of the fast-moving carriage and pointed the ring so that the driver could follow the teal light all the way to True's castle.

"Where is he?"

Marlik pointed across the huge, dark foyer to a cobwebbed staircase.

"Do you ever clean?" she asked, noting the dirt and dust.

"No," said Marlik. "An' I don't cook, neither." He gave Alissa one last look, shook his head, and walked through a set of double doors at the other end of the foyer. Alissa looked up the stairs. Her heart beat frantically and sweat beaded her palms. She hadn't been nervous...not until this moment.

Knowing there wasn't much time, she hurried up the stairs. A long, shadowed hallway stretched before her. There were several doors, but she saw a flicker of light beckon from the far end. She followed the light until she reached the door from which it had escaped.

She didn't bother to knock. Instead, she flung open the door. True stood near a fireplace, his arm on the mantel, his head hung in defeat. In contrast to the rest of the house, the fire was bright and cheery. He looked up, surprised, and she saw the tear tracks on his cheeks. "Alissa!"

"Why do you weep?" she asked as she crossed the room. She grabbed his arm and held on, afraid he might reject her. "I am here."

"I told you—" He swallowed the rest of the words. His fingers drifted across her cheekbones.

"You said you never lied."

"I don't."

"You love me," she declared. "And you said you didn't. That, sir, is a *lie*."

He smiled, but his eyes filled with sadness. "I wanted to protect you."

"Mark me."

"No." He straightened and paced away from the fireplace, into the darkest part of the room. She followed him. He whirled on her, seizing her by the elbows. "Damneth. What does it take for you to understand? You will never love another. You will never desire another. You will be trapped."

"I will be yours." She cupped his face and as she did so, his flesh rippled. Teal scales erupted, their sharp edges slicing her fingertips. He hissed and tried to scrabble out of her embrace. "No!" She held on and though he had the strength to pull away, he stayed.

She watched as the monster form overtook him. His gaze never left hers. With every movement, every change, she loved him more. He had seen *her* beauty, and he could not hide his own — not even under teal scurf.

Within moments, she held not a wizard, but nearly a dragon. He was the same size as the human True, but he had a tail and wings. His clothing had shredded, leaving him naked. Gleaming scales covered every inch of his body. Well, every inch except his ball sac and *two* teal cocks, both which jutted proudly.

"Now, you know," he said in a growly voice.

"And this is what you look like until the wizard's moon?"

He nodded.

"Will I have scales after you mark me?"

"No, you will — *what*?" He blinked at her. "Mark you? Even now, when I'm a monster, you want me?"

"True, my darling. Did you not teach me the value of beauty?" She kissed him, pressing her human lips against his leathery mouth. "I love you."

"Alissa. To mark you, I must take you in this form. Then I will bite you on the neck. There will be pain and magic — "

"And love."

Hope flared in his eyes. Yet, his doubts obviously remained. He waved at the two impressive cocks. "I have to penetrate you with both cocks. Do you understand? You have to accept me both anally and vaginally."

"I hope it's more pleasurable than it sounds." Alissa grinned to take away the sting of her words. She shed her dress and removed her undergarments. Then she wrapped her arms around his neck, pressing her soft form against his scaled body. "Make me yours, wizard."

Chapter Four

Growling, her wizard gently pushed Alissa out of his embrace. The black wrought iron bed she remembered from their dream was to the left. He took her hands and placed them on the top metal rail. "Hold on to this."

She bent over, clutched the rail, and spread her legs. True left her there, gasping and terrified and thrilled. When he returned, he kneeled and crawled under her. With his long, spiky tongue he laved her breasts until they were turgid, then he cuffed each sensitive nipple. With a wicked look in his eyes, he placed a silver ball, bigger than the one he'd used in their dream world, on the middle link.

"Oh!" The weight of it pinched her nipples sharply, creating sweet, undulating pain. Her nipples throbbed as wicked desire pinged from her breasts to her swollen pussy.

"Alissa. My beautiful Alissa," rasped True.

He moved behind her and kneeled. She felt the ginger touch of one scaly finger as it penetrated her sex. She sucked in a shaky breath as that thick, rough finger gently probed the depths of her cunt. He pushed in a second digit, allowing a few seconds for her to adjust to the feel of his asperous fingers infiltrating her. One scaly hand grasped her ass. His talons dug into her hip, his rough scales pressed flat against her flesh as he drove deeper inside her.

"You're so wet," True said in a very sexy growl.

"For you," she whispered, aching deeply for his ingress. She'd be a fool not to be scared about the double penetration he'd promised. Or was that threatened? She couldn't imagine how it would feel to have her ass stuffed with one cock while the other filled her pussy. Even so, the idea of being filled by True that completely made her burn hotter than ever.

"Are you ready, *anonvie*?" He removed his fingers from her wet, ready sex. "Are you sure?"

"Yes! I want you, True. Forever."

He placed a soft kiss at the base of her spine. His leathery lips and scaly skin made her shiver. Then he rose and went to another part of the room. Alissa kept hold of the railing, even though her palms were perspiring and fingers started to cramp. She wanted to please True. And she wanted to free him.

After a moment, he returned.

She felt him position himself behind her. Fear and need wove together in a mystifying desire that clutched at her. Sensation. All wonderful, terrible sensation.

Then True said, "I'm putting lubricant into your ass. It'll make entrance easier." She felt a cold tip pierce her anus then the strange feel of a gelatinous substance filling her. Panting with need, she still felt a zap of cold fear. She trusted True, but she wasn't sure if she could handle the requirements of his mark. What if she failed him?

"Relax, Alissa." He parted her ass cheeks and rubbed the tight star. Then, slowly and carefully, he inserted a finger. She swallowed the knot in her throat and tried to calm down. The feel of his finger sliding in and out of her anus, not to mention the scales tickling her sensitive pucker, took on an arousing quality. She breathed easier, relaxing and, after a while, enjoying the light penetration. *I can do this. I will do this.*

Then she felt something considerably bigger pushing against her ass. Her breath caught and her heart hammered as the top cock pushed into her tight asshole. Tears of the Goddess! She gritted her teeth and clenched the metal rod.

"Stop fighting me, my love." True sounded out of breath. His voice was a low snarl.

Her nipples ached, swelling within their tiny cuffs. The weighted ball swung, causing hot sensation to ratchet through her breasts. With an effort, she loosened up, widening her stance and pushing her ass back to accept True's hard cock.

When he was halfway inside her ass, she felt the tip of the second cock tease her pussy. She wanted, no needed, to feel his cock inside her pussy. Her ass burned, feeling oddly full as True sheathed himself doubly inside.

For a long minute, they gathered their breath, their energy. Joined in the most intimate way possible, pain and passion combined and tore down all the barriers, both physical and emotional.

True wrapped an arm around her stomach to steady himself. Alissa looked down. His gorgeous teal scales were a lovely contrast to her pale skin. He was beautiful. How could he be anything else?

Slowly, he immersed both cocks deeply within her. When he was fully sheathed, she dragged in harsh breaths, anticipation rippling through her.

He leaned over her, his hand joining hers on the rail. The other hand pressed against her sex, stroked the tender swells of her pussy lips. One talon worked magic on her clit. The pleasure built swiftly thanks to her distended nipples and that rough finger tickling her clitoris.

The first full plunge drove heat into her ass, so much so, she couldn't concentrate on the more pleasant sensation of True taking her pussy.

The second penetrating stroke tore a scream from her.

"Alissa?" True sounded both turned-on and anguished.

"Don't stop," she begged. "I want you. All of you."

The ball on its chain swayed, pulling on her tender nipples. Growling, True created a fast, hard rhythm. Soon, she matched his every thrust. Then, she felt nothing but *him*, his claim on her body, on her soul. The scales of his body scraped against her back as he fucked her. The talon pressed and scraped her clit. Goddess, she wanted him. Her body nearly overloaded on sensation, painful and pleasurable.

Joyful tension coiled, low and tight in her belly.

Still, Alissa knew True was restraining himself, trying to protect her from his monster. "Let go, True," she demanded. "Make me yours."

He roared—a sound of terrible possession that shredded her control. Her orgasm unexpectedly burst—a ravaging bliss that seemed connected to every nerve in her body. True roared again, as if her climax was his triumph. He grabbed the rail with both hands and rammed into her, his balls slapping against her as he fucked her thoroughly.

Then his teeth pierced her shoulder and she felt fiery pain. His fangs gouged her and he held her, rutting until he roared a final time and shot his cum deep inside her willing, wet cunt.

They collapsed to the floor, both weeping and laughing. Magic and joy sparkled in the air around them.

When Alissa looked up, she found the human True had gathered her into his arms. He leaned against the foot of the bed and cuddled her.

"What happened?" she asked as she traced his jaw.

"You broke the curse, *an-onvie*."

She frowned. "*An-onvie.* You're pronouncing it differently."

"Because I'm using its second form." He kissed her lightly. "*Anonvie* means precious one. And *an-onvie* means wizard's mate."

"To mark me means to mate with me?"

"Yes. All wizards are cursed, Alissa, until we find the one woman who loves us enough to face our monster and take our mark."

"You mean that you're a monster for your whole life unless you find a mate?"

"Yes. Eventually, we lose the ability to turn into our human forms. Not even the magic of the wizard's moon can help us then."

"What about now? Are you human?"

"The monster is gone, my love. Forever." He smiled. "You saved me."

"We saved each other."

* * * * *

In the dark lands of the Barrens, a heap of rusty metal and crumbling stone flickered into existence. With a groan and a thud, it settled near a clear, blue lake. The sun peeked over the craggy, black mountains, showering the gray land with its warmth and its light.

Some say that wizards have no hearts and that's why they eat those of their lovers.

But the truth is that a wizard cannot find his heart...until his finds his mate.

Also by Michele Bardsley

1-800-SEX4YOU *with Chris Tanglen*
A Taste of Honey
Bride Portal
Redial 1-800-SEX4YOU *with Chris Tanglen*
Shadows Present
Two Men and a Lady *(anthology)*

About the Author

&

Multi-published in several genres, award-winning author Michele Bardsley spends her days creating fictional worlds because, let's face it, reality sucks. A prime example is that no one has yet to figure out how to make calorie-free chocolate. What's up with THAT?

Michele lives in Oklahoma where she is held hostage by her two children, her husband, and three cats. Occasionally her family remembers to feed her, but mostly she's forced to nibble on copy paper while eking out her next story. The manacles make it difficult to type, but she manages.

Michele welcomes comments from readers. You can find her website and email address on her author bio page at www.ellorascave.com.

Tell Us What You Think

We appreciate hearing reader opinions about our books. You can email us at Comments@EllorasCave.com.

RELUCTANT
Lauren Dane

ဆာ

Acknowledgements

ഇ

I have this dude, he makes me coffee every morning and works hard to help me live this dream. He's pretty hot too and I suppose there's more than a bit of him in every hero I write. He's not a werewolf but he's pretty alpha. And he makes a mean latte. Thanks for being my everything.

Ann, thank you for making me a better writer with each book we work on together. I'm a lucky little writer to have you in my corner.

Oh! And to Mr. Kelly, I hope you never read this book ('cause boy would I ever blush!), but I'd like you to know that you nurtured the writer in me and made me believe I could do it. Teachers like you make the world a better place. You gave me my very first copy of Writers Digest.

Kids, parents, beta readers — y'all rock my world but some of you would make me a lot happier if you slept more. You know who you are.

Trademarks Acknowledgement

ഇ

The author acknowledges the trademarked status and trademark owners of the following wordmarks mentioned in this work of fiction:

BMW: Bayerische Motoren Werke Aktiengesellschaft CORPORATION

Brooks Brothers: Brooks Brothers, Inc.

Author's Note

Many of you asked me about Sid and Layla after you read *Enforcer*. I hadn't really planned on writing their story. Not at first. And then I began to think on it and my wonderful editor brought up the Autumn Animalia quickie series and I realized I had the perfect idea for it—a prequel giving you the story of when Sid and Layla meet.

While *Reluctant* is a stand-alone story, Layla is part of a family, the Cascadia Wolf Pack, and you see as it ends, she's in the backyard of now grown-up and mated sister Tracy's house.

You get to meet Tracy and her two mates (yes, I said two!) in *Tri Mates*, the next Cascadia Wolves book.

Chapter One
Seattle, Washington, 1996

ဢ

Layla Warden pulled her brand new BMW into her spot in the parking garage. She'd just gotten the parking spot and the big raise that paid for the flashy new car at the financial firm that'd hired her straight out of college three years before.

Getting out, she headed to the bank of elevators and smoothed down the skirt of the suit she'd picked up from Brooks Brothers the weekend prior. Her hair was perfectly cut every six weeks, without fail, and her manicure was flawless. Layla Warden had a ten-year plan and things were going quite well.

No one she worked with had the slightest idea that she turned furry and ran through the woods hunting rabbits every few weekends, and she planned to keep it that way. Humans tended to get a bit shirty when confronted with the existence of werewolves. Most werewolves she knew weren't very out about it. It kept them all safer.

Her human life was kept separate from her life as a member of the ruling Pack family. Most of her social life was with her Pack and family while her work life was absent that altogether. Her family was not incredibly pleased with the distance she kept her professional life from the Pack. They wanted her to hook up with a male from the Pack and settle down. They felt she could do that better if she worked for one of the Pack businesses. And she could understand their wishes. Who knew what her other sisters would end up doing? Tracy was a wild child at just fourteen and the twins, Megan and Tegan, had decided at eighteen to become part of their older brother Lex's Enforcer guards. Clearly their parents looked to her to continue their line. But they'd have to wait.

The last thing Layla wanted right then was a mate. Ugh. She didn't want that intense connection to anyone just yet. Werewolves didn't just marry each other, they mated. They had an intense chemical and metaphysical bond to their spouse. At some point in the future that would be what she wanted but right then, Layla had plans! Those plans did not include bossy werewolf males meddling in her day-to-day life. She had two domineering, control-freak brothers and enough other male relatives to know that life mated to a werewolf male would not be easy.

She loved her freedom and she liked dating around. Because she may be button-down on the outside, but Layla did love sex, and the thought of getting from just one guy forever? That didn't appeal at all.

Still, she appreciated her roots and her upbringing and she wasn't ashamed of being a werewolf, she just didn't make it her entire life like her oldest brother Cade, the Pack Alpha, did.

"Good morning, Ms. Warden."

Layla smiled at her secretary and took her mail into her office. Her new, bigger, corner office. That hadn't even been due to happen until year five of the ten-year plan and here she was at year three. Booting up her computer with a satisfied sigh, she checked voicemail, looked through her mail and then began to go through her emails.

It was ten-thirty by the time she finished playing catch-up and could launch into her work for the day.

She worked through lunch, as she often did, and left the office at six. She was supposed to meet her best friend for dinner and drinks but she was tired. Still, she had a feeling Tia wouldn't let it go, and she was right.

When Layla got to the front doors of her building, Tia was waiting there, already dressed up and looking amazing, as always.

The petite blonde narrowed her eyes at Layla and put a hand on her hip. "I knew you'd try to get out of tonight. I can see it in your face right now! But we both need the distraction so I'm here to bug you mercilessly until you give in."

Sighing, Layla rolled her eyes and waved Tia through the doors after she'd unlocked them. "How much can I pay you to go away?"

"Shaddup. You're coming out with me tonight. You work ten hours a day! You need to play a little. You're too uptight as it is. So let's see what you have in your closet. I'll pick out an outfit for you while you shower." Tia shoved her into the direction of her bathroom and then headed off to root through her closet to find what Layla was sure would be the most revealing outfit she owned.

Even as she thought it she laughed. Tia Mathers had been her best friend since third grade. They'd gone to college and roomed together and basically shared just about everything. It helped that Tia and her family were part of Cascadia Pack too.

The best thing about Tia was that she knew a side of Layla most people didn't. People thought of Tia as the fun-loving one while Layla was the serious one — they didn't know that Layla had a fun side too. It just got a little lost sometimes, especially since she'd gotten promoted at work.

Going into her bedroom after the shower, Layla saw that on her bed lay a pair of leather pants and a tank top.

"Are you kidding me? That's a Halloween costume!" Layla had gone to a party as Catwoman two years before and probably hadn't worn the pants since. "I'm sure I *will not* be able to get my ass into them now."

"Oh stop crying and try them on. They looked good on you then and hell, woman, I'd be surprised if you even ate today. You're getting skinny since you work all the damned time."

Giving in, Layla tried the pants on and Tia was right. They fit quite well and Layla had to admit she looked pretty sexy in them.

"Okay, okay. But no tank top. I can't wear a bra with one. You know how I hate when straps show and goodness knows me without a bra is a challenge to gravity."

"Fine. Wear this one." Tia tossed her a bright red, shimmery, short-sleeved blouse that was tight across the bodice but loose around the waist.

By the time they'd left the condo, Layla's hair was tousled in a sexy style and she wore red lipstick to match the blouse and teetered on spiky heels.

"Before you complain, we're going to Nautica. I made reservations for us."

Nautica was a werewolf hot spot. Members only. Tia loved it, Layla tolerated it for Tia.

"I thought you said I was supposed to play tonight? Now I'll be hounded by power-hungry males who want to fuck their way into my family."

"Oh my god! Lay! Have you *looked* at yourself lately? You're fucking gorgeous. They want to fuck *you*. Some of them are hot to be married into the Warden family but most of them want to bed you because you're beautiful, sexy and have a good job."

It was an old argument and on most days Layla could believe Tia, but it was hard being from an influential family. People assumed things. They assumed she got her job through her connections instead of the fact she'd graduated at the top of her class, interned and then worked part-time at her company for three years. They assumed her money was family money. There was money there but it was all tied up in trusts. What she and her siblings had they'd all earned.

"Okay. Fine." She knew she was being selfish and she gave in. Tia didn't date too many humans. She didn't think it was fair to have to hide such a large part of herself from them. Werewolf-only clubs like Nautica were the few places she could meet wolf males their age.

"Good. Life would be so much better if you just agreed with me from the start and I didn't have to argue with you. Because you know I'm right."

Layla rolled her eyes when they pulled into valet and flashed their membership cards. "It's 1996! What is up with the mullets?" Layla whispered this quietly to Tia before they got to the top of the stairs leading into the restaurant and lounge area.

Tia looked back over her shoulder at the group of male wolves clustered near the front doors, several with the short on the top, long in the back hairdo that puzzled both women. "Werewolves and their mullets! I don't know, but I'm sure glad Cade got rid of his. Your brother is hot stuff but man did he look stupid."

The two of them dissolved into laughter and the hostess just smiled at them as if they were a bit soft in the head as she led them to their table.

One thing Layla did like about the place was that due to the sheer number of wolves on site, they piped a neutralizer for pheromones through the air circulation system. So there wasn't a whole lot of sniffing going on. She thought it was tacky when some guy she'd just met started sniffing on her.

Across the room, Sid Rosario watched the tall, very busty redhead enter the room and sit down. Her hair was tousled around her shoulders like she'd just rolled out of bed and very big china-blue eyes took in the room around them. And damn, but the woman did leather pants well enough to make him want to lick her like a giant ice-cream cone.

"Who is that?" Sid asked his cousin Adam.

Adam peered around Sid's shoulder and smiled. "The tall one with the red hair is Layla Warden. The petite one is Tia Mathers. Layla is Pack royalty. She's the oldest daughter. Tia's just smoking hot."

"I'm not interested in her pedigree. But I'd sure like to get to know her better. You know either one of them?" Sid could not take his eyes from Layla Warden's mouth with that shiny red lipstick painting it. His cock throbbed in anticipation as a picture of red lipstick marks at the base of it flashed through his mind. Lipstick kisses on his cock, yeah, that worked.

"Ah, it's like that, is it? Well, many have tried and failed. She's a bit cool. But yeah, Tia and I dated a few times. Let's go. I'll introduce you." Adam stood up and Sid followed.

"Ah, so soon?" Tia murmured to Layla. "Adam Rosario. I have very fond naked memories of him. And who is that with him?"

Layla looked up from the menu and locked gazes with tall, dark and dangerous. The man just oozed rebellion. Short black hair, a row of earrings in his right ear. Nautica had a strict dress code but despite the black jeans and the button-down shirt, she was sure the guy lived in ripped jeans and Clash T-shirts.

So utterly not her type. This thought seemed to escape her as she looked into those big hazel eyes.

"Tia, gorgeous. Long time no see."

Tia smiled up at Adam and batted her lashes a bit. "Hi, Adam."

"Hey, Layla. You look great too. Can we join you?"

Tia accepted before Layla could speak. But she wouldn't have refused anyway. Mr. Rebel made her all tingly. And it had been a while. Four months to be exact.

"This is my cousin, Sid. He's visiting here for a few weeks. Sid, this is Tia Mathers and Layla Warden."

Sid shook hands with Tia and smiled at her, but it was fleeting compared to the full-on, deep, soul-shaking look he gave Layla. Taking her hand, he kissed the knuckles and the warmth of his lips shot straight to her pussy.

"It's very nice to meet you, Layla. I like that name. Is it..."

"Yes. My parents were big Eric Clapton fans when I was conceived. Let's speak of it no more."

Her smile was flirtatious and Sid smiled back.

"So what are you doing while you visit? Where do you call home?" Layla felt like she couldn't get enough of looking at him.

The server came and took their orders and Sid watched as she sipped her drink.

He cleared his throat. "I'm doing a mural—I'm an artist. I live in Tucson. And what do you do?"

"I'm in financial services. I do portfolio planning."

His eyebrows rose.

"What? Too Yuppie for you?"

He laughed. "No, not at all. I love smart women. I'm impressed."

She relaxed.

All through dinner she felt herself pulled under his spell. Each time he reached out to grab the salt or his beer, he'd touch her in some small way. His total attention was on her at every moment. His voice was low and seductive, an aural caress. When she spoke, he listened intently, clearly interested in what she had to say.

And she couldn't deny she was fascinated by him. Watched his hands move expressively while he talked about his work. Saw the delightful light in his eyes, making it clear he loved what he did. He flattered her and made her laugh.

There was no doubt for either of them that they'd end up in bed. She liked that his surety wasn't smug or smarmy. He was a sexy guy in town for a few weeks—the perfect fling. She certainly had no plans to stop the inevitable.

Walking out to the cars, he pulled her aside. "Can I give you a ride home? Or would you like to come back to my hotel?"

The salt air of low tide tickled her senses along with his scent. Male werewolf did indeed smell hella good to her, and nary a mullet in sight.

"Where are you staying?"

"The Alexis."

"Let me just tell Tia. I'll be right back."

He watched as she walked over to her friend and hugged her goodbye. Tia winked at her, and Layla gave her the finger, amusing him.

"Let's go."

Adam nodded discreetly and Tia offered him a ride home.

On the way to the hotel, Sid asked if she minded him smoking a clove cigarette. She shrugged.

"I like the smell in small doses."

And it seemed to add to his spice, the very alluring masculine scent of him. God, she had it bad. She wanted to rip his clothes off and climb on his cock right there on First Avenue.

He must have noticed her near-panting and the glaze of desire in her eyes because he took her hand and kissed the fingertips. "I know. I want you too."

She shivered at the near growl in his voice, and when they arrived he tossed the keys at the valet and they headed inside quickly.

"I can't touch you yet," he said in the elevator. "Once I do, it's over."

They walked side by side, just barely not touching as they hurried down the hallway to the door of his room. Which he opened up in record time.

Taking a deep breath, Layla walked inside and he followed her, careful to put the "Do Not Disturb" sign on the door before he shut and locked it.

Chapter Two

ဆာ

A long look settled between them until suddenly he was there, hands on her body, lips on hers. Everywhere he touched, her skin warmed and tingled.

His lips, lush and soft, devoured her in kiss after devastating kiss. Lust and desire drowned her, pulled her under, and she went willingly, giving in to the exquisite sensations.

When his tongue stroked in between her lips like a lover, a deep shudder broke through her. Her nipples hardened to the point of pain and her clit throbbed. His taste, warm and spicy, slithered through her, marking her senses. Her entire body began to vibrate with need. She'd never felt anything like it before. It was overwhelming but amazing too.

Needing to ground herself in him, her hands slid up the wall of his chest and began to unbutton his shirt. He hissed when she brushed against bare skin as she shoved it down his arms. Like most werewolves, he ran very warm and she felt the heat of his skin when his shirt was stripped off. His muscles bunched and relaxed under her palms. Her hands skimmed up his neck and she allowed herself a moment to glory in the feel of the silk of his hair sifting between her fingers.

Stepping back, she drank him in as she reached down and pulled her blouse up and over her head.

He was tall and lanky. Not skinny really. Lots of upper body power there. Lean muscle roped tightly over his chest and arms. His stomach was flat and she grinned when she saw it was tattooed.

"What? Am I your first bad boy?"

"Is that what you are, Sid? I can't wait to see just how bad then." She laughed then and delighted in his gasp as she shrugged out of her bra and ran her hands up her stomach and over her breasts.

"Would it please you to be my first bad boy?"

"Honey, *you* please me. I couldn't care less if you had a line of fifty bad boys at the door because you're here with me right now. And good god your tits are amazing."

Smiling again, Layla ran fingertips around her nipples in slow circles, catching her lip between her teeth for a moment. "My sister would love that tattoo."

"That so? Well, I think I'm with the right Warden sister just now." Taking two steps back to her again, he reached out and pulled her hands away, replacing them with his own.

Her breath caught at his intimate touch as he slowly brushed his palms over the sensitive flesh of her nipples.

"Well, that's good. She's fourteen anyway. But all she talks about are tattoos. And that topic is over now." Her head dropped back as his lips slid over the column of her neck and across her collarbone.

The sound of her zipper sliding down rang through the room and up her spine. He moved away from her neck and stepped back.

"Okay, I'll get my pants off, you get yours off. Meet you back here in a few seconds."

Laughing, Layla shoved her pants — not an easy feat with leather — and her panties down, pulling them off once she'd kicked out of her shoes. By the time she was naked and looked back to him, he'd just tossed his jeans and briefs to the side.

"Well." Her breath rushed out of her as she took him in. Long, lean and powerful muscle covered his body from head to toe. His cock stood so hard it tapped his flat belly. She wasn't sure but she thought she might have made a cartoonish gulp.

Which seemed sort of odd to her. He was so *not* her normal type. She liked her men in suits and ties. This man was all artsy and tattooed. Still, she was quite sure she'd never needed to have sex with anyone more than this man right then.

"If you aren't touching me very soon I might die," she whispered and then he was back against her.

"Oh god!" His words were nearly a moan as their naked bodies touched, skin to skin. If he hadn't taken a fistful of that lush red hair, he was sure his hands would have shaken with desire. Need roared through every single cell in his body. He had to have this woman and he had to have her right then. Tipping her head back, he dipped down for another kiss, this one far less controlled than the last. This one was barely leashed desire as mouths strained against each other, tongues sliding, his imitating the in-and-out motions of sex. Teeth caught bottom lips and breath mingled along with soft sounds of pleasure.

Her mouth felt so good against his, her body fit so right clutched against his that he thought it would be delightful to spend several hours doing nothing more than kissing her over and over. He wanted to spend an entire Sunday afternoon making out with Layla Warden.

But right then, his body demanded a hell of a lot more than long, slow, wet, drugging kisses. "I have to have more," he murmured and walked her backward to the bed, tipping her back onto it. He stopped, stunned at her beauty as he loomed above her. Big blue eyes blinked up at him, her hair spread around her head like a fiery halo, lips swollen from kisses.

He scented her desire and it wrapped around him with great force, nearly bringing him to his knees. He'd never reacted this way to a female, always prided himself in his slow, devastating seduction of his partners. But this one, god, he wanted to eat her up in three big bites.

On hands and knees, he arranged her on the bed so he could kiss down her neck and finally taste her nipples.

Layla looked up at him as he stared down into her face. The need etched into his features took her breath away. Her pussy bloomed, softened and slicked at his perusal. She could smell it, the spice of her arousal, and satisfaction took hold when she watched his nostrils flare and his pupils widen. *She* made him feel that way.

When his hot, wet mouth reached her nipples she thought she'd come right then. Each pull brought the sensitive flesh against the edge of his teeth and he came behind with his tongue, swirling over her nipple to soothe the sting.

She tried to reach his cock but he pulled off her nipple and looked into her face. "No. If you touch me I'll come. And I want to be in your pussy when that happens."

Before she could respond he was kissing his way down her stomach and through the sensitive crease where leg met body. Strong, work-calloused hands spread her thighs, opening her up as he stared.

"But first, I need you to be ready. Nice and wet for my cock."

"Oh!" Incoherence washed through her as he slid his thumbs through the furls of her sex, spreading her honey. "I…I'm wet now. You should fuck me. Oh god." If his thumbs, pressing up and over her clit, felt this good, what would his mouth feel like? She hoped to find out very, very soon.

His chuckle spread over her, warm and sticky. Her nipples hardened and her hips churned, needing him to touch her.

"You'll be even wetter when I'm finished." Leaning his head down, he took a long lick, dipping his tongue deep into her body and then up and around her clit. One of his thumbs slipped into her while the other slid down to stroke over her perineum and ever so lightly against her rear passage.

The tip of his tongue circled 'round and 'round her clit, getting closer to it each pass until he finally began to flick it with gentle, insistent strokes. That wet slide of flesh against her clit shocked into her body, making her back arch.

Layla's fingers dug into the bedspread as her thigh muscles began to burn from the trembling. Endorphins began to flow, her clit throbbed, orgasm was so very close. He ate her pussy like a starving man relishes a meal. She wasn't new to the act but it had never been this good before. Never felt so completely all-encompassing. Never had it rendered her helpless against the sensation.

Low, feral-sounding growls trickled from her mouth, coming from deep in her gut. Her hips began to roll, grinding herself into his mouth. She needed to come. Needed this man to make her come.

And when he grazed his teeth over her clit ever so lightly and sucked it into his mouth, flicking the underside over and over and over, orgasm hit with near violent force. Her back bowed with electric intensity as pleasure swamped her, dizzied her, intoxicated her and made her limbs heavy.

Each time she thought it was over, another wave hit. His mouth wasn't even on her anymore and still the ripples of climax sounded through her.

Dimly, she felt him pick her body up and she blinked herself back to a basic level of attention when he plunged her body down on his cock in one movement. This set off another round of aftershock orgasms, little but deep. A pleasured cry ripped from her gut as ecstasy gripped her again.

When she came back to herself she was wrapped around him, her back against the wall as he fucked her while standing.

Each roll of his hips made his abdominal muscles ripple against her pussy and shudders worked through her.

"Fuck. Fuck. Fuck. You feel so good. I don't know how long I'll last this way." His voice was tight with tension and desire. His cock sliced through her over and over, invading her body even as it welcomed him. She was so hot and wet, every muscle and synapse firing and absorbing the exquisite pleasure he delivered. His scent tickled her senses and drove her to writhe against him.

"Hey, fuck! I'm really not going to last when you do that."

"Potty mouth! And we have all night. Come now. Take the edge off and you can have me again. And again. And again after that." Her lips brushed against the sensitive flesh of his ear as she said it. "You know you want to come inside me. Mark me."

Wolves didn't carry STDs and she was on birth control. She loved the feel of his naked cock buried inside her and she knew without a doubt that she stirred primal werewolf instinct when she told him to come in her and mark her. She was playing with fire and the danger turned her on. She'd examine this completely out-of-character behavior when she got home in the morning but for right then, she'd ride it and him and enjoy it all.

"Oh you're going to pay for that, little girl. I'll enjoy every minute of it too." His voice had deepened and roughened as his wolf came closer to the surface. Layla's own wolf sensed it and stirred within her. Every nerve in her body lit up as their primal selves rose and stroked over the other's while their human skins did the same. Never in her life had sex been so intense and all-encompassing. She wanted more.

Leaning in, she took a deep breath where his neck met shoulder and bit down, hard. A deep growling moan came from him and his cock began to pulse deep inside her as he continued to thrust through his climax. His scent hit her straight in her gut. She wanted more of it. *Needed* more of it.

And it hit her as her wolf wanted to roll around with him all over the floor. It occurred to her just why she'd been so intensely attracted to him, and their eyes met as the bond began to form. Glimmering threads of connection drew their

DNA and their hearts and souls together. She'd just been claimed. By her mate.

Sid Rosario, a man she'd met just hours before and had just wanted a brief, fun fling with, was her fucking mate. How could she not have known? The neutralizer in Nautica, the clove cigarette and her damned lust for this guy had totally blinded her.

"Holy shit," he said wondrously as his knees buckled and he stumbled back to the bed, collapsing on it, still embedded inside her.

"Holy shit?" She tried to move away but he wouldn't let go of her and her legs weren't working well anyway. "Is that all you've got to say? You've just claimed me!"

"Why are you so pissed off? You wanted me to fuck you, Layla. And thank god, because we've found each other."

"I don't want to be found." She heaved a sigh as she felt his feelings as acutely as her own. "I just wanted to have a fun few weeks with a hot guy from out of town. I have plans, Sid."

He frowned and annoyance burst through her as she found that attractive too. His frown changed into a wicked grin and she groaned. Damn it, he'd feel her through the bond. Know how much, even as she was livid, she wanted him to take her again and again after that.

"Oh ho! This bond link thing is pretty cool. Well, we can play the 'fuck the hot stranger from out of town' game all you like, honey. Because you can't buck reality. You're my mate. And I'm yours and you just got served!" He chuckled. "I wasn't expecting it either but I'm not going to lie and say I'm disappointed. You're beautiful and you smell heavenly. I look forward to getting to know my wife better."

Her legs had finally begun to work again and she scrambled away from him. "I'm not your wife!" She moved to grab her panties and her pants and began to get dressed.

"You are my wife. Look, Layla, I get that you're surprised. I am too. But you're a werewolf, you know the realities of our existence. You can't pretend away a mate bond. Especially not once the claiming occurs. Now that I've come inside you, we're united. You need my presence, I need yours. And we'll need the tri-bond to protect you."

The tri-bond? Oh hell no. He not only wanted to claim her entire life but she'd have to have sex with some male of his choosing too? "No, Sid. I'm not going to let this stupid metaphysical shit call a halt to my life. I like my job. I like my condo and I'm not going to move to Arizona, join another Pack and give up everything because I'm a female wolf."

"Layla, you don't have to move to Arizona. I realize your family is here. I'm a fifth son, it's not like I can't move. I paint, my life is easily transportable. And I'm not asking you to give up your life or your job. I haven't seen your condo but we may need to get something bigger so I can have studio space. I'm a male werewolf but I'm not a caveman. I don't want to take over your life. I want to share it."

Why was he so fucking reasonable? Their whole lives as they knew them were now over.

"Look, I need some time, okay? I need to think and I can't do it here."

She got her bra and shirt back on and pulled on her pants, unable to locate her panties. Needing to escape and think, she headed for the door, but he moved to it first. "Where are you going?"

"Home. I'm going to my condo. I need to think. Please."

"Let me drive you."

"No. I'm not that far, I'll catch a cab out front. I know the number here, I'll call you. Just give me some space."

"Space? Layla, you're my mate. The claiming has been made. This isn't something you can think away."

"Look," she struggled to speak without her voice breaking as her world crashed in around her. "I have plans! I can't think here with you...with your scent and your taste in my mouth. It's too much and I have to work this out. On my own." She looked up into his eyes. "Please."

His face softened and he pushed a tendril of her hair out of her face. "Wait," he ordered, and grabbed a piece of paper from the desk and shoved it at her. "Give me your address and your phone number. I'll give you until Sunday. You'll need the tri-bond. The longer you wait, the more dangerous it becomes. For both of us."

Sighing, she took the paper and wrote the info down. "I'm in Queen Anne, just like two miles away."

"I'm a very patient man, Layla, but even I have limits. Neither of us was expecting more than a brief thing, I know that. But you can't fight biology and if you look into yourself, you'll find you don't want to. I'm a good man. I don't want to control you, I want to share my life with you."

Kissing her softly, he stepped away from the door to let her go. She felt how difficult it was for him and before she could stop herself she reached out and caressed his face. "Thank you."

Quickly, before she could change her mind, she left and headed home.

* * * * *

And ended up feeling like shit all day as she didn't answer her phone and tried to think. But she couldn't think about anything other than Sid. The way he felt against her, the way his mouth felt on her, the way his cock filled her. More than the sex, she wanted to smell him, to be with him, to know him. And even though she'd showered off the scent of their sex, the claiming and their bond changed her essential scent subtly and each time she breathed in she was reminded of him.

Damn it! She didn't want to be subsumed into someone else's life. Okay, so she didn't want to want it. But now that she'd been with Sid, she wanted him in her life.

After a day of pacing and reaching to call the Alexis about a thousand times, she drove to Ballard and showed up on Tia's doorstep.

"Whoa! What happened to you last night?" Tia grinned and let Layla into her house. "You're not the one-night-stand type and oh fuck…" Tia's grin fell away and her eyes widened as she scented the bond.

"Yes. Oh god, Tia. What am I going to do?" Layla tossed herself onto the couch.

"What do you mean? Did he treat you badly? That fucker, I'm going to track him down and rip out his throat!"

Layla stopped her whining and looked at her best friend and started to laugh. "No! He's…he's great. Sweet, really good in bed, funny. He's good with the bond. He's happy about it even."

"Wait, you're bitching because of what, then?"

"Tia, I have *plans*! They don't include being mated to a painter! I need to mate with a stockbroker. We'll have two children and live in Maple Leaf or Ravenna. In like, five years." Even as she said it she knew she didn't mean it, never had, really.

Tia snorted and rolled her eyes. "Layla, those plans are not you. You *think* they're you because that's your own way of being different from the other Wardens. I've known you since we were nine years old. You're only button-down on the outside. Not that stockbrokers can't be hot, but your mate isn't one. God, some wolves wait twenty years past maturation to find a mate and you find one at twenty-five and you're complaining? He's hot! And he's good with the bond? And anyway, how did you get away? 'Cause it's hard for me to see a werewolf male just letting you walk away. And oh my, the tri-bond?"

The tri-bond was a ritual whereby a third wolf, a relation of the male mate, or a Packmate who ranked higher than he did, formed a bond with the female. It created what was termed as an anchor bond for two important reasons. To keep the female from losing herself in the emotional and hormonal surge of the claiming and also to keep her alive should something happen to her mate. The bond between mates was so strong that should something happen to the male, without the tri-bond, the female would die too. It was sort of a stabilizing connection. Like a surge protector, her brother Cade always said.

Layla let her head fall back against the couch cushions with a groan. "I know! Look, I'm not saying a threesome with two hot dudes is a bad idea in general. But I just met Sid and now I'm going to have to have sex with one of his relatives or something? Ugh! Adam? No, no, no! I can't have sex with someone you've had sex with."

"Okay, so I get the point about Adam. But you know you need the tri-bond to anchor you. You *know* that. It's not random sex, the anchor is a necessary thing. Without him you'll slip into insanity and that's no joke. The longer you wait, the worse it'll get."

"Why now? God, Tia, I just got this promotion and my life is going so well. This just complicates everything!"

"Oh shut up!" Tia got in her face. "You are *not* this person. Stop whining. Accept reality. He's your mate. Period. And you need the tri-bond or you'll both be in trouble because once you go, he'll lose it too. And for what? This stupid, selfish tantrum?"

Layla looked up at her friend, stunned. Stung, she pushed up off the couch and headed for the door. "I shouldn't have come here. I expected you to support me."

"Support you in what? Being stupid? Not dealing with the thing you need to keep you from going insane? I *am* supporting you, Lay. This guy is your mate. You said yourself that he's funny, good in bed and nice. He's fine with the bond. You're *lucky*! Instead of dealing with it like you usually do, you're throwing a tantrum. You can't change anything with this behavior. This drama queen thing is a sign."

"A sign? What are you talking about?"

"The longer you go unanchored the less rational you'll be. Look at yourself! You're a take-charge person. You rarely ever whine about things. You deal. Period. I'm worried about you, Layla. You aren't yourself right now."

"I'm fine." Taking satisfaction in the sound of the door slamming behind her, she left.

Chapter Three

80

Layla stomped out to her car and drove away. She headed east and tried to think about everything that had happened. She'd worked so hard to advance at her job. It was difficult being taken seriously as a woman in her field. And she was young, another thing she'd had to overcome. A curvy red-haired woman who was young and attractive wasn't something she complained about being in her day-to-day life, hell, it opened doors for her, she knew that. But it was hard to get past in the corporate world.

Three days before she'd been focused on her career and there had been nothing but clear pavement between her and another promotion. But with a mate she now had to navigate around how yet another person would react to her choices. It was hard enough dealing with her mother who never stopped complaining that she spent too much time on her career and not enough time on her family. Now she had to deal with a man. Not a man, *the* man.

And here she was with a big old wrench thrown into her plans by that man! As it was, all she could think about was Sid Rosario. She wondered if he was upset or hurt by her running off. She didn't want this. She wanted her old life where she was free to stay late at work, free to work on a Sunday, free to get up and work in the middle of the night if she needed to.

She wasn't some human who had no idea what she was in for. She was born a wolf, had seen wolves around her mate and watched their lives change in revolutionary ways. Was she ready for that? Did she even want to be? Was she ready for the level of dedication and involvement from her mate? Her DNA was now altered with his claiming of her. She was changed forever.

Frustrated and frightened, she slammed a palm against the steering wheel.

She needed to run. Running always calmed her, and she felt her wolf begin to agitate within her, needing release. Maybe she could think of a way around this mess if she could get a little bit of calm and stop obsessing about Sid for a few minutes.

Pulling her car onto a side road near where Cade's new house in the woods was, she hid her things in the wheel well and went to the tree line to shed her clothing. The scent of the wild teased her senses, soothed her as she fell to her knees and let her wolf take over her body.

Her humanity slid away as her fur rose and the world was black and white and gray and yet sharp and vivid. The scent of her surroundings painted the air—the moss on the trees, the mushrooms in the dead tree trunk, the squirrels and the rabbits that scurried out of the way as they scented her.

Nose up, she drew in the universe through her senses and the world was suddenly right again. There, covered in a pelt coppery and fiery red and gold, things were simple again.

And she ran.

* * * * *

Sid hung up the phone, pissed off. He'd been trying to call Layla for the last day and a half and even had showed up at her place, and there was no sign of her. Her scent, now *their* scent, was cold enough that he could tell she hadn't been around since early the day before.

He paced, his wolf agitated and worried. He never should have let her leave. A newly bonded female wolf needed the tri-bond, and each hour that passed without it happening put her in danger and made her less rational. She was already surprised and stressed out and that would only be exacerbated by the lack of the anchoring bond.

He picked up the phone and dialed Adam, who told him where Tia lived and that he'd meet his cousin there.

Not knowing what to expect, Sid was happy Tia seemed so happy and supportive of the bond. He was less happy to hear about Layla's agitation and that it seemed so far out of her normal character.

It wasn't just that he wanted to protect her—he *needed* to protect her. As a male werewolf, the mate bond was the ultimate commitment. Her needs were paramount. Knowing she was out there somewhere, upset and agitated, tore at him.

"Do you have any idea where she could be?"

"She always runs when she's upset and Cade, my Alpha and her brother, has a big house on a lot of acreage. She may have headed up there."

"Will you show me? Adam, will you go back to my hotel? I'll need an anchor and I'd be honored if you were our tri-bond."

"No! Look, part of what had Layla upset was the thought of having sex with someone I've…had sex with. Do you have any other cousins or family members who could help? Any other Pack members who outrank you?"

"Oh, I hadn't thought of it that way." Sid looked at Tia and thought. "Adam, call Shane please. He's on break from school visiting Aunt Jennifer down in Portland. I just talked to him a few days ago. Will you ask him for me? I need to go and get her."

Adam agreed and said he'd arrange for their cousin Shane to meet them at Sid's hotel room for the tri-bond.

They took Tia's car and drove up to where she thought Layla may be, pointing out Cade's new house.

"She won't have gone up to the house. They'd scent her and know and make her deal. I'm going to take you down this back road here to see if her car is around. You'll have to do the rest. There're about forty acres of forest here."

"I'll scent her if she's here." He meant to bring her back and make her safe, one way or another.

Tia swore when she saw Layla's car. "There's her car right there. Do you want me to wait?"

"No. Because if she gets away from me, I'm going up to that house and enlisting her family to help me."

Tia laughed. "You're gonna be just fine, Sid. She's a good person. Strong. Her family is important to her. Be gentle."

"She's my mate. Of course I'll be gentle. And yeah, I can tell she's a good person. Thank you."

He got out of the car and quickly disrobed, getting to all fours and letting his wolf surface. Nose up in the breeze, he caught her scent, spicy and rich, and tore off into the trees to track his mate down and bring her back.

Layla lay next to a small stream, breathing in the deep loam of the forest floor. The calm she'd had when she first ran was leaving her. As she'd run she'd thought. A lot. Realized that all her reasons, well, most of them anyway, for resisting the mate bond were work-related. And she realized she didn't want her life to be all about work any more than she wanted her life to be all about a man. There would be a way to find a middle ground. If anyone could, Layla knew she would do it.

Moreover, Tia was right. All of her whining and drama were not part of Layla's normal behavior pattern. Her grasp on things became more tenuous the longer she went without the tri-bond. And she missed Sid.

But despite knowing she needed to get to Sid and take care of the tri-bond, worry that he'd be angry at her and not want her anymore ate at her. The weight of the fear held her in place.

She was so lost in her thoughts she didn't even sense his approach until he pounced, teeth at her throat to hold her still.

Panic filled her and her back legs levered up to push off any male but hers, until he growled, a mixture of comfort and warning. She drew in a breath and scented him. Her mate. *Hers*. She relaxed and he let go and licked over the spot where he'd bitten her.

A soft whine brought her head around and her heart pounded at the sight of him there. So large and majestic. The most beautiful wolf she'd ever seen. Reaching in, she rubbed her face along his and growled softly. The sound was filled with desire and longing.

He took her there, quick and feral. Large body over her smaller one. His need to have her and mark her as a wolf as well as a man overwhelmed her. After, they lay side by side, her muzzle resting on his back as they let the forest calm them.

After some time she transformed, human eyes looking up at him.

Moving to her knees, she reached out and ran a hand over his ebony fur, thick and soft. Putting her arms around his neck, she hugged him tight and breathed him in. Loved the smell of him. "Such a gorgeous wolf. I'm sorry I ran."

And only moments after she'd spoken, his skin was smooth and hard as he transformed back and held her with human arms. "It's okay. Shhh, it's okay. Let me take care of you, honey."

He pulled her against him, into his lap, and kissed her mouth. He felt like he'd come home in her taste. The way her hands felt as they slid up his arms and into his hair, against his skull, burned into him.

"I want to be inside you again. But we don't have a blanket so will you come back with me? To any place with a bed? We can talk afterward. We've got to get the tri-bond dealt with, and today. You understand that?"

She nodded, her eyes clear. "I was afraid you wouldn't want me anymore. That you'd be so angry because I ran."

Kissing her again quickly, he added, "Oh, honey. God, it's so good to hold you. I've been crazy without you. I'm not angry. I was worried, yes. And I'd have brought you back kicking and screaming if I had to. But there's no way on earth I wouldn't want you. You got scared and things got a bit over your head. It's okay. I'm here and we're going to get through this together. From now on, we'll take turns freaking out so one of us will always be the strong one. You ready?"

And it was the most perfect thing he could have said. Sharing their burdens instead of shouldering them all himself — that last knot of concern in her gut eased from her softly.

"Yes. Oh yes." She allowed him to help her up and they changed again to run back to where her car was parked.

A short trip to his hotel and they practically ran to his door.

Turning on the hot water in the shower, she let his lips capture hers once again as she discarded her clothes and tossed them aside. A sense of deep rightness followed when his ended up with hers in the same pile. So odd that something so simple would make her feel her connection to him so deeply but it did.

"Come shower with me, I'm all dirty."

His lips slid into a naughty grin. "I like you dirty. It's my favorite."

Laughing, she pulled him into the stall with her, moving so he could share the hot water with her. His hands slapped hers out of the way as he took over the job of soaping her up from head to toe.

"My. I think I'll be the cleanest wolf ever when you're finished."

"As long as your insides stay dirty, I'm fine with that."

"Yeah?" A soap-slicked hand wrapped around his cock and began to slowly ride up and down the shaft.

His eyes dropped closed as he lazily accepted her touch. She added a second hand. Each hand slid up from the root of him, over the crown and head, and as the other followed to make the same path the seeds of his orgasm were sown and sensation began to build. Her scent rose on the steam, tightening his body.

Her sole focus was on him and pride burst through his senses. This beautiful, vibrant woman gave herself to him, made his pleasure her goal, and he'd never felt more amazing.

"Honey, let's get into the bedroom." His need to be inside her ramped up and his control hung by a thread. Knowing he'd have to share her, even for something as natural and necessary as the tri-bond, drove his need to have her, mark her, before his cousin arrived.

She stepped out and toweled off as he picked her up. Wrapping her legs around his waist, she teased them both, sliding her pussy over his cock.

"Still naughty on the inside, I see." Sid tossed her on the bed and she laughed as she bounced.

"With you, I seem to have a limitless supply."

"Oh good. I'm glad to know I bring the goods into this relationship."

She held her hand out to him. "Come on then. Do me before I start going crazy."

Shaking his head, he fell to the mattress next to her. "Don't joke! Damn it, Layla, I was so worried about you. Tia told me where you were. She's worried too. My cousin will be here. No, not Adam. Shane. Shane is a good guy, probably my closest male relative other than my oldest brother. He spent many summers with us when I was growing up. My brothers are all much older than I am, Shane was one of my only other cousins who was near to my age. I trust him with my life, god knows he and I got into enough trouble as teenagers. His mom is human, his dad is a werewolf. He didn't really grow up in a Pack so my parents were sort of in charge of his education as a werewolf. It's a very long story but she—his mom—lives in Portland and he's been visiting her on break from school. He goes to medical school at UCLA. Anyway, he's on his way up from Portland. We've got some alone time for now."

Pushing him back against the bed, Layla rolled atop him and rained kisses on his neck and over his chest. "Okay. I'm not happy about this. I know, I know it's necessary and all. I can feel myself losing my grip already. I'm more irrational than I normally am. But you know, I'd rather have a fun threesome, not some rigid, forced thing."

"Layla, after this, there'll be no more threesomes." His voice was a growl and the ferocity of it sent shivers down her spine. "You're mine. I don't relish the idea of you being with anyone else either. But it's our reality and what we need to do to keep you safe if something should happen to me. And so let's just make the best of it. I'll stay here if you don't mind. I can't bear the thought of it happening and not knowing."

Shimmying down his torso, she let her hair trail over his skin as she kissed and licked over his stomach. She surrounded his cock with her breasts and he groaned.

His hands slid through her hair and cradled her skull. "You're suddenly so important to me. Three days ago I didn't even know you and now you're everything."

"Hmmm. A girl could get used to hearing stuff like that." Moving down further, she licked the head of him, tasting the salty spice of his pre-cum.

"Oh yeah, well, a guy could get used to that too."

Moving to kneel between his thighs, she bent on all fours and took him into her mouth. She loved the taste of him, the feel of his skin as she licked over him.

The hot slick of her mouth on his cock began to pool sensation at the base of his spine. He'd never felt anything like it, the slide of her tongue against him. Watching down his body, he was mesmerized by the dreamy sway of her ass, each knob of her spine down the curve of her creamy back. She was exquisite, the sexiest thing he'd ever seen and felt.

He let her continue to suck his cock, watching her mouth, feeling his balls tighten against his body, knowing his climax was approaching. Each draw of her mouth and swirl of her tongue was another step higher.

Waiting until he teetered just on the edge of coming, he gently pulled her back. "Wait, honey. I want that sweet pussy around me when I come. Ride me, Layla."

Scrambling up his body quickly, she knelt over him and reached back to guide him true. That moment, suspended just above him, her hand around the girth of his cock, the expectancy of it, was sweet. She felt the heat of her pussy just above her hand and the hardness of his cock would soon fill her.

She let the anticipation build, feeling herself grow even wetter, her clit throbbing in time with her heart. Catching her bottom lip in her teeth, she looked down into his face, watching his pupils widen and the steady beat of his pulse at his neck.

"You're going to kill me."

"Wouldn't want that. I need you alive for your cock." Her voice was teasing as she slowly sank down onto him.

Sensation shot up her spine. Pleasure filled her, electric and hot, his cock the source. She arched her back to take him deeper, feeling the head nudge against her cervix as she lowered herself down on him over and over.

The muscles in his abdomen bunched and released against her inner thighs. His hands stroked over the skin of her thighs and up the curve of her waist. Her wolf pressed against her human skin and brushed against him. In answer, his wolf did the same and her skin felt tight, nearly too small as the feeling filled and filled and filled her until she thought she'd explode.

Panic began to edge against the pleasure but his soft touch and murmured words calmed her. "Shhh, honey. It's just us. Let it be." Big hands held her hips and she let go, let his calm wash over her. "That's the way, honey. I love the way you feel around me."

Her palms moved over his chest as she pulled his cock back into her pussy, deep and hard. Over and over.

Hands held her breasts, thumbs lazily moving back and forth over her nipples. Her breath hitched as she caught his gaze, looking at her with deep hunger. More deep than sexual hunger. He devoured every detail of her face, the line of her neck. His hands on her breasts were reverent.

Her honey, hot and sticky, brushed against his groin, scalded his cock. The superheated walls of her pussy gripped him, pulled him back into her body even as she rose up on her thighs and withdrew.

The sight of her, like a goddess above him, burned into his soul. One hand slid down and he drew his fingertips through the wet and swollen folds of her pussy, bringing her honey up and around her clit in big circles.

She gasped and he groaned when her pussy fluttered around him as her body readied itself for orgasm.

"You're pretty good with all your appendages there, Sid. I think I'll keep you around just to see what you can do with your elbows and nose."

A surprised laugh came from him. "So essentially, that whole suit thing is like your Clark Kent disguise?"

He sped up the fingers on her clit, moving them from side to side so it took her long moments to find words. "You have to know it's a bit hard to concentrate on your questions when you do that." She tightened herself around him and raised a satisfied eyebrow when he gasped. "Clark Kent? 'Cause I'm so super in the sack?"

"Among other things." Things shifted between them and it became a competition to see who could make the other come first. "But what I mean is that underneath the tailored clothing there's this whole other layer to you. I gotta tell you, it's pretty intoxicating."

She paused, incredibly touched, and then burst into tears.

"Honey? That was a compliment." He sounded confused and slightly worried but she noticed he didn't stop his fingertips over her clit.

"I know. I'm not usually like this. I...what you said, it just touched me. It was a lovely thing to say."

Shane couldn't get there fast enough for Sid. He knew the tears and uneven emotions were due to it being so long without the tri-bond. Still, he watched her pull herself together and relief poured through them both.

Increasing the pressure over her clit, he matched the intensity of pulling and rolling fingers at her nipple. Moaning, her head dropped forward and she began to grind herself against his fingers as she sped up her pace on his cock.

"Oh, it's like that, is it?"

"Show me what you got," she panted.

And he did, gently squeezing her clit over and over between thumb and forefinger. "Come on, hot stuff, show me what your cunt feels like when it comes around my cock."

She moved so that she was directly above him, levering back on his cock instead of sitting astride him. Over and over she slammed her body back against him. He wasn't going to last much longer, but neither was she.

He reared up and bit her then, where neck meets shoulder, and pushed her into climax. Which tipped him over right with her. Blinding waves of pleasure shot through him and through their link he felt her climax as well. Ricocheting back and forth between them, their united orgasm went on and on until he was sure he couldn't take another second of it.

Finally she fell to the side, his cock still inside her body.

"I win," she mumbled.

"Hey! I won. You came first." He brushed the hair out of her face.

"Exactly. I won."

They lay there, hands all over the other, legs tangled, for some time. No talking, just taking simple pleasure in the other's presence.

The phone in the room rang and Sid leaned over her body to answer it. The conversation was short and Layla got out of bed to clean up a bit. When she came back he'd hung up.

"That was Shane. He'll be here in a few minutes."

She sat with a sigh. He smiled when he noted she was wearing his robe. "Okay."

"I know you're upset about all of this. I wish it could be slow. So you could get used to the idea of being with me."

"It's not so much being with you. I *like* being with you. Look," she stood up, needing to move while she worked through it all, "it's about the suddenness and then this whole tri-bond thing."

"You think it's easy for me? I have a life too, Layla!"

Her first response died as she clenched her teeth. She wanted to yell at him but it wasn't fair. "I know you do, Sid."

His anger drained from him as he saw her rein her impatience back. Getting up and going to her, he pulled her tight against his body. Her arms encircled his waist and she put her head on his chest.

"We'll make it work. I actually really do love it up here. And I've got family in the Northwest obviously."

"After we complete the tri-bond, you need to check out of this hotel and move into my condo. We'll start looking for something with studio space for you soon. We need to move forward to the next stage of our life together."

Relief. Relief that they would make it work flooded him. Now that she accepted it, he could revel in finding his mate. The thing that werewolves wait so long for had happened.

And his mate was beautiful and strong and smart. It would be all right.

"Good. I hate sleeping in hotels. The last two nights, knowing you were out there but I couldn't find you, drove me crazy."

A knock sounded on the door and Layla stiffened.

"Hold on, honey. Shane's a good person. I wouldn't trust your tri-bond to just anyone." Sid went to the door and let his cousin in.

It wasn't like Layla could complain. Shane was tall and broad and shared the same black hair that Sid and Adam had.

Without preamble he approached her and hugged her, kissing each cheek. "Welcome to our family, Layla. I'm honored to serve as your Anchor."

Layla blushed like crazy. "Thank you, Shane."

Sid watched her, saw how uncomfortable she was. "I have an idea. Honey, I can tell you're really nervous about this whole thing. I don't want it to be some stilted, horrible experience. I don't want you to feel embarrassed about liking what Shane is doing. You should enjoy it."

She narrowed her eyes at him. "Okay. So what's your idea?"

He turned and rustled around in his suitcase and came back with a long silk handkerchief. "My mother. She has a thing about handkerchiefs. This one is long enough. She refers to them as 'werewolf size'."

"Long enough for what?" Her voice went up an octave as he approached. Shane just watched his cousin with interested eyes.

Sid chuckled. "To blindfold you. That way you can enjoy yourself without guilt. You won't have to worry about who is touching you where and how to respond. You just have to feel and enjoy." And he wouldn't have to watch her eyes meet another man's as he made her come either. He held the red handkerchief up. "What do you say?"

"That's a great idea, Sid!" Shane grinned. "Layla, would this work for you? I know it's not easy. I'm a stranger and heck, Sid's not much more than one. But I'm standing here making my promise to you to be your Anchor and to step in when and if you need me. In some ways, you'll be my mate too. I want this to be okay for you."

Layla looked at them both, strong male wolves bending over backward to make her feel better about having sex with two of them. She laughed. "Twist my arm. Okay, I'll have sex with two hot werewolves while I'm blindfolded. But I have to give Tia the details. She'll kill me if I don't."

Sid started for a moment and then rolled his eyes. "Okay. You ready?" Layla nodded and he moved to her and kissed her softly. "I don't know if you're ready to hear this yet or not, but I love you."

She gulped air and nodded. "Ready or not, it's still true. I love you too."

He tied the kerchief around her head, not too tight but snug enough it wouldn't slip off and no light got in.

Layla's skin suddenly felt a hundred times more sensitive. She could smell both men and hear the rustle of clothes being removed. And then the brush of fingertips as her robe was slipped from her body.

A hand at her shoulder and lower back guided her back in the direction of the bed. Suddenly, lips brushed over the back of her neck as hands slid up her stomach. Most likely, she would have felt odd about reacting depending on who was doing what if she'd seen who was touching her. But with the blindfold, she was free to just accept the touches and relax.

A soft sigh slid from her lips and Sid murmured, "Let's get you on the bed, honey."

Two sets of hands helped her onto the bed and onto her back. It was a bit disorienting to feel things and not see them coming. With the sense of sight gone, all she had to do was feel. Feel the warm swirl of a tongue through her navel and down through the crease where her thigh met her body. She'd wanted to reach out and touch a few times but when she'd tried to move her hand, Sid had taken her wrists and put them above her head, saying, "If you touch us, you'll know who's doing what. Let it be a mystery."

So she'd left her hands above her head and lay there as mouths and hands began to caress and touch her everywhere. Her foot was lifted and strong hands kneaded, thumbs sliding over her instep. Then a mouth laid openmouthed kisses over her ankle and the very erotic spot between her ankle and the back of her heel.

Shudders wracked her body then at the intensity of feeling. Strong hands moved up her calves, massaging and caressing. She'd fallen under the hypnotic feel of that when lips closed over her left nipple.

With a gasp, she arched and both men chuckled. If she'd really paid attention she'd have been able to figure out whose mouth was on her nipple by the laugh, but she left it all alone, falling back into the maelstrom of building pleasure.

Lips drew on her nipple in a wet suck and then nibbled, over and over again. Her breath began to come short and her hips churned absently. Until the caressing hands on her thighs found her pussy and fingertips trailed their way through the wet furls of her cunt.

Then a mouth on her for long moments, eating her like there was no tomorrow. Broad, wet licks, hungry dips into her gate with a tongue. Fucking her with it. With her eyes covered, the intensity of feeling was much greater and she was quickly on her way to another climax.

But two sets of hands turned her over and she found herself on hands and knees, ass high in the air. Excitement roared through her at being handled like that. She'd never been blindfolded before and she made it a point to remember to ask Sid to try it again with her sometime, when they were alone.

Someone moved so that he lay beneath her, his cock at the level of her mouth. Her legs were spread to either side of his legs and the other man settled in behind her, mouth on her pussy that way, fingers holding her open to his hungry licks and nibbles.

A cock tapped her lips and she took it into her mouth. She realized it was Sid beneath her at that moment but it didn't freak her out. She felt safe and secure as well as desired like a goddess with these two men.

A thumb, wet with her honey, pressed into her ass. She gasped at the invasion of it and the taboo of that part of her being breached. Moments later, teeth grazed over her clit and climax consumed her. A deep, guttural cry came from her lips, around Sid's cock.

Sid groaned beneath her and began to roll his hips, thrusting into her mouth.

And suddenly a cock, much wider than Sid's, pressed into her pussy. Hands held her hips in place as he continued to push into her until she felt his groin and the soft slap of his balls against her mound.

He waited there for a moment while Sid continued to stroke into her mouth gently but surely. When the thrusting into her cunt started again, it quickly found rhythm with Sid.

In and out of her mouth, in and out of her pussy. Her body held in place as these two men sought their pleasure. As both had given it to her. The tri-bond wasn't a scary thing at all anymore but something deeply special and important. Shane was pledging himself to her with his body and with his bond. Sid loved her enough to open their relationship up and allow this third person to create the stability she needed. It was beautiful.

Sid's hands, long-fingered and graceful, cradled her skull as he rode her mouth. With his body spread out underneath her, she felt as if it were *him* that served as an Anchor. The emotions of the bond swirled through her, dark and light, but they weren't confusing and terrifying anymore, they were enormous but wonderful and she opened herself to them, knowing she wouldn't drown because neither of these men would allow it.

And things felt *right*. After the confusion of having her carefully made plans totally fall apart, the rightness of the bond and her connection to the man beneath her body clicked into place and she knew without a doubt that they would make it work because it was meant to. Corner office at work and with this wolf at her side at home, she'd continue on a path she could feel proud of achieving. She could still be her own person within something larger than that. She could be a Warden and still be Layla. She could be Sid's wife and mate and still be Layla. She could be a successful businesswoman and still be Layla.

That revelation seemed so totally simple, even as it had eluded her for twenty-five years.

"Oh, honey," Sid murmured, pleasure tingeing his voice. He'd felt her emotions through their bond and then her satisfaction and resolution. She could feel his joy at that.

Moments later, Sid's hands in her hair tightened as he came with a long groan. Her hands cupped his balls and fingertips pressed into that sensitive spot just behind them. His taste flooded her, consumed her senses.

After he finished, she kissed his softening cock and laid her head on his thigh, arching her back as Shane continued to stroke into her pussy.

The broad girth of him filled her in a different way than Sid did. Stretched her. Sid's hands moved to her shoulders, pushing her back into Shane's thrusts. Shane reached around and pressed two fingers into her mouth, wetting them, and moved them to her clit.

She wasn't sure she could take more but his touch was just the right amount of pressure, his thrusts into her giving the friction against his touch rather than his fingers doing it.

"Come around his cock, Layla," Sid whispered in a hoarse voice. "He'll only taste you this once, let him feel how good it is."

With a deep cry, Layla began to come again, this orgasm a deep, muscle-wrenching climax laced with emotion as well as physical pleasure.

She heard Shane's stuttered curse behind her and his thrusts got harder and deeper as he fucked into her body with ferocity.

Her nipples brushed over the wiry hair on Sid's thighs with each stroke Shane made into her. Holding on, her fingers dug into Sid's hips as Shane's cock jerked and began to pulse with his orgasm.

And when his semen began to fill her, the cacophony of the lack of the anchor bond that she'd been managing, silenced. A moment of disorientation and then it all clicked into place. She felt the fullness of her connection with Sid but also that small part that was bonded with Shane.

Gently, they helped her down to the bed and she reached up and took the blindfold off. Craning her neck, she looked up at Sid and smiled as he leaned down to kiss her. Getting to her knees, she moved to Shane and hugged him, brushing her lips over his briefly.

"Thank you both."

Sid reached over and handed her the robe, which she put on, and Shane chuckled. "Layla, it wasn't a chore by any stretch of the imagination."

Sid stood and shook his cousin's hand. "Thank you, Shane."

Shane nodded at his cousin. "I'm going to take a shower and then why don't we get all your stuff moved to Layla's. Unless you want me to go right away?"

Layla shook her head. "No. I'd like to get to know you better. Plus, I'd like for you both to meet my family. They're going to be mad enough that I did all of this without telling them, you two can protect me."

"Oh great. That's the way to start off as a son-in-law!"

"No, they'll be mad at me. But we should take Tia over there too. I need to thank her for helping you to find me and for telling me off when I needed it."

After they'd given up the hotel room to Shane and moved Sid's stuff to her condo, they picked up Tia and headed out to Cade and Lex's house for a family dinner Layla had hastily arranged.

As predicted, her family was angry she'd waited so long for the tri-bond but they all seemed to really like Sid, especially fourteen-year-old Tracy, who wouldn't stop talking about tattoos and piercings.

Epilogue
Ten Years Later

ဢ

Layla watched as her children played in a now-mated, twenty-four-year-old Tracy's yard. Sid and her brothers and brothers-in-law ran around with the kids and a wildly barking three-legged dog.

"Isn't it funny how this fate thing works?" Layla murmured.

"Yeah. We all lucked out in a big way, dontcha think?" Lex's mate Nina watched him hungrily. Layla was sure she wore the same look whenever she watched Sid. The desire for him hadn't waned one bit in ten years.

"And to think you didn't want him at first!" Tracy laughed as Sid allowed the kids and dog to tackle him.

"I wanted him from the first time I laid eyes on him. My body knew exactly what needed to happen. My wolf knew. It was my brain that was reluctant."

"Well, two kids, ten years and a minivan later, you're the happiest werewolf soccer mom I know."

Layla threw her head back and laughed. Sid heard it and turned. Heat flared between them as their gazes locked. Thank goodness all parts of her were now on the same page. She'd want Sid Rosario until the day she ceased to draw breath.

Also by Lauren Dane

୬

About the Author

Lauren Dane been writing stories since she was able to use a pencil, and before that she used to tell them to people. Of course, she still talks nonstop, but now she decided to try and make a go of being a writer. And so here she is. She still loves to write, and through wonderful fate and good fortune, she's able to share what she writes with others now. It's a wonderful life!

The basics: She's a mom, a partner, a best friend and a daughter. Living in the rainy but beautiful Pacific Northwest, she spends her late evenings writing like a fiend when she finally wrestles all of her kids to bed.

Lauren welcomes comments from readers. You can find her website and email address on her author bio page at www.ellorascave.com.

Tell Us What You Think

We appreciate hearing reader opinions about our books. You can email us at Comments@EllorasCave.com.

SPIRIT OF THE PRYDE
TJ Michaels

ഔ

Trademarks Acknowledgement

§

The author acknowledges the trademarked status and trademark owners of the following wordmarks mentioned in this work of fiction:

Hummer: General Motors Corporation

Chapter One

ഇ

Neesia glanced back and rolled her eyes up to the rain-clouded sky with a groan. Pinning her younger sisters with a hard glare, she growled right into their minds. They were obviously more occupied with their trip to New York tomorrow rather than the possibility of getting their asses pounded in a fight tonight.

Kotara, Koreas, pay attention. Get your heads into this hunt or I'll skin your backsides when we get back to the house!

Sorry, Neesia, they demurred, their words as identical as their looks. Eyes downcast and unmistakably sheepish, the two youngest Pryde twins quietly caught up with their oldest sister.

Hey, Niah called, *I've got his scent.*

Stay put. We're on the way. Neesia moved swiftly toward the rolling hill a half-mile from where she and the younglings hid in the brush. Without a word, Kotara and Koreas trailed along, headed toward Niah who was out scouting ahead.

Niah motioned to the spot where the old, almost gagging scent was strongest. *The scent is strange. I've never smelled anything like it.*

Kotara eased forward, eyeing the grass cautiously. There was no blood, but something had definitely been here. Dipping her head, she took a whiff and jerked her head back in disgust. *Definitely an animal, but what kind, I have no idea. Whatever it is, it's rank. It reminds me of rabid Were.*

And, Niah added, *the scent came from the Clarks' ranch onto ours, then trails off to the east.*

What the hell? Neesia cocked her head in question.

Yeah, my thoughts exactly, grumbled Niah.

This mystery got stranger by the day. Mutilated buffalo carcasses on Pryde lands? And someone or something brought the damned things onto their land, half eaten, and left them to rot. This one was a mass of stinking, slimy gore, partially hidden under a thick bush that did nothing to keep it out of the early spring rains.

Neesia looked toward her sister, still stalking silently through the high brush. Ears pricked forward, a low growl emanated from her chest. Niah's edginess was almost tangible. Nervous energy coursed through their twin bond. If Niah was rattled, that was really saying something. The woman was all logic and reasoning. If it couldn't be parsed or dissected on her computer, it didn't exist and was easily dismissed. But there was no mistaking the flash of concern pulsing through their psychic connection. Niah was worried.

A setup, Niah?

It's beginning to look that way, sis.

Neesia sent comforting thoughts along the special bond shared with her twin and spoke privately to her. *Don't worry, Niah. It'll be all right. Let's just do what we do best. Hunt.* The two sisters peered into each other's amber eyes with silent agreement.

Okay, ladies, Neesia called to all her siblings, *let's catch this bastard so we can get on with more important things.*

Together, their locations strategically chosen, four African lionesses stalked out into the Wyoming brush.

* * * * *

Damn. Just when he thought he was actually going to get a vacation, the emergency beacon on his secure cell phone lit up. What now? He'd just closed his last case, was packed and ready to head to the coast for some well-earned relaxation. Well, if the little red light was any indication, he wasn't headed anywhere anytime soon.

"DiCaplis!"

Damn, his captain had signaled only moments ago. For her to make it down six floors and to his desk so quickly meant trouble. And lots of it.

"Yeah, Cap," Jason replied, packing equipment into his gear bag. Laptop, secure wireless network cards, extra USB storage, mini video cams...

"I want you in my office in ten minutes. Better yet, come with me right now. Leave the rest of your packing for later."

Boy, was *she* in a foul mood. Standing at five-foot-nothing, her long black hair pulled back into a severe knot emphasized the blaze in her deep gray eyes. The woman was a formidable shifter, a good leader, and all of her agents respected her. Without a word, he followed behind her small frame, holding his questions. Once behind her soundproof office doors, the briefing began.

"Cap, what's going on? I'm scheduled for vacation starting in, uh," he looked down at his watch, "about five minutes from now. What's with the emergency beacon?"

"I know, DiCaplis, but this is urgent and it can't wait. When we're done talking, go home, pack fast and sleep faster. You're to be at this address at five o'clock tomorrow morning, ready to work."

Jason took the little piece of paper from Captain Johns. His eyes narrowed with a tilt of his head. What the hell?

"Cap, this is the private airstrip where all the bigwigs keep their private jets. What the hell am I supposed to do there?"

"I'll answer your questions after the briefing. Now sit your ass down and don't say a word. Don't breathe until I'm done."

He snapped his mouth shut with a glare. But he sat.

"Look at these pictures and tell me what you think," Captain Johns said, switching off the light. A large screen lowered silently from the ceiling and was immediately filled with the most gruesome, sadistic pictures Jason had ever seen. Clamping his lips together, he bit the inside of his cheek and fought the urge to blow chunks.

"Well?" Johns pushed, lips sternly set and eyes lit with anger. Jason took a deep breath and applied his skills at deduction and observation to the photos on the screen.

"Buffalo, slaughtered by a large animal. First guess would be a mountain lion, but the claw marks are too deep, meaning the wounds were caused by something larger. The bite marks are typical of a larger cat, a fully grown lion perhaps." Or a Were. But there was no way in hell he would say so. Not without proof.

"Not bad, DiCaplis. The carcass was found on the lands belonging to Pryde Ranch, but the buffalo is from a neighboring spread. It was hidden, but not well enough to keep from being spotted."

"Who found the carcass?"

"Actually, this is the third. The first two animals were reported lost by the owners, neighbors of the Prydes. The local sheriff found them. The Prydes found the third, but didn't report it to local law enforcement. We found out anyway. We think it's a rogue."

"You really think a shifter or a Were is responsible? Can we be sure it wasn't these Pryde people?"

"The Prydes are two sisters who own a seventy-thousand acre spread in Wyoming. In addition to running a huge estate, they're professionals in their chosen fields of science and technology. They're also bounty hunters."

Jason's eyebrows rose at that little piece of information. "Bounty hunters?"

"Yes, DiCaplis, bounty hunters. For us."

"What?" Jason exploded out of his chair and paced furiously in front of his superior. "We've stooped to using humans?" he thundered. How dare they endanger the very people they were supposed to protect! Humans shouldn't have a clue about the existence of shifters and Weres. The Shifter and Weres Armed Tactics, S.W.A.T.'s, sole purpose was to protect humans from rogues, and protect themselves from discovery.

"Sit. Down. DiCaplis." When he didn't immediately comply, the sparkle and flash in her silver eyes that warned of an impending shift made him sit. After all, the captain was no punk bitch.

"Look, DiCaplis, you're the best agent we have. You also have the highest clearance. No one, and I mean no one, is to know the Prydes work for us from time to time. And the Prydes are not to know you work with us at all. Understood?"

At his stiff nod, she held out two black-and-white photos. He practically snatched them from her fingers and froze.

"The first picture is the young lady you'll meet tomorrow. Her name is Neesia Pryde. Twenty-nine years old. Five-foot-eleven. A hundred eighty-five pounds of lethal genius. The technical brain of the two."

A soft whistle left Jason's lips. Wow, what a beauty! Eyes riveted to the small picture, he almost missed the rest of the briefing.

"Neesia is the oldest. Degree in business management and a Master's in marketing. She runs the ranch and does most of her technical consulting from there. The second picture is her younger sister, Kotara, a veterinary scientist and biochemist. She engineered the cure for FIV, a disease similar to HIV but only affects felines and is usually fatal to domestic cats. Right now, she's out of town at a biotech conference in New York."

"So, what do you think this means, Cap?" Jason asked tightly, turning away from the gore in front of him. He'd never seen anything so disgusting.

"What I think, Agent DiCaplis, is you're going to Pryde Ranch and find the rogue that did this."

After the briefing, Jason DiCaplis walked out of S.W.A.T. headquarters shaking his head over this turn of events. Instead of a relaxing vacation, he was walking into the possibility of losing his head on a Were hunt. If he didn't love his job so much, he would have almost been disappointed.

Chapter Two

80

The land below took Jason's breath away as the pilot pointed out the beginning of Pryde lands. When the jet landed, he had yet to see the boundary marking the end. He'd never seen such beautifully wide-open spaces. The place seemed to go on forever. The land was green with trees, plenty of scrub and grasses that swayed with the wind. The Medicine Bow River wound its way through the property and sparkled under the morning sun as if it the fast-running waters were full of diamonds.

The second they touched down on the private airstrip, he popped the hatch and found a set of jetway stairs already rolling toward the opening.

At the bottom of those stairs stood a goddess.

"Hi, I'm Neesia Pryde. Thanks for bringing this equipment on such short notice."

The woman's voice flowed over him like rich chocolate. The sweet confection was obviously named after her beautiful cinnamon skin, which was clearly visible, compliments of a formfitting white tank top. She was dark, velvety and surely delicious. The thought of tasting her made Jason's tongue dance around in his mouth until he snapped it closed. Lips, full and ripe, had him swallowing hard. And the golden hue of her eyes was simply arresting, like little orbs of the purest honey. The woman was, in a word, fine as hell. Well, that was three words, but it summed her up pretty well.

But judging from Neesia Pryde's strong and fit physique, she'd probably deck him if he stepped up and started licking the side of her neck. With a mental shake, he reminded himself that he was here to do a job.

"Mr. DiCaplis, right?" she asked, probably wondering if he was some kind of dimwit, staring at her for at least thirty seconds without a word.

"Uh, yes, hi. Sorry, I'm not usually up at dawn and I'm a bit slow this morning," he said with a bright smile. He extended his hand, noticing her strength as she firmly pumped it up and down. It had been a long time since he'd been with a woman. Most of the ones he came across were simpering annoyances. But Neesia seemed far from being such a woman. Damn, he would love to get to know her. And since he wasn't investigating Neesia, there was nothing unethical about tempting the temptress, right?

By the way, had the gods invented blue jeans? Hers fit like a dream. The light blue fabric accentuated a trim waist and a firm, wide ass tapering down to endless legs. Damn, had he ever seen such a nice ass? Physically restraining himself, he practically shook with the urge to reach out and touch. Her rich, sinful voice snapped him out of his musings.

"Broglio here will help you unload the crates," she said, motioning to an older, salt-and-pepper-haired man sitting on a small forklift. She held out her hand and jangled something on the end of her long fingers. He looked down at her hand and gulped.

Snap out of it, idiot. Hell, he was practically slobbering on himself, imagining the feel of those fingers. Mentally slapping himself in the back of the neck, he focused on her words and tried not to look at the yummy lips speaking them. If he kept this up, he'd blow his cover. Among other things.

"Here are the keys to the jeep over there," she said, nodding her head toward a sporty-looking four-wheeler parked off to the side. "Just tell Broglio which crates you want brought up to the house and he'll help you get them into the jeep. There's plenty of storage space, but you don't have to take it all up right now. Load whatever you don't immediately need on the flatbed over there and bring it up to the house later. All right with you?"

"Sure, thanks." She turned to walk away and his mind scrambled for something to say, anything to keep her from leaving. What the hell was wrong with him? Certainly he couldn't be this hard up for a woman? Hell, who was he fooling? This was a terrible time for his cock to remind him how horny he was.

"Oh, I forgot," she said as she stopped and turned to pin him with her light, tawny stare. Jason's heart practically beat out of his chest. "All the wiring and setup for the new surveillance system is going to take a couple of weeks. We told your employer it would be best if you stayed here. Just follow Broglio back to the main house and we'll get you settled, all right?"

"Uh, yeah. Sure. Thanks," Jason mumbled, sounding like some goofy schoolboy as he dragged his eyes away from her smile. And those lips. Tempting was such an inadequate word.

"We'll start tomorrow with the grounds around the house, then move out onto the ranch. A schematic is in the jeep for you to study."

Waving at the captain who'd come out of the cockpit to help unload the cargo, she called out as she headed back to her own vehicle.

"Thanks for flying on such short notice, Harry! Come up to the house and get a bite to eat before you take off!"

The pilot grinned like a loon and bounded down the stairs. "Come on, boys, let's put our backs into it."

But Jason knew the man's eagerness to get the unloading done had more to do with Neesia's invitation to visit the house rather than a desire to get back in the air.

He couldn't blame the man one bit.

* * * * *

Broglio had been good company and a fountain of information. In fabulous shape at fifty years old, he'd known the Prydes since the girls were children. Jason put his subtle interrogation skills to work and learned quite a bit about the family. Originally from East Africa, Neesia's parents had been killed as innocent bystanders during an uprising in a neighboring village. Neesia and her sister were brought to the States as toddlers and brought up by their grandmother. Working together, the two had earned a sizeable fortune for themselves. Good, solid educations, innovative ideas and hard work had paid off big time. The huge estate he'd spent part of the day wandering around was proof of that.

Late that afternoon, they finally made it up to the house, which turned out to be more of a mansion-sized rustic lodge. They parked the jeep in the eight-car garage, and Broglio showed him up to his room, then back downstairs for dinner.

When they passed the empty formal dining area, Jason stopped to admire the room. The design was elegant and tasteful. One entire wall was made up of screened windows that allowed the orange glow of the setting sun to fill the room. A lacquered white pine table for eight sat in the center, with little cushioned benches off to the side against the opposite wall.

"This way," Broglio said. "Unless the whole family is here, we usually eat in the kitchen. If you can call it that."

Whole family? Jason pondered the man's words until they walked into an all white and stainless steel room almost as big as his whole apartment. This was a kitchen? It looked more like chef heaven.

"Neesia loves to cook. She's the head of the family and makes sure everyone is well fed," Broglio said with a proud smile.

Hmm? Strange way to describe a family with only two women in it. Too hungry to pursue the issue, Jason followed the older man past the stove, several industrial-sized refrigerator-freezers, a tile-topped gourmet block large enough to butcher a whole cow, and over to a big bay window.

On top of a quaint country-style table sat a feast

presented so nicely, he almost hated to eat it.

There were bowls of steaming white rice, a platter of grilled tilapia fish with a light sweet sauce, a big bowl of fresh greens sprinkled with a light ginger vinaigrette, and a small crock of some kind of clear soup.

Famished, his stomach was immensely grateful as he practically inhaled the meal. With every bite of the delicious Japanese-style fare, he imagined Neesia's exotically beautiful face and her lithe but bountiful body laid out in front of him. During dessert, Jason wondered if she was as succulently sweet as the light lemon cake covered with lemon curd and fresh strawberries she'd so thoughtfully left for them.

His lust was beyond misplaced, but his cock didn't care. Here to solve the mystery of possible rogue Were attacks, the more he thought on how nicely her full breasts filled out the tank top she'd been wearing earlier, the more his blood pounded in his ears. He had to see her.

"Broglio, where do you think Ms. Pryde is? Does she always skip dinner?"

"No, the family eats early. Ms. Neesia usually relaxes in the library before she heads up to bed," the older man answered, a knowing, protective look in his eye.

"Which way is the library?" Jason asked, his expression bland as he gathered his dishes and headed to the sink.

Moments later, he walked into a huge, cozy room practically filled to the ceiling with books. He didn't see a single one. Instead, he zeroed in on his target. Neesia.

* * * * *

Good lord above! Every techno-weenie she'd ever met, with the exception of her twin, was a total nerd. But Jason was a hunk and a half with a sexy voice and even sexier body. And so tall! Would she have to get up on her tiptoes to wrap her arms around his neck? Whoa, where'd that come from? She wasn't supposed to wrap anything around him. The man was here to do a job. And she was supposed to help him? Not good.

"Look, Niah," she hissed into the phone. "If I pretend to be you for more than ten minutes, I'll blow it. You know how important this is. You were supposed to be back yesterday, damn it. You knew this shipment was coming in."

God, she was a wreck. Always able to play a cool and logical Niah, but not this time. Something about this Jason person had her usually level head giddy and nervous all at once.

"Neesia, will you take a second to breathe? It's not my fault the fugitive gave me a hard time."

"But it's all wrapped up, right?" Neesia asked anxiously, hating when any of her sisters went after a bounty alone.

"Yep, wrapped up and tied with a bow. He's in S.W.A.T. custody."

"Good, now hurry up and get here so you can help Jason. He was told we'd help get all the surveillance equipment up and running. Won't he think it's odd when I can't tell one damned wire from another?"

"Oh, relax, will you? I'm on my way. Is something else going on? It's not like you to be so wound up, Necie."

"No, everything is fine. And no other carcasses have turned up. Let's hope it stays that way."

"Good. So the equipment guy's name is Jason? What does he look like?"

How was Neesia supposed to answer the question? How about handsome beyond words with dark, golden hair, hazel eyes, the wide-chested body of a god, and a tight ass?

Instead she said flatly, "He's tall, about six-foot-six, brown hair, hazel eyes. Why?"

"Since you and I can't be seen together, I'll be meeting him by myself when I get home. It wouldn't do for me not to know him since you two have met," Niah said around a yawn.

Thank goodness one of them had some sense right now.

"Look, Necie, I've gotta run. Harry just got here to fly me home. I'll be in sometime tonight. Don't wait up, all right?"

"Fine, just hurry up," Neesia ground out and quickly hung up the phone as her keen ears picked up footsteps crossing the hardwood floor in the hallway. Seconds later Jason strode into the library.

She looked up from her reclined position on one of several plush loveseats and painted on a thin smile. Her tongue stuck to the roof of her mouth. The man was all buffed perfection, and eyeing her like a piece of candy. Oh lord, she should really make a run for it! Damn it! Too late.

"Hi, Jason. Find everything all right?"

"Definitely."

Hold the door! Was he stalking her? In nothing but the tight tee shirt and jeans he'd worn off the plane, she could see every movement of muscle. He looked like a predator if she'd ever seen one.

Placing her book on the coffee table, she sat up and tried to appear calm. "How was dinner? Everything okay?"

"More than okay. It was all...quite delicious."

The determined look in his twinkling eyes made her insides quiver. A parched throat kept a reply from leaving her mouth as she tried to figure out what to do with her hands. What the hell was wrong with her? Where was the tough, down to earth and down to business, Neesia?

Garnering her strength, she commanded her stomach to stop flopping all over the place. Just as she swung her feet to the floor to get the hell out of there, her way was blocked by the devastatingly handsome, tawny-haired man. His expression brought to mind something she'd seen on the Discovery Channel about hunters and prey.

"Jason, I-I, uh." Now this was new. Neesia at a loss for words? The world must be ending any minute now.

"Neesia, there's something I need," his voice was deep, stirring.

"What's that?" she said on an unsteady breath.

The next thing she knew the man was on his knees in front of the loveseat, kissing her like an old lover who'd been away too long. Raising her hands to push him away, her fingers sent a message to her brain that the firm set of shoulders under her hands felt good. The play of solid muscle as he wrapped her securely in his arms and leaned her back against the cushions was even better.

His lips were firm, his kiss gentle yet hungry. And he tasted like berries and cream. She closed her eyes, took in the feel of his delicious mouth moving over hers, and reveled in the blaze of hot ice his touch created in the hollow of her womb. Decadent and devastating all at once, taking everything she had, then reaching inside her soul for more.

He moaned into her mouth, obviously enjoying the contact as much as she. But when he broke it off so his hot lips could travel along her jaw and nip at the sensitive skin just below her ear, Neesia's world spun as her womb clenched wildly.

Oh, god, it was too much. But why? There was no way she could be this far gone over someone she'd just met. Unless she decided to become a liar, there was no denying the strong attraction between them. But she could—no, *must*—deny the sudden need.

Gently, but with firm resolve...oh who the hell was she kidding? Her resolve wasn't any firmer than week-old pudding, but she managed to push against his oh-so-nicely built chest to get his attention.

"What?" he asked, somewhat dazed.

"Jason." Breathless? Since when did she do breathless? "I think I'll go up to bed now. Alone." He backed off and gave her some room.

"What's wrong?"

"I don't usually get intimate with men I don't know. It's just not something I do. I'm sorry."

"Well, precious, I'm very interested in getting to know you." He brushed his lips across hers again, this time gently, as if he wanted to ease her. A single finger stroked just underneath her jaw, teasing the area near her ear. "I'm going to take a shower and catch up on some work. I'll be back down in about an hour. Maybe we can talk?"

She didn't trust her voice to answer. First off, she had no idea what to say. Second, even if she did, the zing his touch produced from playing near her ear destroyed her ability to think. The moment his head dipped for another kiss, Neesia scrambled from the loveseat and practically ran out of the room.

She couldn't afford to get mixed up with a man right now. Especially a man like Jason—too virile, too male, too much! The man wore no façade, was as real as the day was long, and completely honest about wanting her.

And this strange zing between them was just…what?

It didn't matter. She was the oldest female of her family and responsible for her siblings. It was up to her to protect her sisters. She couldn't afford to have anyone uncover their secrets. Besides, what kind of example would she be if she went around humping every beautiful, towheaded hunk that came out to their property? Especially in the middle of trying to figure out who was setting them up for killing off the neighboring herds.

So no matter how much he filled her thoughts and made her body ache and hum, the pride came first. Well, a cold shower first, then the pride.

Chapter Three

හ

It was so good to be home. Niah had been positively relieved when Harry, after one of Neesia's home-cooked meals, of course, had flown directly to Las Vegas, picked her up, and brought her home. The flight was, thankfully, uneventful after such a long day spent chasing down a nasty rogue Were for S.W.A.T.

From their teens, all four Prydes had been trained in military tactics at the express request of their grandmother. She'd been careful when risking their exposure to S.W.A.T., making sure only two of them were seen at any given time, and only by those responsible for the most covert activities. So far, it had been a decent trade-off. The fact that S.W.A.T. kept their very existence a secret, even within their own organization, allowed them to live as normal "humans". In exchange, the Prydes took down some of the most lethal and dangerous outlaws in the shifter and Were communities.

Niah sighed and slipped further under the water in the deep tub, and winced at the burning sting of the hot scented water over her skin. Lord, she was tired. Glad the hunt was over, now she could do something she enjoyed—installing the new surveillance equipment around the property. Hopefully it would help catch the bastard who had it out for them, or at least let them get a good look at it, whatever *it* was.

After a delicious soak, she dunked her head beneath the suds and washed it clean, loving the squeaky-clean feel after the sweat and dirt were washed away.

This hunt had been particularly nasty. She'd chased that damn Were across California and up through the Sierra Nevada mountains, dodging humans and shifters alike. The whole episode reminded her of a song they used to sing as children, "Over Hill, Over Dale", and something about dusty trails as Niah kept rolling along.

Finally pinning him down near Las Vegas, she'd pulled her favorite weapon, one she'd designed herself—a gas-compressed projectile weapon that fired tranquilizer rounds from an electronic crossbow. Once the Were was secured, she called in the coordinates for S.W.A.T. to pick him up, erased all traces of her presence and disappeared into Sin City. When Harry called her private number and informed her he was at the airport, she'd never been so happy at Neesia's overbearing interference. The woman had sent her a ride home!

Soothed and relaxed by the bath, she dried off with a thick, soft towel. The floor-to-ceiling mirror in her bathroom revealed the source of the stinging along her shoulders and arms—a few bruises and scrapes. Examining the cuts from the earlier hunt, she rubbed her dark skin down with creamy shea butter, noting it was already healing.

She donned a soft, green silk robe, embroidered on the back with the family crest—a fierce lion hunting with his mate at his side. Making her way down to the library, Niah realized she'd never seen nor heard tell of any other lions in the States. No one had. And they were careful to keep it that way. Prolific, deadly and feared for their tendency to completely dominate and expand their territories, news of four strong African lionesses in the States would be cause for alarm. Because of that, even S.W.A.T. wasn't aware of all their secrets.

Picking up her favorite book, *Grimm's Fairy Tales*, she settled down on one of the many loveseats, and tucked her legs beneath her, wrinkling her nose on a wince when the bruise on her thigh throbbed a bit.

The house was quiet, everyone in bed. Now she could relax and try to figure out why Neesia was so anxious about the man who'd delivered the surveillance equipment. Born a few minutes before her twin, as the oldest, Neesia was the glue of their little family. After Grandma died, she'd kept them together, kept them focused, made them all work and study harder. Thanks to her, they'd become successful in everything they'd put their hands to. For Neesia to be shaken by anyone, especially a man, was really saying something. What had she said his name was again? Jason? Yes, that was it.

Her book closed with a snap as she looked up from her seat through her lashes. What was that smell? It enticed her breathing to quicken, her fingers to tremble. It smelled almost as good as Neesia's homemade cinnamon rolls. Like pure male.

Then he was there, his scent preceding him into the room as he stood in the doorway of the library. Her light amber-brown eyes clashed with his hazel ones and her stomach muscles clenched, and remained tight and hard. My god, he looked like walking candy! Beyond yummy in a loose-fitting tank top, she got more than a glimpse of sculpted pecs and rock-hard shoulders, all covered in golden, tanned skin. His even looser sweatpants did nothing to hide the pole of an erection straining against his groin. Tastefully cut tawny reddish-brown waves graced his head. A strong jaw, with a hint of shadow, made him appear to belong out here in this wild, untamed land near the Rocky Mountains. And damn he was tall, with a heavy frame laden with thick, roped muscle. Good lord, no wonder Neesia didn't want to be alone with him. Men like this stripped away all desire to play nice and just play nasty.

Moving away from the doorframe, he stalked into the room. It was the only way she could think to describe the way he moved. Smooth muscles bunched and released as he made his way toward her, his powerful body a mix of strength and primal grace.

The man was simply overwhelming. An urge as old as time pulled at her typically effortless restraint and overpowered her will. Resisting was impossible. And he hadn't said a word! Geez, he'd walked into the room, took one look at her, and the temperature of her body skyrocketed.

Strange, even with all the fluttering and dancing of her nerves, there was no possessiveness to her body's craving. He didn't feel like...hers. But close, very close indeed.

"I'm glad you changed your mind," he said in a silken deep tone. If her breath came any harder, she'd hyperventilate.

"Changed my mind?" she croaked, not sure what he meant, but not sure she cared.

Standing over her he bent down until he was a breath away and inhaled deeply. "Mmm, you smell good. I'm glad you came back down after your shower. Now, how about that talk?"

"Talk?" Niah said, breathlessly. "What talk?"

"I'm with you, precious. Let's talk later," he groaned and knelt on the floor, pulling her to the edge of the loveseat. Her robe fell open as his wide chest settled between her legs as his fingers dove into her hair to pull her into a wicked kiss. Wow, she'd never had the hair on her little pinky toes singed off before.

Her eyes slipped closed as a large, slightly calloused hand caressed her thigh. Right on top of one of her bruises. Ouch.

He must have felt her stiffen, and let out a frustrated groan when he broke the kiss, leaned back on his knees and gazed at her barely clad thighs.

"What the hell happened to you?" he asked, all care and concern, staring at a big purple and blue oval spread across her upper thigh. A bruise delivered via Were-Asshole-of-the-Month.

"It's just a little bruise. It'll be gone by morning." His gentle massage of the sore spot caused her breaths to come out short and fast as a pleasure-pain sensation traveled up her leg and puddled between her thighs. Oh, what a nice touch.

"Neesia, are you sure?"

Niah cocked her head, locking eyes with his. The man thought she was Neesia? Well, duh! Nobody could tell them apart except their sisters. The man was ready to make love to her because he thought she was someone else? Now why didn't that bother her?

His fingers inched higher up her thigh to stroke the skin right where her short cropped curls began. Instinctively, her hips rolled forward, wanting his caress just a little lower. A single finger dipped into those curls and tickled her plumping lips. Niah's mind went blank. His touch was magnetic. Now, if only he'd kiss her again. "This bruise looks nasty," he said, smoothly. His mouth kicked up into a lopsided, very evil grin as he teased her flesh. "Should I get you some ice, precious? I can—Ooomph!"

With her hands full of his hair, Niah took a split second to revel in how soft and thick it was. Okay, time's up. She slammed her mouth down over his, inhaled the sweet, rich scent of his skin and tasted the sweetness of his tongue.

When he settled more firmly between her thighs, the kiss deepened as he tilted her head back for his ravishing.

Niah did something she'd never felt compelled to do with a male, human or otherwise. She submitted.

When he'd come into the library moments ago, he couldn't have been happier to see the woman of his dreams sitting in the exact spot he'd found her earlier. She seemed astonished to find him standing in front of her. Hadn't she believed him when he'd said he would come back down to talk with her?

The urgency he'd felt when in her presence earlier had eased somewhat, but not completely. There was still an unreasonable urge to have her. And, god help him, once he got a good look at her long, shapely legs, barely covered by the delicious, silky confection that was supposed to be a robe, the last thing he wanted to do was talk. Talking was good. Tasting was better.

Kneeling between her legs, listening to her heart run a

chariot race, caused his pulse to speed up, striving to match hers. But at least this time he had some semblance of control, and took his time exploring her mouth. Tilting her back onto the loveseat, the soft little pants and moans she made as he wrapped his tongue around hers sent a tingling shiver through his body.

Her hair was damp, the coolness of the blacker-than-black strands contrasted wildly with the heat emanating from her skin.

He groaned with loss when she broke the kiss.

"Jason, listen, you don't know me," she panted. But he'd already heard this song earlier, and didn't particularly want to hear it again. With a single finger over her lovely mouth, he peered deeply into her eyes and met a genuinely troubled expression that pulled on his heartstrings. When her lashes lowered, and a deep blush covered the high cheekbones of her lovely face, he stroked her gently across her lips.

"Ssh, just listen to me a minute." At her reluctant nod, he continued. "I know we've just met but I'm drawn to you in a way I've never experienced before."

"I bet you say that to all the girls," she smiled, her tone light and playful while he'd rather have her breathless and needy.

"Actually, I don't say that to all the girls. I'm being totally honest, baby, I want you so bad I can practically feel my cock sinking into that lovely body of yours. I swear I just can't help it." His words ended on a whisper. Each one brought his mouth closer to hers and Jason literally felt when she gave herself up to his care.

The kiss started out gentle enough, a sweet meeting of the mouths, but quickly escalated into a hot give-and-take. She gave and he took.

Breaking away to remove his shirt, he tossed it aside and unashamedly rubbed his chest against her lush breasts. Licking and sucking a path down her throat, he reveled in the tight clench of her fingers digging into the muscles of his back, holding him tight.

She was burning up, skin so hot it practically sizzled the light sheen of sweat popping up over his skin as he tried to control his need. God, his manhood throbbed and his balls were on fire, but something made him back off just a bit, to give her a little bit of time to get used to his touch.

Her beautiful breasts filled his hands. The warm, swollen globes begged for his kiss as he deliberately rasped his thumbs over the tight, puckered nipples. Unable to resist a moment longer, he lowered his head and wrapped his tongue around one and was rewarded with a deep gasp. Her chest rose and fell rapidly. Her taste and texture exploded in his mouth and were permanently imprinted on his senses for all time. She was all cinnamon and chocolate lust as her strong thighs wrapped tighter around his waist. Jason suckled her lovely breasts until her body undulated with each deep pull.

One hand left her lovely mounds and slid over the trembling muscles of her stomach, then down along her hips to tease her there. Her hips rolled wildly and her words were no longer tentative or concerned, but full of desire.

"Oh, your touch is magic, Jason. Please. Touch my pussy."

"I can do better than that, precious. Much better."

Lifting and spreading her lovely thighs until they were draped over his shoulders, Jason leaned forward and inhaled. Mmm, she smelled delicious. Her pussy was allspice and cream, a dewy delicious treat just waiting for him to eat it up. A soft breath over her slick heat had her quivering in his arms.

"Jason, please!"

Never one to keep a lady waiting, with gentle fingers, he spread her open and dove into her cunt, lapping and sucking on her engorged, sensitive lips until she rode his face with abandon. The wild movement of her hips, the erotic steam of her words, and the sweet nectar pouring from her body seemed to reach into his sweats and pulled on his cock until it throbbed painfully.

But he wasn't finished with her. Not by a long shot.

So sexy, he hummed his appreciation while slipping a long finger into her soaking-wet depths.

The woman grabbed a pillow off the loveseat and slammed it down over her mouth as a spine-grabbing shriek left her mouth. And when his tongue left her pussy lips, encircled her clit and sucked firmly, she just kept right on screaming as a firebomb ignited in her womb.

The sound was pure erotic heaven. And the feeling of her tight pussy muscles clamped around his fingers as he worked in her body while she came was beyond divine.

His cock urged him to lose the sweats and take her this instant, but his mind reached back to the concern he'd glimpsed in her eyes earlier. The words touched his heart and he knew there was more to them than what was said.

Tonight would be for her to learn to trust him with her body, her feelings and her needs.

Easing her down from her climax, he stroked her hair, closed her robe and gently kissed her good night.

Besides, he'd already decided he wasn't going anywhere anytime soon.

Chapter Four

ಐ

Six a.m. and the scent of cooking bacon and freshly brewed coffee was delicious enough to get him out of bed. He'd never been an early riser, but he had work to do. A good meal was plenty of incentive to get to it. After a quick shower, dressed in a denim button-down shirt, a pair of black jeans and his favorite work boots, Jason headed downstairs.

The sight of a nearly naked Neesia bending over, half her body inside the fridge as she foraged for something, made his gut clench like someone hit him square in the stomach. He got a good glimpse of strong, long legs where her royal blue robe rode up to just below her tempting backside. It made him smile that her feet were bare.

The wild urgency to take her was back. Shit.

Leaning against the counter directly behind her, he cleared his throat. She kept right on looking for whatever she was after.

"Excuse me?" he called, stuffing his hands in his pocket to keep them off all the cinnamon-colored skin showing.

With her head still in the fridge, she said, "I heard you the first time. Just a minute."

He grinned at the impertinent woman. So she'd heard him, eh? He'd given her a cataclysmic orgasm in the library last night and she was telling him just a minute? Not!

Pushing away from the cabinet, he walked right up behind her, took her by the waist and settled himself behind her, and nestled his rising cock right in the crack of her luscious ass with a not-so-subtle grinding motion.

Biting his tongue to keep from laughing, he watched her

move like greased lightning, bumping her head on one of the shelves trying to get out of that damned refrigerator and away from him.

Eyes wide, she seemed almost shocked that he would do such a thing.

"What the hell are you doing?" she growled at him. Head lowered she watched him like a bull ready to charge. What was wrong with her? Was she suddenly shy now that the sun was up and she stood facing him in the light of day?

"Neesia, why are you shying away from me, baby? Do you regret last night?" he asked calmly, palms up as he walked slowly toward her. After all, he didn't want to make the woman feel threatened if she'd decided during the night that she'd rather not be with him. He'd just have to change her mind.

"Last night?" she queried, at once nervous, then confused, then...knowing? "I mean, about last night. Well, you and me. We, uh, did we?"

Jason's eyes narrowed. He watched her closely, but was unable to keep up with the barrage of emotions crossing her lovely features. And her scent was a little different, like she'd spent the early hours of the morning eating a sweet fruit of some kind. Last night she'd smelled spicier, like rich vanilla and cloves.

"What are you saying? I left such a poor impression you don't remember last night, Neesia?"

"No, it's just that. I didn't. Oh, hell," she said, slapping the butter she'd dug out of the freezer section of the fridge down on the counter so hard, the rock-hard brick broke in two. Damn, remind him never to piss her off.

"Come here, Neesia."

She didn't move. Just stood there frowning, shifting her weight from one foot to the other while a frustrated growl bubbled up from deep in her throat. Was she upset, embarrassed, or what? He couldn't tell, but whatever it was, he wanted — no, *needed* — to comfort her.

"Neesia?" he called her name quietly and moved slowly toward the object of his desire. Holding out a hand to her, Jason released a pent-up breath when she grasped it and went willingly into his arms.

"Jason, I…" she started.

"Sssh, it's all right. Just kiss me." He didn't give her a chance to refuse. Instead, he pulled her into his arms and claimed her lips in a scorching kiss. Moaning at the taste of her — fresh berries and cream — he moved closer, pressing his body intimately against hers.

The response to his nearness affected her as much as it had him. Her arms wrapped around his neck and full firm breasts pressed against his chest as she abandoned herself to the kiss. He could practically feel the round globes swell, burning into his skin through his shirt.

Unable to resist, he slipped his fingers into the neat bun at the nape of her neck and eased the hair tie loose until her hair spilled over his fingers. The soft, black strands were like the most decadent silk. He hadn't noticed it was this long last night.

His free hand strayed down around her ribs to stroke the undersides of a plump breast, weighing and caressing until she squirmed against him, so hot for his touch, she broke the kiss and tilted her head toward the ceiling on a loud moan.

The robe became a puddle on the floor. Jason buried his nose between her breasts, then pulled one taut nipple into his mouth and suckled greedily. She was flame and flood, spicy and sweet. And after he'd tasted her succulent mounds to his heart's content, it was time to feast.

Lifting her by the waist, Jason sat Neesia on top of the gourmet island. He pushed her legs wide, prepared to gorge on the dewy treasure laid out before him. Lowering his head, he buried his nose in that luscious treat. Honey, cream and a hint of spice.

"Wait! Jason, what are you doing?" she shrieked.

"Surely you know, beautiful," he murmured against her clit, coaxing the little bud out of its cowl to play.

"But...oh, dear lord!" she gasped as his tongue laved between the silken folds of her soaked cunt. "What if, oh god! What if somebody comes?"

"It's okay, baby. Broglio is already out unloading crates. There's nobody here but us." Her shyness was endearing, but he couldn't accommodate her. Not today. He felt like a damned satyr, an insatiable, lust-filled male in rut.

"Besides, I can't wait to have you, and the bedroom is too far away." With that he buried his face again, reveled in her scent, her flavor. His lips wrapped around the sensitive bundle of her clit and sent her hurtling toward a blistering climax.

Reveling in the pleasure-pain of her fingers yanking at his hair, Jason knew he was tormenting her, pushing her toward another orgasm before she'd stopped trembling from the first one.

The need to mate with her, to bury his painfully erect cock deep inside her sweetly scented core rode him hard. So hard he shook with it. But her pleasure was imperative. He wanted to drive her beyond absolute mindlessness.

"Jason! Please, I can't take any more." Breathless and pleading, she pulled harder on his hair, trying to yank him away from her sensitized flesh. She'd never experienced such wild abandon. Damn, her toes tingled from the orgasm — correction, multiple orgasms — he'd wrung from her. But she wanted some good, hard cock. Right. Damn. Now!

Ripping his denim shirt from his shoulders, certain she'd find a few of the buttons in the sugar bin later, she couldn't help but gape at the slabs of flexing pecs and rippling abs. So much sun-kissed skin dusted with the lightest brown-sugared downy hair. The fuzz on his chest was as soft as the hair on his head, enticing her fingers to play in it. But the urge passed the second a jean-covered erection pressed against her soaked core, sending a jolt of pure lust streaking up her spine.

"Do you want me, Neesia?" His voice was tight, gritty and sexy, on the verge of losing control. "Tell me you want me, baby."

Her own words sounded just as raw. "Oh, Jason. Yes, I want you."

The jeans hit the floor, and his proud cock jutted up to meet her.

Looking down between their bodies, her nerves fluttered at the sight of his engorged shaft. The veined ridges pulsed in time to the beat of his heart. Huge and imposing, it looked almost angry. Hungry. He positioned the weeping head of his cock at her slick entrance when a familiar presence brushed against her mind. Niah.

Looking out toward the sitting room, she expected to see her sister standing in the doorway. No one was there. What the hell was going on? While she couldn't hear Niah's thoughts, her presence was unmistakably hot and edgy. But why?

Pushing the worry away, she glanced down again, eyes glued to Jason's strong fingers wrapped around his turgid flesh, sliding over the velvet-covered steel, up and down, up and down. The fat head brushed her clit, then paused, threatening to ease inside. Suddenly an unexplainable heat bloomed and grew until every cell of her body was aflame. That monstrous cock was to blame, and she wanted it more than anything she could remember craving in life. Craved it more than a midnight run under the stars. More than the thrill of the hunt. Hell, she wanted Jason more than Belgian chocolate! It was like a yearning in her blood, an unexplainable need flowing under her skin from her head down to her toes. Her hips surged forward, seeking what would satisfy.

But nothing prepared her for the feeling of his wide, hard flesh sliding into her body. It had been years since the last time she'd given herself to a man, and none had been as well endowed as this one. The stretching, burning sensation was quickly replaced by liquid lust. It poured through her aching pussy, across her clenching butt cheeks and down the back of her thighs.

"Keep looking, baby. Look how wet you make my cock," he rasped, moving deeper, then pulling practically free so she could see how she covered him with her juices before easing back inside. "Uhh! Aah! So tight. So wet."

His erotic speech, combined with the sight of him sliding in and out of her sopping core, was the most titillating thing she'd ever experienced. Until she looked up into his face. His eyes burned into hers as the rich gold deepened to a smoky brown. With each stroke, his lips parted on a whoosh of breath. His ripped, solid chest heaved. Packed stomach muscles tightened and rolled like the ocean tide.

"Neesia, god, baby, your pussy feels so good wrapped around my cock."

And he felt more than good filling and taking her. Something primal lurked just below the depths, wanted to break free and revel in her sensuality until she was mad with pleasure. He seemed to instinctively know, sense the wildness, and plowed into her tight depths with firm strokes. Harder. Faster. Deeper. Oh, yes.

Picking up the pace even more, he laid her back on the gourmet block. The tiles should have been chilly against her skin, but did nothing to cool her off.

"Oh, god, Jason! Soooo good. Ooooh!"

Strong fingers dug into her hip and held her still for his ravaging until she screamed with each thrust.

"Ah, yes! More!"

"Your wish is my command," he panted into her ear, taking her with a force that practically raised her body from the countertop island and threatened to leave her undone.

Her thick mass of wavy hair whipped around her head as

141

she panted and thrashed underneath him. His eyes were glued to her little pink tongue as it journeyed across her parted, plump lips. He wanted to suck on those lips. So he did just that and leaned forward to capture her bottom lip like a plump cherry. But it wasn't enough.

Grabbing the nape of her neck in a hard grip, he left her delicious mouth and licked the length of her long neck like a lollypop. Shaking his head, he wondered what the hell had come over him. He'd never been rough while having sex with a woman, but the urge to bury his teeth in this one overwhelmed him.

When her back arched up off the gourmet block as she screamed for him to fuck her harder, he couldn't resist dipping his head and burying his teeth in the soft flesh.

The second his teeth made contact, the honeyed walls of her tight channel fluttered and tightened, milking him, squeezing so tightly, his back bowed forward as he clenched her neck harder, sucking furiously at the flesh there. After long moments, he released her. Looking down at his handiwork, Jason's chest filled with satisfaction. The skin wasn't punctured, but there was a fat, purple hickey on her lovely cocoa skin. *His* skin. *His* mark.

Mine! his mind screamed as he rode her through her orgasm, burying himself in her pretty pussy over and over. The energy gathered inside her body, ready to burst forth and bathe them both. She came again.

The slick, raw heat practically pulled his seed from his balls. He pushed as deep as he could get and threw his head back with a primal roar. One he'd never heard in his own ears before, but would make sure he heard again. With her.

Panting like two over-aerobicized gym rats, Jason laid his head on Neesia's heaving chest trying to catch his breath. Even in his sated state, he couldn't resist pulling an enticing nipple into his mouth and laving it with his tongue.

She tasted so good. God, he wanted to taste her

everywhere. Touch her everywhere. All day. All night. Maybe after he caught whoever was behind the herd killings, he could take her somewhere remote where no one would hear their screams.

Damn, for the first time in his life, he couldn't wait to be done with work so he could make his way to a woman's bed.

Rising up on his elbows, he took in her dreamy, wistful expression. Pride filled his heart, mind and soul—she was well loved and completely satisfied. A lone finger traced one of her perfect black brows as his lips captured hers in a tender kiss.

"That was beyond fantastic," he whispered. A cheeky grin was her answer as she closed her eyes and sighed like a kitty filled with cream. "Well, I guess I'd better get to work. I'll meet you at the garage after I have my breakfast, okay?"

"Mmm-hmm," she purred, letting him help her up off the gourmet block to stand on wobbly legs. Damn, he'd really laid it on her.

"I didn't hurt you, did I, Necie?" he asked quietly, gently pulling her robe up over her shoulders. The silk felt nice against his rough hands, almost as nice as her smooth skin.

"Oh, no, you didn't hurt me. It was wonderful," she said softly, traipsing a finger down his sweaty cheek. "Besides, handsome, I'm not that easy to hurt," she sighed, and walked away.

Completely entranced, he watched the sensual sway of her hips as she made her way across and out of the kitchen and through the sitting room before turning to go up the wide staircase.

All the while, he stood next to the large island in the middle of the kitchen, bare-chested, pants down around his ankles and his cock waving after her.

Chapter Five

ဆ

Energized by his bout of loving with Neesia, Jason flew up the stairs and hit the shower. Changing into a tee shirt, fresh jeans and a light jacket, he grabbed his utility bag full of tools and headed to the garage.

Wow, these Pryde women knew how to pick their vehicles. Standing in the garage, he eyeballed three sport utility vehicles, a military-grade Hummer, the jeep he and Broglio used yesterday and a few luxury cars fit for the stars. For a second, he wondered why they kept their jet at a private airstrip off the property. Surely the garage was big enough for it.

"Hey, handsome."

He turned to watch the woman who'd just screwed him into oblivion walk in the door and across the huge room. And she looked more delectable than she had only half an hour ago. While rummaging through a locked cabinet for the keys to whatever machine they would take out to survey the property, he took the opportunity to eye the fit of her jeans. Bad idea. So he closed his eyes and spoke to his stiffening cock instead.

Stop it, you greedy bastard, he scolded his twitching rod. *Come on, man, you were just knee deep in that pussy and you're horny already? Give it a rest or I'll die from blood loss to my brain!*

"Jason, you all right?" she asked as a perfectly arched brow inched up her beautiful forehead.

Hell no, he was far from all right! Obviously, a taste of her goddess body wasn't nearly enough.

"Jason?"

"I'm fine. Let's just head out already." Geez, his voice

sounded tight even to his ears, ears that happened to be burning with embarrassment at no way to hide the growing erection in the front of his pants.

With a shrug of her shoulders and a knowing look, the woman and her tight-assed jeans climbed into the Hummer. Damn, he'd like to wipe that smile off her face, but all he could think about was kissing her again. Hell, it might just work. At least her smart-assed smile would be gone.

Tools tossed into the backseat, he hopped into the passenger seat and avoided looking at anything that would encourage his wayward cock. But her scent filled the cab of the vehicle. Again, he noticed it was a little different than just a little while ago in the kitchen. She smelled more like she had last night—damned good, and even with the windows down the fragrance swirled around him before floating out into the chilled morning air. Damn, there wasn't a thing he could do about it, except stop breathing. And that just didn't seem to be a viable option.

The vehicle came to a halt at the bottom of a hill. She hopped out, her long legs carrying her a bit further up the rise where they could see the surroundings for miles.

"There's the first tower," she said, pointing to a tall steel structure just on the other side of the hill. "I want a closed-circuit camera we can operate wirelessly. And one on each tower off that way. They're about a half-mile apart and enable us to get cell service out here, among other things."

Jason's nose twitched as he looked away, trying to find the offending odor. *What the hell is that smell?* Though faint, it reminded him of old, rotting meat, like something died out here. He needed to investigate without Neesia on his heels.

"This place is beautiful. I don't think I've ever seen this much land in one stretch. You mind if I look around a little?" he asked, sounding merely curious of the layout.

"Sure, have at it," she said, her tone just as calm as his as she moved back down the hill and toward the SUV. Something in his gut screamed that she was more than a little concerned. Did she smell it, too? No, impossible. She would have to be a...

"Shit!" she exclaimed the moment she reached the bottom of the hill. Jason was right on her heels when she took off running. Less than fifty yards from where she'd parked their ride, partially hidden under a scrub brush, was a carcass. A freshly killed carcass.

Damn.

After a quick examination of the bloodied hunk of flesh, they stood together looking down at the mess.

"What do you think did this?" she asked, her face drawn tight with anger. Fists clenching open and closed at her sides, the woman looked mad enough to fight.

"Something big," was all he could think to say. He had other ideas, but couldn't voice them without giving away being more than a simple tech installation guy. "I'm definitely going to look around now. Don't go far. We have no idea if whatever killed this animal is still around," he said.

She nodded her agreement and strode away, eyes alert and shoulders stiff.

As soon as she was out of sight, he walked to the truck, pulled a private frequency videophone out of his utility bag, and spoke into the voice recognizer. Seconds later, Captain Johns' stern voice filled the line.

"Cap, it's Jason. We have a problem. A carcass turned up just now. Fresh kill. Not more than a few hours old. I'd say just after dawn."

"Damn it. He's getting too reckless. Find him and take him down, DiCaplis. Today."

"Who is getting reckless, Cap?" When his superior didn't respond, he pushed a little harder. "Cap, who am I after?"

"No need to tell you that, DiCaplis. Trust me, when you find him, you'll know." He knew that tone well enough — take care of the problem first, ask questions later.

"Fine. I'll check in with you later."

"Get rid of the body, Jason. The one you found just now, and the one you catch later."

"I'm one step ahead of you, ma'am." With that, he clicked the phone closed, and headed in the direction Neesia had disappeared.

* * * * *

"Hey, it's me," Niah spoke quietly and quickly into the mouthpiece of her wireless headset. "We've got a problem, Necie."

"Correction. We've got two problems. And one of them is named Jason DiCaplis."

"Aaah," Niah said with sudden understanding. "We've, uh, sort of met."

"Yes, I know you met, damn it. I wasn't even aware you'd made it home last night until I was jerked awake by the sudden feeling of, uh, of…"

"Of hot, wild animal sex?" Niah was nothing if not direct.

"Oh, damn it, Niah. It was disconcerting to wake up to a blistering orgasm and realize I was in bed alone. And I knew exactly who you were with and where. That's never happened between us before."

Niah's logical brain immediately reasoned out what was going on. Neesia had met her mate. It was the only thing that made any sense. Sure, as twins they had a special psychic bond that allowed them to sense each other's feelings. As shifters, the bond was even stronger, allowing them to speak telepathically when in their pelts. But they'd never felt the other making love to anyone before. Ever.

"Deduction says he's your mate. My reaction to him is strong, but yours is off the charts."

Protesting in an unusually loud and shaken tone, Neesia griped. "But he's human! He can't be my mate."

"And how the hell do we know he's human, Neesia? Besides, it would certainly explain the nasty thoughts coursing through my mind this morning while I was in the shower and you were..."

"In the kitchen with Jason! Oh, lord! That's just not possible, Ni! It can't be!"

But Niah knew better. All the signs were there—along with something neither of them ever thought to experience.

"Neesia, I think Jason's presence has thrown us into heat," she whispered, trying to look nonplussed while her heart leapt up into her throat at the sight of the sexy man moving up the hill toward her. She shivered with longing and willed her thighs to stop flexing. "I can feel it."

Just then Neesia inhaled sharply. "What are you doing, Niah?" her sister challenged, as if this were all her fault.

"I didn't do anything. I glanced Jason's way and my pussy went haywire." Niah cocked her head to the side, knowing the answer before she asked the question. But logic required her to gather facts, not assumptions.

"You felt what I did just now, just like you felt us last night? Is that why you yelled at me?"

"I did not yell, damn it!" Neesia yowled, then backed off with a frustrated "shit" into her sister's ear.

"Shit, indeed," Niah said breathlessly as Jason's scent wafted on the morning breeze and tickled her nose. There was something about the musky clean whiff of pure male that made her insides clench in conjunction with her thighs. Bad timing.

Neesia's firm resolve and even firmer words pulled her out of her musing.

"Look, Niah, we'll figure out this Jason zing thing later. Now, tell me why you really called," Neesia said.

Her sister's no-nonsense tone was like being doused with ice water. With those few words, her big sister's turbulent mood slammed through their bond and delivered an effective dose of self-control. Hell, she'd heard that tone all her life and knew it was time to get down to business. Niah's breathing calmed and her skin stopped burning as she pushed the flaming reaction to Jason's nearness to the back of her mind and delivered the bad news.

"We've come across another carcass. A big buffalo bull, at least fifteen hundred pounds."

"And?" Neesia asked slowly. Niah could picture her pacing around the football field she called a kitchen, eyebrows practically meeting in the middle of her forehead from a deep, fierce frown.

"Claw marks made by something bigger and more powerful than anything naturally roaming this area. The deep teeth marks and puncture wounds obviously made by long canines, a predator. The animal is practically torn apart. Looks like a pack of lions, Necie. Big, bad-assed African lions."

"But that's impossible," her sister exploded. "The only African lions around here are…"

"Us. Yes, I know." Damn and double damn.

Was there another lion shifter around they didn't know about? If so, they had to find the idiot who risked them all with his stupidity and recklessness. Judging from the size of the bull, the killer must be massive. Niah couldn't think of any circumstance where she or any of her sisters could have brought the animal down without help. Maybe there was more than one?

What fucked-up timing. With Kotara and Koreas in New York, she and Neesia would have to handle this on their own, without involving their potential mate.

"Tonight, we hunt," Neesia said, her voice strong, sure and royally pissed. "Whatever or whoever is trying to set us up is a dead man walking."

"You've got it, sis. Look, Jason's almost within earshot. Gotta run," she gasped, trying desperately to squash the newly awakened butterflies dive-bombing her cunt.

"Yeah," Neesia's breathlessness reached through the phone. "Oh, lord, this is insane," she groaned. "Find out what you can and check in with me privately when you get back to the house. I'm going to hit the shower."

"But you showered this morning. Again?" Niah asked.

"Yeah, again, damn it. A cold one this time."

And there was nothing Niah could do to help her sister. She was in the same sorry shape—instantly horny.

Chapter Six

ஐ

After a long day of wiring and testing, with yearning just beneath the surface all damned day, Jason joined Neesia for a late dinner. Feigning tiredness with a very real yawn, he gave her a quick kiss on the lips and rose from the table. At the confused, hurt look on her face, he eased her into his arms.

"Baby, you're the most beautiful, desirable woman on the planet. I want nothing more than to carry you upstairs, strip you naked and dive into your tight pussy." Nuzzling her neck, he yawned again, exhausted from working literally sunup to sundown. Her reassuring smile warmed his insides as she shooed him off to bed.

His alarm went off at one a.m.

Slipping away from the sprawling house, he headed back to the spot they'd found the carcass, hoping a return to the scene of the crime would get him some answers. And perhaps, an outlaw Were.

They had yet to install any surveillance out in the surround. Glad he wouldn't be seen, Jason prepared for an all-out hunt and checked his weapons before getting out of the jeep—a shotgun with shells powerful enough to leave a hole big enough to drive the jeep through, plus a semiautomatic pistol with several magazines of explosive rounds filled with thermo-gel. *Let's see how the bastard liked being shot, blown up and burned all at the same time.*

Cautiously, he surveyed the area, senses fully in tune with the night. Keen eyesight spotted nothing other than the long grass waving under the cooling breeze. But his nose picked up the rank scent of old meat and wet dog—a rogue.

Most Weres were clean and courteous. Typical family

members with jobs and careers like everyone else. The only difference was they were under the jurisdiction of S.W.A.T. law enforcement instead of the humans', and strove to live under the radar. For some reason, the outlaw Weres didn't give a rat's ass about fitting into society and were almost rabid. Dirty and filthy were the words of the day when it came to the bastards. Even their scent was different from normal Weres. You couldn't tell a law-abiding shifter from a human. But rogues? You could scent them anywhere.

Quietly stalking through the thick brush on full alert, he passed a copse of evergreens and ducked inside for a look around. Nothing in the grass-covered clearing except a hint of pale moonlight. He moved, noting his position at about five miles south of the Pryde lodge, and a couple miles east of where they'd found the last dead animal.

Out here was so still, quiet. In fact, too quiet, enough to make him uneasy. And the closer he got to the Medicine Bow River, the more apprehensive he became.

A low, muffled scraping sound caught his attention. So faint he'd almost missed it, even with his acute hearing. Then he caught a scent that made him spin around, draw his pistol with blinding speed and drop down to his knees in anticipation of a long, hairy arm swinging for his head. But no blow came.

He knelt a second, wildly searching with his eyes for his enemy, then eased down on his belly. Crawling through grass so high it almost completely hid his body, Jason made his way closer to the river. Right in front of his eyes, no more than twenty feet, was Devon Lane.

Captain Johns was right—he did recognize the rogue. Devon Lane, number twelve on S.W.A.T.'s twenty most wanted list. Huge, even in his human form, he sat on his haunches, happily crunching the bones of a full-grown buffalo, as at home as he pleased.

Just then a stiff wind blew out of the west. Jason stiffened as the outlaw picked up his scent, turned cold, black eyes on him and charged.

"Shit!" Jason growled, getting off a shot. Damn, it went wide, only grazing the Were's ear. The round hit a tree off in the distance and exploded, leaving a big charred hole in the trunk.

The buffalo carcass forgotten, Devon's roar of rage filled the night.

Jason rolled away and the Were's big clawed feet landed where his chest had been seconds before. His weapon flew out of his hand and landed in the tall grass. There was no way he'd find it in time. The shotgun was free of its harness and raised just in time for...

His head exploded with blinding pain as he spun into darkness.

* * * * *

Did you hear that? Neesia stopped in her tracks and glared toward the eerie sound. *That's a fucking Werewolf!*

And it sounds pissed! Niah growled as they broke into a mad dash toward the snarled screams.

Hitting their bellies at exactly the same time, their golden brown coats were camouflaged by the grass and brush. Instinctive hunters, they moved into position for a coordinated ambush.

Neesia lifted her head, got her prey in sight and prepared to take this asshole down. One good look at his ugly maw explained plenty. Devon Lane. Hell! A bounty they'd hunted and nearly caught until a freak accident saw him take a tumble off a cliff in the Appalachian Mountains. They thought he'd died in the fall. But here he was, in the flesh. Son of a bitch.

Too much attention on Pryde ranch was detrimental to their very lives. And this idiot had done plenty to shine the spotlight on them. And nobody, *nobody* endangered her sisters!

Whoa! What the hell was Jason doing out here? The Were

landed a staggering blow, and was now moving in for the kill.

Hold, Niah! It's Jason! Neesia spoke urgently into her sister's head.

I see him! Niah gasped. *What the hell is he doing out here?*

We'll ask him after we save his ass. Let's go.

The sisters attacked. Neesia's muscles bunched powerfully as she sprang into the air, massive teeth and claws bared. Flying into the rogue Were, she threw all of her heavily muscled bodyweight into the blow. Hitting him square in the chest, she sank her teeth into his throat as Niah plowed into his legs, taking him down.

Biting, tearing through the thick, tough flesh of the raging beast. Blood loss and severe injuries soon had him facedown on the ground gasping as his lifeblood ran into the dirt.

Done playing around? Niah panted with a quirky grin only a lioness could deliver.

Definitely. Let's finish this, Neesia growled. Together they moved in on the downed Were and relieved him of his head. He shifted back to his human form just as his heart stopped beating.

Chapter Seven

Jason awoke in the copse of trees he'd passed earlier. His head throbbed, but he was none the worse for wear. No bite marks, no deep gouges. How did he get here? And why wasn't he Were-food?

With a groan, he sat up and froze.

A fully grown African lioness lounged not six inches from him. Next to the majestic-looking creature was...Neesia? Buck naked? Jason blinked, then blinked again. Were his eyes deceiving him? Maybe he was really asleep — or worse, dead — and imagining all of this?

Then she spoke and her voice had the same effect on him it always did — instant heat.

"How do you feel?" she crooned softly, as her fingers eased gently over his brow.

"I'm fine. Surprised, but fine. What happened?"

"We came up on you fighting a rogue Were," she said, matter-of-factly.

"We? You mean you and your sister?" he asked, closing his eyes and sucking in a deep breath. It was all he could do to concentrate on the conversation with her luscious body on display.

"What do you know about my sister?" she asked warily, but still idly stoking his skin. In light of the fact they'd saved his ass, he didn't see the point in following Captain Johns' order to keep his affiliation a secret. He owed them his life.

"I'm S.W.A.T., Neesia."

"What?!" She stiffened and started to move away. His hand shot out, grabbed a wrist and held fast while he spoke even faster. He needed her to understand, needed her close.

"I'm not supposed to tell you this, but I was sent here to find the rogue that was setting you up as the ones trying to wipe out the other ranchers. S.W.A.T. didn't want attention on you or your sister, Kotara. And I know all about you working for us from time to time."

"So you weren't sent here to investigate my family?"

"No, precious, I came to take down a Were. But seeing I'm still alive, someone has already taken care of it. What happened?" he asked, rubbing the hard, sore knot on the side of his head.

"We took him down, and dragged the body to the edge of the property. We'll send the coordinates to S.W.A.T. when we get back to the house. They'll fly in and do a snatch-n-grab. They never see us. We never see them."

"I don't like S.W.A.T. using humans to take down Weres, Neesia, but in this case it seems to be a nice arrangement."

She didn't answer, just looked at him with those beautiful, light amber eyes like a woman with a yummy secret. The breeze ruffled her hair, lifting it up off her neck. Her scent filled his nostrils and his self-control slipped. Unable to resist, he released her wrist and allowed his nails to scrape lightly up her arm. The second her perky nipples tightened and puckered, Jason had to touch. The backs of his fingers rasped over the luscious peaks, and delivered an achy jolt of awareness straight to his balls.

Neesia straddled his body and settled in his lap. The heat of her pussy seeped through the crotch of his jeans, searing the flesh down to the bone. A wild craving slammed through his blood with the potency of rare, aged rum. And she wasn't immune. He felt the answering blaze in every flutter of her stomach, every clench of strong thighs tightening around his hips. God, he wished he could touch her everywhere all at once.

His mouth fell open when his already torn shirt was

shredded from his body. The woman pushed backwards until the cool blades of grass caressed his skin, then raised herself up to turn her back to him. His shaft throbbed fiercely as her swollen pussy oozed nectar down the inside of her thigh. Deft fingers unbuttoned his pants. Free at last! Her smooth cheek brushed against his cock as it bucked uncontrollably from sheer anticipation. When Neesia's creaming center was a few scant breaths from his face, he gently spread her swollen lips and the scent of creamy coral cunt made his mouth water. Jason wasted no time and thrust his tongue deep into her sweet, weeping pussy, swirling his tongue in and around, lapping up every dewy drop.

Neesia shoved his pants down around his knees and plunged her luscious mouth over him so fast he shouted into her cunt at the same time his eyes crossed. Her talented tongue wrapped around the fat head of his cock and pulled with a delicious suction. Then she took him to the very back of her throat with a low moan of satisfaction. That hum worked its way from the base of his engorged cock, up the shaft and tornadoed around the sensitive head until he was dizzy with pleasure. Damn, the woman knew how to suck a cock!

God, he wanted to gobble her up, eat her until she became a part of him, inside and out. He slipped a single finger into her creaming channel, loving the way her pussy gripped it as she swiveled her hips. So he slid in another and reveled in the smoothness of those strong inner muscles tightening hungrily, grabbing at the digits as they slid in and out of her flesh. Then he added his tongue to the mix, and wrapped it around her unhooded clit, sucking fiercely. Each pull of his tongue was rewarded with a maddening vibration around his cock, compliments of Neesia's hungry moaning.

His wild need for Neesia had him in such a lust-filled haze, he'd completely forgotten about the big cat lying just out of reach. The lioness growled deep in her chest, eased closer and licked the sweat-slick skin on his thigh, grooming him. Jason waited to be repulsed by the animal's tongue moving over his skin. Wait? What was an African lioness doing in Wyoming?

He had no idea why, but the combination of Neesia blowing his cock, the scent of her drenched cunt, and the rasping groom of the lioness's tongue against his thigh, felt so good he gritted his teeth and tried not to explode.

Protesting with a whimper when his woman eased away from his face, Jason reached up and tried to pull her hips back to his mouth. Agile and quick, Neesia evaded even his fast reflexes. Placing the entrance to heaven over his iron-hard shaft, she plunged down and took him fully inside with a single stroke and screamed.

"Oh yeah, baby, ride that cock. Give me that pussy," he howled. Yes, this is what he needed. To be buried inside her, to blast her full of his cum, to make her his in every way.

With a hand buried in her wavy locks, he pulled Neesia down until they were practically nose to nose.

"You're mine, Neesia," he practically yelled into her face. "Now and always. Mine!" With a subtle shift of his grip, her neck was bared to him. Biting down on the sleek muscle between her neck and shoulder, he sucked and nipped as she bucked on top of him, moaning her pleasure in breathless gasps.

Fingers dug into her hip and held her to him as he plunged deep, stuffing her full of his cock, filling her until he bumped against her cervix.

"Yes, Jason. Oh, yes, give it to me. Fuck me!" she screamed, cried and yelled as he pummeled into her welcoming body. And he gave it to her until she was a trembling mass of arousal and her pussy tightened around him in a death lock. She fell apart in overwhelming orgasm. Not until she sprawled in a boneless heap across his chest did he release her neck.

"Neesia!" he bellowed as he hit a wall of arousal so powerful his body shattered, then went up in flames. The blood boiled in the thick veins along his shaft and he wondered if he would survive it. One final, long stroke inside her addictive pussy pulled his full balls tight against his body. His own eruption traveled the length of his cock at light speed and burst through him with violent velocity.

His cock exploded. Jason saw stars, and they weren't the ones filling the pre-dawn sky overhead.

"Damn, baby, that was beyond wonderful," he whispered into her hair as she lay on his chest, her succulent channel still wrapped around him.

Abruptly, she sat up. Steady fingers smoothed her hair behind an ear as she gifted him with an unsteady smile.

"That was good, Jay," she crooned, "but there's more."

"More?" He wasn't sure he could take any more.

"Oh, yeah," she grinned, easing off his semi-hard cock with a loud sucking sound. The exquisite slide of her cunt pulled a raw groan from his throat. He sat up, fully intending to reach for her again.

When Neesia joined the lioness lounging in the grass, both females pinned him with a serious stare. He sat frozen to the spot, out of self-preservation or sheer curiosity, he couldn't tell.

Suddenly the lioness's body shuddered. Powerful shoulders twitched and shortened. The unmistakable pop of bones crunching and rearranging was heard in their little tree-surrounded haven.

Before him stood Neesia and...Neesia? Two Neesias?

Realization hit him like an unexpected right hook.

"Wait a minute," he gasped, "you mean, there are two of you?" Hell, one Neesia was almost more woman than he could handle. But two of them? He was going to die, he just knew it.

Jason sat up shaking his head, a silly lopsided grin on his face. How the hell had he missed something his agent's training should have caught on day one? Now it all made sense. This explained why her scent seemed different from time to time, because she *was* different. Hell, not just different, but two different people! And S.W.A.T. had no idea their secret bounty hunter had a secret of her own—practically a damned double!

"So, which one of you is really Neesia?" he asked, wondering aloud.

The woman who'd sexed him up moments ago stepped forward and his libido went off the chart. His skin was suddenly too tight and his body shivered from head to toe, and not from the cool breeze off the river. His cock was instantly on full alert.

Gently running her fingers through his hair, her wicked pink tongue slid over her lips as she whispered, "I'm Neesia."

She moved back as the other woman approached. She too let her hands play in his hair. Her touch rang his bells, but the skyrockets didn't fire. "And I'm Niah Pryde. And you," she said with a smile, "are my sister's mate."

Niah returned to her sister's side and remained quiet. Jason's cock began to sing their praises. He was, after all, a very lucky man.

He understood the insanely strong reaction to Neesia. While his attraction to Niah was definitely there, it wasn't as frantic. The ridiculous urge to fuck Neesia from sunup to sundown made sense. She was a lion shifter. And his mate! And since Niah was her twin and part of the pride, it was normal for him to be attracted to her. But Neesia had his heart.

"I can see in your eyes that you understand what's happening," she said quietly, waiting.

Jason knew his head was nodding, but was still incredulous and so damned happy he could barely stand it. His mate was a strong, shifter, fine-as-hell woman!

"I never expected to mate since there are no male lion shifters in the States. And I certainly never expected to mate a human. But you are mine, so let me make one thing clear. I don't share," she said, hips swaying seductively as each word moved her closer to his itching fingers.

"But, Niah and I already..."

She cut him off in a tone so sultry it damned near singed the hair off his body. Jesus!

"Yeah, I know about that night in the library, but you've only made love to me. Now, I'll gladly share with my sisters under, shall we say, special circumstances."

"Sisters, plural? What the hell are you talking about?" he asked impatiently. The closer she got the more he wanted to jump up off the ground, grab her by the waist and drill her silly.

"Yes, three. Niah, you've met. The other twins, Kotara and Koreas, are out of town," she explained.

God, please let her hurry up and finish talking so he could sink into her luscious pussy, he whispered to the sky as both women stalked, their looks hungry and determined. Then another thought popped into his head. Was Niah's pussy as sweet as Neesia's? He'd tasted, but damned he'd love to feel. And there were two more he hadn't even met? The thought just made him hotter.

"So what are the special circumstances?" he growled, reaching for Neesia.

"Your presence has thrown us into heat, handsome," she purred.

Oh, so *that* was the special circumstance she'd alluded to? Heat? Shit!

"So, what are you gonna do about it?" Niah asked, eyeing him like a perfectly cut, rare filet.

His wayward cock became a ramrod. Yep, he was definitely going to die. But he'd die fucking happy!

But not before he sprang a little secret of his own. The two beauties stood over him while Jason toed off his boots and kicked his pants from around his calves. Rolling over onto his stomach, he allowed the change to ripple through his body. Limbs stretched and pulled. The familiar sound of a body rearranging itself hissed and crackled in the peaceful copse of trees.

Jason tossed his head and looked up at the two women, who were now speechless with mouths gaping. The unmistakable roar of a fully grown, majestic male lion echoed in the dark hours of the morning near the winding Medicine Bow River in Wyoming.

The women joined him in the change, shifting right away. The second they were in their pelts they tried to play hard to get, but Jason was beyond horny and wasn't in the mood to play. Without warning, he pounced. Neesia, immediately captured under his big body, growled with pleasure as his cock slammed home. Jason's sharp canines clamped down on her neck as he took her fast and fierce while Niah paced restlessly. When his woman lay licking her paws, sated and content, Jason turned blazing eyes on Niah. She sprung away and evaded him for all of six seconds.

In heat? Excellent!

Also by T.J. Michaels

∞

Gift Wrap Optional
Jaguar's Rule
Primed to Pounce

About the Author

∞

Born into a musically eclectic family, TJ's first love is music. She sings, even outside of the shower. She also loves to read. You'll find her with her head buried in a book every day of the week, whether it's her own creation or something snagged at the bookstore.

So, where does this writing stuff come from? Working for a pretty interesting organization allows her to interact with even more interesting customers. With an imagination expanded beyond belief after the birth of her two (now teenaged) children, spinning life's experiences into tales is a blast! And now that books have caught up to technology, TJ's eBook reader is shown no mercy, forced to entertain her at all hours of the day or night. Even in the dark!

Her favorite compositions are multicultural romances in various genres, some naughty, none nice. With several works in the wings, TJ loves to spin, create, and explore whatever world her mind decides to conjure. She currently lives in Colorado with her two children, and enjoys working as a technical resource with a company that provides analytic solutions to large pharmaceutical manufacturers.

T.J. Michaels welcomes comments from readers. You can find her website and email address on her author bio page at www.ellorascave.com.

Tell Us What You Think

We appreciate hearing reader opinions about our books. You can email us at Comments@EllorasCave.com.

FIRST MOON RISE
Tielle St. Clare

ରେ

Trademarks Acknowledgement

✌

The author acknowledges the trademarked status and trademark owners of the following wordmarks mentioned in this work of fiction:

Glock: Glock Gesellschaft

Prologue

ಐ

"Dammit, Fallon, you can't just go off half-cocked and hunt this guy down."

Fallon Myers, Alpha wolf of the Northern Pack, stared down at the tall, sleek woman who challenged him. None of the females in his pack would have dared. But she wasn't in his pack...and that was part of his problem.

Clenching his teeth, he inhaled a long, intoxicating breath, filled with the scent of cookies — chocolate chip cookies, freshly baked. And dammit, the scent was coming from her. Oh, this was bad. His wolf — who had been suspiciously absent since Fallon's wife had died a year ago — was practically howling with the need to taste and scent and fuck the woman before him.

It didn't seem to matter that she was human and that as Alpha Fallon was expected to re-mate advantageously. To form a mate-bonding with a Luna wolf from another pack.

His wolf wanted Tate — Sheriff Tatum Bryant. Recently transplanted from down South, Fallon had noticed her on a number of occasions — what man in his right mind could have ignored the tall figure with such interesting curves? Particularly her ass and the way her uniform clung to it. His palms heated with the thought of holding that ass as he pumped inside her. His cock twitched in fervent agreement.

But even though he'd seen her, talked to her, he'd never let himself get too close. She was a townie and he knew better than to get involved with her.

Now it was too late — the wolf had chosen her.

"Fallon."

He snapped his head up and realized the three other people in the room were waiting for his response.

"The wolves died on my land, Sheriff," he said softly. Four wolves, killed with silver bullets. That meant someone knew their secret—and someone was hunting the werewolves in his pack.

Tate folded her arms across her chest and stepped in front of him. "I'm telling you—don't go after this guy." Once again the challenging lift of her chin made his cock harden. She would be a delicious fuck—strong and sensual. His wolf growled low in his mind, his hunger for the woman growing.

"I wouldn't think of it. But I might take a walk across *my* land."

Tate hooked her thumbs onto her gun belt and stared him down. She wasn't going to back off. Well, neither was he. They watched each other for a few long seconds—giving Fallon ample opportunity to observe the tightly controlled emotions move across her face. Finally, she shrugged. "Fine. If you decide to go for *a walk*, invite me along."

Fallon watched her suspiciously. That seemed a little too easy.

"I'll do that, Sheriff." He nodded his goodbyes and followed Misha and Luc to the street.

Misha faced him, his eyes alight with concern. "You aren't seriously planning to let her go with you."

"No."

"Good. We don't need humans interfering. The pack is worried. And with the First Moon Rise so close, *you* need to handle it." Fallon raised his eyebrows at the subtle command in Misha's words. Misha lowered his eyes. "Forgive me, Alpha. It's been a tough year, for all of us. Permission to speak?" Fallon nodded. "Some in the pack have expressed concern that you're not able to push through your grief. This is a chance to show them, everyone, that you're still the right man to lead us."

Fallon considered Misha's words. He hadn't heard any rumblings himself—but maybe he'd had his head buried too long.

"I'll take care of it."

Misha smiled, visibly relieved.

"Before we go back to the compound," Fallon said, "Let's stop at the bakery. I'm really craving cookies." It wasn't what his wolf wanted but it would have to do for now. Until he could get the sheriff alone.

Chapter One

ຂາ

Fallon dropped his head back and drew in a breath of clean fresh air—and something else. Something sweet and tasty. Cookies. His body pulsed, feeling alive. Alive like it hadn't been in more than a year.

Without opening his eyes he catalogued the rest of the scents and said, "Sheriff, what are you doing here?"

"Just making sure one of my residents doesn't get himself killed."

The serious tone in her voice prompted him to open his eyes. Plus, he wanted to see her face, the dare in her eyes. The arrogance in her stance. She wasn't in uniform today—choosing instead a pair of shorts that fell to mid-thigh and a crisp khaki shirt. Her feet were encased in solid, hard-working hiking boots.

"You're on private property, Sheriff."

"Which I'm allowed—when I think someone is in imminent danger of being harmed."

He shook his head, hoping he projected a casual attitude he didn't feel. "Just going for a little hike. I'll be back in a few hours."

She nodded toward the shotgun he had resting against his car. "That's pretty heavy firepower for a day hike."

"I like to be prepared."

She tapped the Glock strapped to her hip. "Me too."

He looked at her for a long time and then sighed. "I'm not going to get you leave, am I?"

"Nope."

He smirked. "Well, then let's go, Sheriff. I don't want to be out after dark." *There are so many other things I'd rather do*, he thought, *including the sexy sheriff.*

Tate grinned at Fallon's back as he hiked up the hill. It was the perfect day for a walk in the woods—sun shining, a slight breeze and a man with the perfect ass walking in front of her. But she wasn't there to enjoy the scenery. Despite Fallon's claims, she knew he was searching for the wolf killer—and she wasn't going to let him go alone. Too dangerous.

Fortunately, Fallon's sister Rebecca agreed with Tate and warned her when Fallon was taking his "hike".

She wondered for a minute if Rebecca was trying to play matchmaker. Tate hoped not. Not that Fallon wasn't gorgeous—short dark hair, bright blue eyes and a body that just screamed to be plastered across a billboard dressed in nothing but pair of boxer shorts—and nice, respectful. Shortly after Tate had first arrived in town, she'd flashed her eyes at Fallon. He'd shown no interest in her light flirtation so she'd backed off. She could take a hint.

It would have been a bad idea anyway. She was the sheriff—an appointed position but still open to scrutiny—and he was a community leader. They could hardly have a wild affair. And from all reports Fallon was still mourning his wife.

"Are we going somewhere in particular?" she asked after a while.

"Just walking."

"Right toward the area where those wolves were killed," she pointed out. He shrugged. "Speaking of that..." She lengthened her stride to keep up with him. She was in good shape but he had a lot of power in those legs. And it was mostly uphill. "Why didn't you send one of your minions to *look around?*"

He stopped and turned—his eyes flat and a little cold. "Minions?" he bit out.

"I don't know what else you'd call them. The five guys who hover around you, ready to do your bidding."

"I call them employees. And cousins."

With that brusque answer, he walked away.

Right, cousins. The whole damn county was related to him. Thank goodness Rebecca had welcomed her and they'd become friends or Tate was pretty sure no one else in town would talk to her.

Tate quickly caught up with him just as he turned south. Fallon seemingly followed a path that only he knew. At random points he would change direction, sometimes taking them deeper into the trees, sometimes leading her up the hillside. They took a break, munching on granola and sipping water—but Fallon seemed anxious to get moving so Tate didn't linger.

Clouds moved in shortly after noon and the breeze grew. Her legs, bare to her mid-thigh, were a little cold, though the sturdy shirt she wore kept her top warm. She thought about the lacy little bra and panty set she wore underneath. Totally inappropriate for hiking but when she'd dressed that morning, she'd been thinking about Fallon—and the insane chance that she might have the opportunity to undress for him, *with* him. Same reason she'd taken the time to shave her legs with extra care.

It was unlikely but hey, a girl had to have her fantasies. For the past two years, that was all that had kept her warm.

Midafternoon, Fallon stopped and glanced over his shoulder. "Do you have good shoes on?"

She looked at her hiking boots.

"They're good enough."

"Good. We need to hike upriver for a bit." He pointed to a shallow stream. "We're going to get our feet wet."

She looked up at the sky. Ominous clouds warned of rain. "That's not all that's going to get wet." He grunted in response and started to hike. The river got deeper as they walked, splashing against her knees, cold snowmelt from high in the mountains.

"There's a cabin a couple miles upriver. We'll go there to get warm."

Tate nodded feeling the first shiver run up her spine. Between the river, the rain and the wind that had kicked up, she was feeling the cold.

Fallon stopped and looked like he was sniffing the air. The angry look that crossed his face made her curious and she stepped closer. Her foot hit a rock and slid, sending her down into river. The water grabbed her legs, dragging her down, drenching her in icy water.

Cold consumed her, leaving behind a brutal numbness. She lifted her head and shook back the short strands of hair that clung to her face. Seconds later, a hand clamped around her wrist and pulled, yanking her out of the crippling water and into Fallon's arms.

Fallon carried her to shore and set her down. Wind wove through the material of her shirt and Tate shivered.

"Baby, are you all right?"

She nodded, amazed at how fast the cold had invaded her body.

"We've got to get you dry and warm," Fallon said.

"Fast," she agreed. Hypothermia could set in so quickly and the temperature of the water put her at immediate risk.

"The cabin is close. Want me to carry you?" Her shiver turned into a shake of her head.

He grabbed her arm and started walking, dragging her behind him. It was a bit caveman-like but she didn't care. She wasn't sure she could have made it on her own. The mountain breeze made every inch of her skin ache like it had been dipped in ice.

Her steps were awkward. Only Fallon's hold on her and intense concentration made it possible for her to walk.

They turned the corner and the tall grasses that had lined the path disappeared. She looked up. A wooden shack that looked like it was being held together by prayer and gravity filled the clearing.

"Cabin?" The word erupted from her frozen lips.

"It sounds better than broken-down shack."

He rubbed her back. "Now let's move it. We need to get out of the wind and get out of these."

She laughed awkwardly as she stumbled behind him. She'd thought, imagined, fantasized about taking her clothes off for Fallon but never when she was dripping wet and freezing.

He led her into the cabin and went immediately to the fireplace. A fire was already laid out and he grabbed a match, igniting the tiny timbers at the bottom. Tate followed him, sinking down onto a hard, stiff-backed chair.

"No. Get undressed. We've got to get warm and we'll need body heat." He and pulled her to her feet. "Come on, honey, strip. I'll grab blankets."

Her fingers trembled, refusing to cooperate when she tried to open the buttons. Frustration made her grab the edges of her blouse and pull. It took two hard yanks but finally the buttons popped free. She let the shirt fall to the ground. Her shorts came off easily and when Fallon returned, she was waiting in her panties and bra.

"All of it." He stacked two blankets together and laid them out in front of the fire. Bracing himself for the sight of her delectable, naked body, he looked up. Tate stood there, fumbling with the front clasp of her bra, her eyes glassy and she was weaving slightly. Damn, he had to get her warm.

"I can't make my fingers work." She threw up her hands in frustration.

"Come here, baby." She came to him and he slipped his fingers between her breasts and undid the hook. A groan broke from low in his throat. Tight hard nipples pressed forward as he dragged the soaking-wet lace from her skin. Damn, he could spend hours licking and sucking those perfect nipples. His cock pulsed and his wolf growled. He gave himself a shake. That was for later. When she wasn't shivering.

Clamping down on his urges, promising his wolf that he would have her soon, Fallon grabbed the waistband of the thin scrap she probably called panties and pulled them down. Her cool, damp skin kept him from lingering.

"Get under the blankets, honey." Once she was settled he stripped off his own clothes and crawled in beside her. She instantly turned to face him. "That's it. Cuddle up. We've got to get warm."

She nodded but he was pretty sure she would have agreed to anything he said. Her drooping eyes and sluggish motions worried him.

He placed his hand on her ass and eased her toward him, drawing her leg up and over his hip, trying to ignore the close proximity of their bodies, hoping she wouldn't protest the erection pressing against the V of her thighs.

She sighed and shifted closer.

"This wasn't how I imagined the first time we were naked." Her words were drowsy and slow and he wasn't sure she knew she'd said them aloud.

His cock twitched in response but shivers racked her body and he pushed aside all sexual thoughts. His first concern was getting her warm.

Then he would satisfy the needs of the wolf who wanted its mate.

* * * * *

Tate awoke slowly with the realization that she was warm...and pressed against the hottest, hardest body she'd

175

ever imagined. Fallon. A large hand cupped her ass, holding her close, one leg high on his hip, opening an intimate space between her thighs. Her mind took a moment to recognize the pressure between her legs. He was hard and thick and a heartbeat away from entering her.

Her pussy clenched and a flow of moisture dampened her flesh, as if her body rushed to prepare itself. Wanting that heat and strength inside her, she pressed closer, easing her breasts against his chest, needing the light brush against her nipples. She turned her head, blindly finding his lips with hers, silently telling him she wanted this, wanted him.

Fallon pressed his cock up, easing the tip into her opening. The thick head stretched her as he penetrated, slow and deliberate. Her pussy was damp but not quite ready to accept all of him. She whimpered in feminine distress but couldn't find the desire to draw back.

"Shh, shh," he whispered against her mouth. "Let me in, honey."

He claimed her slowly, thrust and retreat, each time going deeper, the delicate pain fading as she grew slick, her pussy creaming around him. It felt so good—to have him inside her. She'd been empty for too long. Her fingers gripped his shoulders—holding on to him as the one solid point in her world.

His hand tightened on her ass, holding her as he pushed deeper, sinking the rest of his cock into her. She moaned and Fallon whispered soft, soothing words, placing light kisses along her jaw, a wicked lick of his tongue across her lips, asking for entrance into her mouth the way his cock filled her pussy. She opened her lips and let him inside, savoring the tender kisses as he slowly pumped his cock inside her, his hand keeping her thigh pressed high and tight around his hip.

It was lazy and sensual, so soft that Tate had to wonder if she was dreaming, imagining the delicate thrusts, the breath-stealing kisses, the way his hands skated across her back, her ass, trailing his fingers between her cheeks and teasing her sensitive flesh, a promise and a warning in his touch.

Heat built inside her, flowing through her pussy, the wicked pressure building in a long, slow rise.

Tate moaned and rocked forward, meeting his shallow thrust with one of her own, telling him she wanted more. She loved the slow delicious fuck but she needed to come.

He seemed to hear her silent plea and shifted, guiding his cock higher. He still moved in slow, shallow thrusts but every entry pressed against her clit. She moved against him and was rewarded with a quiet dangerous growl. She raised her eyes and looked at him for the first time. He stared at her, the heat and hunger visible in his eyes as he fucked her pussy.

"Come for me, baby," he commanded with a soft kiss. "Let me feel you come." As he spoke, he pressed forward, sliding long against her clit, giving her the caress she needed. Her pussy clenched and contracted, sending a warm sparkling climax through her core.

"Oh, yes, baby." He smoothed his hands down her back and held her to him as he pumped into her, a little deeper and a little faster. His hand slid between their bodies and he rubbed his thumb across her mound, finding the precise pressure to rocket her sensitive clit to another orgasm. As her cunt grabbed him, he thrust into her one final time, pouring his cum into her pussy.

Fallon groaned and kissed her. The wolf rumbled low in his chest. Being inside her had soothed the animal but it wanted more. It wanted to mount and ride its mate, hear her scream his name.

Tate closed her eyes and her head dropped forward, falling against his shoulder. Asleep.

A wave of tenderness filled his chest. Even the wolf calmed at the sight of Tate, asleep beside him, a soft, satisfied smile curving her lips.

Chapter Two

ಜಿ

When Tate came awake the second time it was with two realizations—she'd fucked Fallon…and despite the fact that no body lay beside her, she wasn't alone.

Awareness prickled the hair on her neck. She was being watched, hunted. Moving cautiously, she rolled to her back and scanned the room. It took only seconds to find him— crouched in the darkest corner, his eyes practically glowing as he stared at her.

The flight instinct tightened her body but she held herself still, knowing that would be the worst thing she could do. Power surrounded him like a wild animal—a purely sexual beast stalking its prey.

The fire flicked brief glimmers of light across his skin and she could see the strong line of his chest, the tight ripples across his stomach…and the hard erection standing between his legs. Her pussy fluttered in response to the blatant desire— in his eyes and in the thick hard cock she knew fit perfectly inside her.

But he didn't move. He watched and waited—his body strung tight, his gaze hot.

Keeping her movements slow and measured, she eased the blanket back. A cool shiver raced down her spine as the air hit her skin but it was quickly overcome by the desire surging through her body. Her nipples tightened and puckered, silently begging for his mouth. Tate let her sensual instincts guide her, knowing if she wanted him, she needed to break the fierce control he wielded over his body.

She slid her hands up her sides, cupping her breasts, rubbing her thumbs over the taut peaks. A delicious ache built in her sex and she moaned softly, letting him hear her pleasure. His hands looked almost like claws as they dug into the floor beside his knees.

Wicked pleasure flowed through her chest. This man—so strong and powerful—wanted *her*, wanted to fuck her.

She kept her gaze on him, watching his eyes track her hands as she smoothed her palms down, across her stomach, her hips. Her stomach trembled as she swirled her fingers over her skin, along her thighs—the scenario very much like one she used to masturbate. Fallon, watching as she touched herself, sliding her fingers into her pussy, tempting him with her own pleasure. She reached up and pinched her nipple, loving the sharp little bite of pain. His eyes tightened and she heard a low snarl from the corner.

Sensual power to match his poured through her, making her feel strong and sexy in a way she hadn't in years. With her hands wandering across her skin, she let her mind free, imagining how it would feel to have him inside her again. Hard and deep, fucking her with the desperate hunger she sensed. Cream melted inside her cunt and crept down her pussy lips.

She drew her knees up, baring her sex to him, wondering if he could smell her need. In the dark, he never took his eyes from her, even as he gripped his cock and began to pump, his hand sliding up and down his shaft. The delicious sight made her ache, wanting her fingers wrapped around that thick rod.

Harsh breath filled the room and she knew it was hers and his. Anticipation flooded her pussy. The way he watched her, the barely constrained need made her want more.

She thrust two fingers into her pussy, moving her hand in time to his strokes, imagining it was his cock filling her. The shallow, narrow penetration of her fingers was good but not enough. She needed Fallon. All of him, all of that thick hard cock pushing inside her. Sitting up, she pumped her fingers into her cunt, driving as deep as she could but wanting more.

The tension in Fallon's body seemed ready to snap. With movements that looked pure animal, he crawled forward on hands and knees, his stare focused on the hot space between her legs.

He stopped, inches away from her knee. There was something animalistic in the way he sniffed the air and licked his lips — as if sampling the atmosphere with all his senses.

Caught in the sensual web that surrounded them, she pulled her fingers from her pussy and offered her hand to him.

"Taste me."

Fallon's growl filled the room even as his lips covered her fingers, sucking the two she'd had inside her into his mouth. His teeth scraped her skin as he licked and lapped her juices, swallowing her flavor. The delicate roughness of his tongue teased her skin, warning her how it would feel against her clit. Heat poured from his eyes as he drew back, leaving one final bite on her fingertip as if to reprimand her for tempting him.

But Tate wasn't finished. Not yet. She didn't want this powerful man to crawl on top of her and *slowly* slide into her. She wanted to be fucked. Hard. The power surging through her body would allow for nothing less. She wanted him out of control.

With a wicked smile, she rolled over, coming up to her knees and placing her elbows on the blanket. Butterflies battled in her stomach as she thought about the picture she made — ass up, pussy open. An animal waiting to be mounted.

Fallon stared at the erotic image before him — and felt the beast claw at his throat. The wolf howled its victory. This was his mate, open and eager for him.

She arched her back and presented her cunt to him, offering him her pussy like a bitch in heat, her legs spread wide, her juices dripping down the insides of her thighs. The taste of her cunt lingered on his lips. He wanted, needed to bury his face in her pussy and taste every inch, drive his tongue into her until she screamed, but the sexual sight before him was too much temptation. The slow tongue fuck would have to wait.

The wolf drove him forward. He bent down quickly, licking one long hot stroke up her slit and nipping at the rounded curve of her ass before he gripped her hips. He placed the head of his cock to her opening—fighting for control but needing her cunt as much as his wolf. With a human growl that blended with the animal's, he drove inside, her tight walls gripping him as he pushed through the resistance. She cried out and buried her head in her hands.

The sound dragged him back from the edge and he stopped, hilt-deep inside her, his cock pulsing, his hips fighting the compulsive need to thrust. He waited, gauging her pain, caging the wolf that demanded he fuck.

"Tate," he whispered, his mind barely able to form the word.

She moaned and rolled her hips forward—as if she would slide him out of her cunt. His fingers bit into her hips but he fought the urge to restrain her. Then she moved again, driving back, fucking herself onto his cock.

"Hard, Fallon," she whimpered as if her thrust wasn't enough. "Fuck me hard."

Red covered his mind and the wolf spirit invaded him, consumed him. Holding her in place, he pulled back and plunged forward, slamming into her, claiming every inch of her pussy. Again she cried out but he recognized the sound—knew it was pleasure. He fucked her—hard—just as she'd begged him to.

She moved with him, timing her strokes perfectly to his as he pounded into her. Long and deep, each thrust forced him closer to a climax that he needed but wanted to delay. He placed the heel of his hand to her mound, teasing her clit with his fingers. Her cries turned to whimpers and groans, the rhythm of her hips growing erratic as she struggled for her orgasm.

He angled his hips up, driving his cock into her sheath and felt the first ripples even as she screamed. The wolf inside him went insane. He fucked her harder, wanting more, wanting to feel it again. Before the sweet contractions were done, another set stronger and deeper began.

Tate moaned as if she'd lost the strength to scream.

The squeezing of her cunt along his cock was too much and Fallon shouted as he drove into her again, his cum filling her, flooding her.

The strength sucked from his body, Fallon struggled to stay upright. He widened his stance and held himself deep inside her. The hard length of his cock was barely weakened, despite the orgasm he'd just experienced. It had been more than a year since he'd fucked and his wolf wasn't going to let Tate go until he was fully satisfied.

Exhaustion tugged on Tate—the seductive lure of sleep after such delicious orgasms was almost too much to resist. She tried to slow her pounding heart, draw enough oxygen into her lungs. Her cheek lay against the rough blanket—but her ass was still in the air and Fallon was still buried inside her.

He pulsed forward, as if to remind her that he belonged inside her pussy, then withdrew. She moaned as he slipped out of her—from regret and the strange sense of being empty without him.

She started to collapse onto the blankets but Fallon's hands stopped her, guiding her onto her back. He lifted her leg over his hips so that he continued to kneel between her thighs. Her throat grew tight as she watched him. His cock was hard—even though she knew he'd come. Hell, the evidence was leaking out of her. He leisurely stroked the inside of her leg.

"This is how I imagined you," he whispered as he caressed her. "Relaxed and satisfied from having my cock inside you, your pretty legs spread and my cum dripping from your cunt."

Her heart skipped a beat at the sexy words and the revelation that he'd imagined fucking her.

Tired but happy, she smiled as he moved over her, his cock pressing against her pussy but not entering her. Fallon wasn't done with her yet. Supporting himself inches off the floor, he bent down and kissed her—soft at first and then deeper. Tate ran her hands up his chest and around his neck, savoring the long drugging kisses, the gentle bites, the deep strokes of his tongue.

Breathless, she pulled back. He nipped her lower lip, gently punishing her, then moved lower, his hips against hers as his mouth opened over her breasts. Hot slow laps of his tongue ignited new warmth in her pussy. He circled one nipple with the hard tip of his tongue before drawing the peak inside and sucking—gentle pulsing motions that matched some internal rhythm, making her pussy throb. He worked her slowly as if testing her, finding the pressure she liked.

He sampled each breast, spending glorious minutes touching and tasting—the hypnotic caress of his tongue arousing and soothing at the same time. Tate slipped her fingers into his hair and held him, unwilling to let him go just yet.

Finally, he lifted his head. The hungry need had returned to his gaze. His stare holding hers, he reached between their bodies and guided his cock to her opening, the thick head stretching her again.

"That's it. Take all of me," he encouraged as he steadily sank into her, her well-used pussy protesting for a moment before it eased and accepted him.

Once he was inside, he stopped. "All right?"

She nodded, not sure what to expect, not sure she was up for another hard fuck—though she didn't think it would take long to convince her body.

Fallon pressed her knees down so her legs were straight and then shifted, moving so his knees were outside hers. The movement pulled his cock from its deep penetration, but left most of the thick shaft inside her.

"Is that okay?" he asked, rocking his cock inside her pussy.

Tate ran a quick inventory of her body and nodded. She wasn't ready to fuck but she loved the sensation of having him inside her.

"Good. I'll give you a bit of break."

Her eyes snapped open. "*This* is giving me a break?" She rolled her hips upward. The shallow thrust rubbed his cock along her clit.

They both groaned and she watched Fallon's eyes glaze over. Pleasure shot through her core—that *she* was capable of creating that look on his face.

"Compared to what I want to do with you, yes, this is a break," he groaned.

Tate laughed softly—and she realized she was happy being with him. It wasn't just the sex—though she'd come harder with him than any man—it was him. He was the kind of strong, reliable man who made a woman feel safe—even when she could take care of herself.

"How do you feel about kids?"

Tate flinched at the abrupt question.

"Uh, kids are fine," she offered hesitantly. "Why?"

"I have two of my own."

"Yes."

"And I've just come inside you twice—with no protection." He smiled. "And before the night is over, that will likely happen again." He brushed the stray piece of hair away from her forehead and placed a quick kiss on her nose. "I'm not worried about disease — we're immune —" Tate didn't have a chance to ask about *that* comment. "But considering the last few hours, a child is a real possibility."

She shook her head. "Nothing to worry about."

"You're not on the Pill —"

"How do you know that?" There was no way he could know that unless his sister — who was also *her* gynecologist — had told him. Tate would ream Rebecca's ass when they returned.

"I just do. Now, answer the question."

Tate's heart caught in her throat. She knew just how she'd feel if they conceived. But they wouldn't.

"Don't worry. I can't have kids." Her voice was steady and calm. She's spent years making sure she could say those words without tears.

"What?" He looked down at her, his eyes concerned, not condemning — and she found herself talking.

"My husband, my ex —" she clarified when Fallon tensed up. "We tried for years to have a baby." She looked into the fire but Fallon cupped her cheek and turned her face to him, concern and affection in his eyes, his touch gentle.

"Tell me, honey."

"Nothing to tell. I couldn't conceive. We did tests and they couldn't find anything specific wrong with either of us. Eventually, Sam gave up and left."

Tension zipped through his body and Tate braced herself for its onslaught. But as soon as he opened his eyes, she knew all the anger was directed at Sam.

"That bastard left you because you couldn't have kids? He's never heard of adopting? Thousands of kids are born every day without parents and he skips out because he can't have one with his genes?"

He sounded so pissed that Tate actually laughed.

"It wasn't just that. I don't think I was the wife he was expecting." Fallon raised his eyebrows, silently commanding her to continue. "We met in college. I was majoring in criminal justice, not sure what I was going to do, never expecting to become a cop. Sam didn't expect it either."

The fierce light in Fallon's eyes faded and amusement filled his gaze.

"Tell me the rest," he encouraged.

"Well, I did become a cop and found I really liked it."

"He wanted something else?"

As he spoke, Fallon pumped his hips as if to remind her he was there. A delightful shiver ran up her spine at the subtle penetration and silent statement in his movements. He wanted her.

She smiled ruefully. "I think Sam's perfect image of our marriage was me, on the front porch, wearing a floral-printed dress, waiting to greet him when he returned from a hard day at work."

"I like the idea of that myself."

She rolled her eyes. "All men want that."

"Maybe," Fallon conceded. "But you see, in *my* perfect world, you're waiting on the porch, in the floral-print dress...and you're not wearing any panties." The seductive teasing sank into her sex. "And your nipples are hard, waiting for my mouth to suck them. And that sweet pussy." He groaned like it was a treat he was anticipating. "So wet, dripping with your need. You've spent the day waiting for me, legs spread, wanting my mouth on your cunt, my cock deep inside you."

Every word was like a tongue caressing her pussy. She rocked against him, trying to move him inside her.

"That's it, baby. That's what would be waiting for me on the front porch. Your hot, wet pussy. I'd fuck you right there."

"What about the neighbors?" she gasped trying to concentrate as he moved.

"Let 'em watch. Let 'em see what a pretty cunt you have."

She couldn't stop the shudder that raced through her body—something primitive in her responding to the caveman way he claimed her.

"I'd bend you over the porch railing and fuck you so they'd all know you belong to me, that only my cock gets to slide into this tight pussy. Only *my* seed fills you."

With each phrase he pumped inside her. He couldn't thrust hard or deep but the shallow, slick ride and the tight grip of her thighs gave a new caress to her clit. Tate groaned and hid her face in his shoulder as he wrapped his arms around her.

The pressure was perfect, wonderful…but it wasn't enough.

"Please, Fallon." She bit his jaw, needing to express the violence that surged through her veins. He growled as her teeth nipped his skin and the light flared in his eyes.

He pulled back, drawing his cock all the way out of her body.

"No!" She sat up and reached for him. He met her, greeting her mouth with hot, harsh kisses—but not giving her what she needed.

"Do you want my cock?" he teased her. "Want me to fuck you? Slide back inside you?"

"Yes!" There was no other answer.

"Lay back, my pretty little bitch. Lay back and spread your legs. Show me how much you want me."

Any other setting, any other man, she'd have slapped him silly and walked out, but this was Fallon—and she wanted him, needed him.

He watched as she lay back and bent her knees, lifting her hips, offering herself. The deep pink of her pussy called to him.

He reached between her legs and thrust two fingers into her cunt. "Is this what you want?"

"Nooo." The sound was more moan than word.

He loved her desire—the way she was so blatant in her hunger for him.

And he was pleased to see the haunted look in her eyes had faded. If he ever met her bastard ex-husband, he would pound him into the ground but for now, the best revenge was making Tate forget she ever knew the man, that any man but Fallon had ever been inside her.

She pumped herself up, fucking herself onto his fingers, moisture coating his hands as she worked herself against him.

He cupped her breast, tweaking the nipple knowing she was too far gone to accept a light touch. The firm mound filled his palm to perfection and he squeezed gently.

"Tell me what you want."

"Your cock," she moaned, still moving against his fingers. "I want your cock."

"And my cum. Do you want that?"

"Yes."

He stroked his hand down between her breasts, smoothing over her stomach, imagining his child growing there. The wolf sensed she wasn't fertile yet but soon he'd plant his seed inside her.

With a growl, the wolf drove him forward and he lifted her hips, raising them high on his thighs and placing his cock to her opening.

He pushed his shaft inside her, snugging her legs up around his waist. Tate groaned and locked her heels together, pulling him into her.

Fallon raised his head, smiling as he filled her. "Greedy, little thing, aren't you?" He drew back, loving the sweet way her cunt drew him inside. She groaned and tried to pull him deeper but he resisted, fighting her and his wolf for control. She was going to be sore when he was done with her. The least he could do was pleasure her along the way. He slipped his thumb into her slit, loving the wetness that greeted him. He rubbed a slow circle around her clit and felt her pussy squeeze him as the sensation moved through her cunt. "You want more, don't you? Want my cock? Only *my* cock?"

"Yes! Fallon!"

The edges of his control wavered and he thrust in deep, savoring the shocked cry that burst from her lips as he drilled his cock into her, the delicate ripples of her orgasm initiating his.

The climax ripped through his body, pulling his cum from inside him and pouring it deep into her pussy. *His* pussy.

He spread his fingers across her stomach, feeling her body relax as he held himself inside her. She opened her eyes and looked up at him, the dazed sated stare he'd learned accompanied her orgasm clouded her gaze. With a slow smile, she pumped her hips up, subconsciously pressing him deeper.

Mine. The wolf staked his claim. This body, this cunt belonged to him.

Chapter Three

જી

Tate awoke with the sunlight on her face—and feeling like she'd been run over by a truck. Between the hard floor below her, the hard man who'd spent most of the night on top of her and the hard cock that had been inside her, her body felt beaten and battered and never more satisfied.

With a groan, she sat up. The fire had died out, leaving a morning chill in the air. She pulled the blankets up around her shoulders and looked around. Sometime in the middle of the night, Fallon had hung up their clothes, letting them dry. She reached out and grabbed his shirt off the thin line that hung above the fireplace.

Standing was a challenge. Her legs ached. Muscles not used in a long time protested as she arched her back and tried to walk. The main room was empty but Tate was pretty sure there was a bathroom in the back of the cabin.

Each step reminded her of the previous night—and Fallon. Through the night, he'd made love to her, fucked her—call it what you wanted—but he'd been desperate for her. He'd allowed her moments of rest and brought her food and water but even then he'd continued to touch her. And when she'd fallen asleep—exhaustion finally winning the battle with desire—she had a vague memory of an orgasm waking her in the middle of the night and Fallon's voice whispering her back to sleep.

She went to the bathroom and cleaned up a bit. The cabin only had cold water so she contented herself with a sponge bath, washing away the sticky remains of Fallon's cum from her thighs. Memories of his loving assaulted her. He'd been relentless, loving her, fucking her.

But now it was morning.

She walked back into the main room, buttoning his shirt as she entered. Fallon sat at a rickety kitchen table, wearing his shorts, his chest deliciously bare. As she entered, he looked up, his eyes scanning her body. It made her feel wonderfully feminine to have him look at her with such fire and hunger, the dominant male wanting his woman.

Without speaking, he held out his hand. Part of her wanted to reject the silent command but twelve hours of absorbing the pleasure he provided made her more compliant than normal. She walked forward, putting her fingers in his and letting him pull her to his side, her knees pressing against his thighs.

She waited — an anxiousness filling her chest when he didn't speak. He reached up and opened the shirt she wore, drawing it down her arms, leaving her naked, her nipples tight and plump.

He leaned forward and placed a light kiss on each tip, teasing her taut flesh with a quick flick of his tongue. Sensitized from the night, she gasped, the caress like a spark against her clit. Her whimper crept through the silent cabin as Fallon opened his mouth on her and began to suck, slowly drawing her nipple deep into his mouth. Her knees trembled as he lapped and sucked, unhurriedly, like he could spend the day worshiping her breasts.

"Are you sore?" he whispered against her skin.

She shook her head. His fingers skimmed the inside of her thighs then moved up, teasing the hot folds of her pussy. He slipped two fingers into her passage and she couldn't stop the hiss as he stretched the sensitive flesh. He drew back and raised his eyebrows.

"Maybe a little," she admitted.

The edge of his mouth pulled up in a self-mocking smile. "I'm sorry about that." As he spoke he turned, facing her and drawing her down so she straddled his lap. His fingers still stroking her, light, whisper touches. "Next time, I'll give you a break."

She shivered at the promise that there would be more, then wrapped her arms around his neck—completely comfortable straddling his thighs, naked while he was dressed.

"Yes," she said with a teasing laugh. "I remember how you gave me a break."

He had the courtesy to blush. "Last night was different. I needed you." His hands rubbed up her back as he pulled her close, hugging her against his chest. It wasn't sexual but it was intimate. "Needed to know that you would take me."

Tate nodded and she tried to think of what to say. *I love you.* The words filled her mind but she erased them. It was too soon. Just because he'd spent the night inside her didn't mean he'd attached any meaning to it besides a good fuck.

The crack of a gunshot jolted them both upright. The sound was distant but clearly recognizable.

"Fuck." Fallon's soft curse matched Tate's. He lifted her off his lap and they ran for their clothes. Tate pulled on her shirt but realized she'd ripped the buttons off last night. With a growl of frustration, she tied the shirttails together beneath her breasts.

Fallon looked over and she recognized the heat in his eyes as he saw the black lace of her bra barely covered by her shirt.

"At least the day isn't a total loss," he said with a grin. Tate laughed as she bent down and forced her dried boots onto her feet.

"Here. Use this." He put the spare pistol from his pack into her hand.

She shook her head. "I'm good with mine." She indicated the Glock she'd had strapped to her hip yesterday.

"Use this one. It has silver bullets. I doubt yours does."

"Uh, no." She laughed uncomfortably. "I wasn't expecting vampires."

"Werewolves."

"What?"

"You kill vampires with wooden stakes. You kill werewolves with silver bullets."

"And you think we're hunting a werewolf?" Disbelief laced her.

"Yes."

Questions filled her gaze but he ignored them. There would be time later to explain — after they caught the man who was hunting his pack.

They left the cabin and ran uphill, leaving the trees behind them. Paths crisscrossed through tall grasses but Fallon seemed to be tracking by some unknown sense.

Suddenly, he reached out his arm and held her back. He crouched down and she followed. A furry mound was stretched across the path and Tate's heart dropped to her stomach. Another wolf.

"Stay here. In case he's not dead." Tate nodded and remained behind, mostly hidden by a large rock. Fallon crawled to the wolf's side, putting his hand on the animal's shoulder.

Fallon straightened, standing beside the body.

"It doesn't make sense. He'd cold. He's been dead for—"

Another shot shattered the air. Fallon cried out and blood streaked across his side. He dropped to the ground to a soft groan. Keeping low, Tate ran forward, kneeling beside him.

A line of red stained his waist. She ripped open his shirt and saw that the bullet had burnt his skin as it tore by. It was a surface wound. Painful no doubt but not life-threatening.

Fallon hissed as she touched the skin near the wound.

"Sorry. It probably hurts like hell."

"Silver bullet," he groaned.

"How can you tell?"

193

"I can feel it." The effect of the silver in his blood was almost immediate. It was already sapping his strength. He grabbed her hand. "Whoever shot me is likely coming to make sure he finished the job. You need to get out of here."

"I'm not leaving you." She drew her weapon instead.

"No. I won't have you involved in this. Go." He nodded toward the trail. "Head down that path. Take the left trail. You'll be back at the cars in two hours."

"I'm not leav—"

"Do as you're told, dammit."

The angry snarl seemed to shock her but he couldn't let himself care. He had to get her out of there. Whoever was hunting his pack was coming for him and he needed to know she was safe.

Her lips tightened and she backed away, staying hunched over as she headed down the trail. As soon as she was around the corner, he rolled to his side and fingered the burning wound. His sister could cure him, if he could get down the hill in time but until then he couldn't take his wolf form. That meant he had to face the killer as a human.

Giving his would-be killer a target, he lay still, waiting.

A footstep snapped a twig and Fallon looked.

A man stood before him. A boy, really. The kid's eyes were wild and frightened. Hell, the gun was practically shaking in his hand. Fallon had seen him before—Daniel, if he remembered correctly. His parents were members of the pack but for some reason, their child hadn't ever joined.

He raised the pistol, the barrel pointed in the general direction of Fallon's chest. It didn't matter if the kid couldn't shoot. At this distance, it would kill Fallon.

"At least tell me why," Fallon asked calmly.

"You're going to kill me."

"I barely know you. Why would I kill you?"

"Because I can't change. I'm not one of the pack. At the First Moon Rise run I'm supposed to be sacrificed."

Fallon shook his head, letting his confusion show. "The First Moon Rise is a new year's celebration—that's all. We don't sacrifice anyone. And why the hell would I care if you can't change?"

Daniel's hand clenched the grip of his gun—his finger wasn't even on the trigger. There was a good chance Fallon could talk the kid down.

"He said you—"

The end of his sentence was cut off by a cry as Tate appeared from the trees and knocked the gun away. She swung her elbow back, connecting with Daniel's jaw. He crumpled to the ground. The soft slick of Tate drawing her gun made Fallon smile.

She hadn't left him to die.

She also hadn't obeyed him.

"I told you to get your ass to the car."

She glanced away from Daniel long enough to roll her eyes.

"This is your guy?" She didn't sound like she believed it any more than he did.

"I think someone's pulling his strings."

The silver weakened his muscles but Fallon got to his feet. He had too much to live for to let himself die on a mountainside.

Tate searched Daniel and came up with a knife and a cell phone.

"What's this about?" She held up the ornate knife.

"Silver dagger."

"And tell me again why silver is bad?"

"It poisons a werewolf's system and we can't change into our wolf form."

She looked at him for a moment — the questions in her eyes but also the realization that *now* was not the time to answer them. She hung the dagger on her belt loop and flipped open the cell phone, scrolling through the menu.

"What are you doing?"

"This kid was shaking so hard I'm surprised he could hold a gun. I'm thinking he called his boss beforehand to boost his courage."

She clicked through the recently called numbers. There was one — dialed minutes before they'd heard the first shot.

"Recognize this number?" She turned the screen to Fallon. His lips tightened and he nodded.

"Unfortunately, yes."

Fallon nudged the kid with his foot. Daniel groaned and looked up, his eyes widening when he saw his Alpha standing over him.

Fallon handed the phone down. "Call him. Tell him you finished the job."

"But I—"

"Call him." The command allowed for no disobedience. Daniel gulped and took the phone.

"It's me. It's done. Yeah…" He looked up at Fallon and swallowed deeply. "Yeah. His wolf form. I'll carry it to the roadside." He looked up at the Alpha wolf. Fallon took the phone, dropped it on the ground and crushed it under his heel.

"Did you shoot the other wolves?"

Daniel shook his head.

"I was just supposed to shoot you. But you were supposed to be alone." He glanced toward Tate.

"Change of plans. In three days, bring your parents and present yourselves to me."

Daniel tensed and showed a little backbone. "Don't hurt them."

"Do as you're told. Like a good wolf. Three days. You and your parents." Knowing he would be obeyed, he looked at Tate and tipped his head toward the path. "Let's go." He stalked off, Tate following a few feet behind him.

"What now?" she asked as they started downhill.

Fallon's hands curled into fists as he thought about what waited for him.

"Now, I kill the wolf who is trying to steal my pack."

Chapter Four

ഔ

Misha stood before the small crowd of Fallon's Betas, their mates and the elders. With all eyes forward, Fallon slipped into the back of the room, staying in the deepest shadows, knowing the presence of so many wolves would mask his scent — at least long enough.

"Another wolf is dead," Misha announced.

A rumble of dismay ran through the crowd.

"Where's Fallon?" Luc asked.

Misha shook his head and the pain in his eyes was almost believable, even to Fallon.

"I can't reach him. His cell phone is dead." He raised his eyes and tears glittered in the pale light. "He went up the mountain yesterday to find this killer." He smacked his fist into his palm. "Dammit, why did I let him go alone?"

"No worries," Fallon announced from the corner, stepping into the light. He knew the picture he presented, blood dripping from his side, the pale skin warning of silver poisoning. But damned if he would turn over control of his pack. Not until his carcass was dragged from the room. "I took a friend." With perfect timing, Tate walked forward. "It's a good thing, because when your killer tried to finish the job, Tate was able to stop him."

"*My* kill —? What are you…?"

"It was a brilliant idea. Send me up the mountain. Alone. And you stayed behind, ready to pick up the pieces of the pack."

"Alpha, I don't know what you're talking about." Misha looked around to see if his pleas of innocence were being believed. The suspicious looks on the faces must have made him change his tactic. He scoffed. "And why not? You're not fit to lead. In the past year, you've ignored the pack. So trapped in your grief your wolf won't appear." He sneered at Tate. "And now this? Our females aren't good enough but you'll rut between some human's legs?"

Tate tensed and Fallon placed his hand on her shoulder, simultaneously comforting and cautioning her.

"Be careful how you speak of my mate — your new Luna."

Misha spat on the ground. "A human, leading our pack? I'll see you dead first."

"Is that a challenge?"

Misha hesitated long enough to gather his courage. Finally he nodded. "Yes."

The crowd moved back, instinctively forming a circle to watch and contain the fight. Fallon tried to keep track of Tate, warn her to stay near Luc, but she wasn't behind him.

With the silver running through Fallon's body, he couldn't take his wolf form but that didn't mean he couldn't win. And there was no way he was letting Misha steal his pack.

Misha ripped off his shirt and threw it behind him. He smirked at Fallon, glancing at the still-bleeding wound on his side.

One thought consoled Fallon. Even if Misha won this battle — he wouldn't live long as Alpha. Luc or one of Fallon's cousins would challenge the bastard before the blood was dry on Fallon's body.

But that was only if Fallon lost. And he had no intention of losing. Not with Tate watching. Not when he had so much to live for.

Misha rolled his shoulders back and stretched his chest wide, preparing for the change to wolf.

Ignoring Misha, Fallon scanned the crowd. He found Tate standing behind his opponent, her jaw set and her eyes like flint. A faint smile curled her lips as she pulled the dagger from her belt loop. He tipped his head in silent question but she moved before he could shout a warning.

With one quick swipe, she slashed the silver dagger across Misha's waist, a wound almost identical in length and depth to the one that marked Fallon's side.

Misha cried out and clutched his side, his eyes glowing as he spun around. Fallon lunged forward but Luc grabbed him and held him back.

"Let her handle it," he advised.

Tate raised her chin and stared Misha down. She nodded to Fallon. "Silver bullet." She held up the dagger. "Silver dagger. Now at least it's a fair fight."

"She's interfering," Misha accused. "It's supposed to be a fight between me and the Alpha."

"All she did was level the playing field," Luc announced. Fallon sensed rather than saw the agreement of the wolves around him. He was focused on Tate, the brave, defiant way she'd faced his enemy. Faced him to protect her mate.

His wolf howled its pleasure and Fallon knew it was time to finish the fight and return to his woman.

* * * * *

Fallon stalked down the hall—fire pounding through his veins, the wolf lurking a breath beneath his skin. The combination of the nearing moon rise, the challenge and the woman made the animal difficult to control. The wolf wanted its mate.

With neither Fallon nor Misha able to change, the fight had been long and bloody—until Misha had finally collapsed. Luc had dragged the fallen wolf away while Rebecca had treated Fallon's wounds and given him something to counteract the silver in his system.

Caitlin, Luc's human mate, had taken Tate in hand and brought her to Fallon's rooms. He stepped inside—his eyes drinking in the sight of his woman, mud coating her legs, dust smeared on her cheek. She was perfect. His wolf howled its desire, clamoring for his mate.

Fallon watched for a moment. Tate paced the far side of the room, her head bent forward, arms wrapped around her waist, thumbnail between her teeth. The jerky rocking motion warned Fallon that she was on the edge.

He curled his hands into fists, physically containing the beast that sensed freedom now that Rebecca's elixir was working. The silver was being leached from his body and with its departure the wolf could return. Would return to claim the woman.

Fallon knew he had to get some distance—either physical or emotional—before that happened. Tate had to be freaked out by everything that had happened.

"Tate—"

She jumped at his low call as if she hadn't heard him enter the room. Her eyes widened as she stared at him, looking down his body. Damn, he should have changed before he'd come. Bloodstained shorts and the bandage were his only coverage.

He walked forward, keeping his movements slow—like he was approaching a wild animal. As he drew closer, she stepped back, inching toward to the wall—farther from him. The wolf growled its disapproval.

"Tate? Are you all right?"

She swallowed deeply and shook her head, continuing her subtle retreat, her body trembling. The wolf's growl turned into a mental howl.

"I can't seem to—" Before she finished her sentence, she wrapped her arms around his neck and pulled him down, her lips covering his in a hungry, desperate kiss. Her tongue drove deep into his mouth as her fingernails bit into his skin reminding him of dainty little claws. She lashed her tongue around his, barely giving him a chance to respond before she leapt away.

"I'm sorry." She scraped the fingers of one hand through her hair. "I know you're hurt and probably still pissed at that guy. Sorry."

"Tate?" he asked, giving her space to explain.

She turned and started pacing again. "I've got this adrenaline spike going here and I can't quite calm down. I should go." She started by him but he grabbed her arm, yanking her back, pulling her hard against his chest.

"You're not afraid of me?"

"Did you want me to be?"

"No." He spun her in his arms, plastering her body against his, his cock easing between her thighs. He clamped his hand onto her ass and pulled her up hard, driving his erection against her clit. She cried out and arched her back, pushing her breasts into his chest and rubbing her pussy against him.

She wasn't frightened. She was aroused.

"I thought you might be—after what you saw. Misha—"

Her fingers tightened on his shoulders and he felt the delicate bite of her nails. "That bastard. I can't believe he—"

"Don't worry, baby. You didn't let him. We took him down, together."

Her chest rose and fell in long, heavy pants and he realized she was pissed—for him. For the danger.

Pride and lust flooded his chest. He pulled her up and kissed her—dominating, commanding, giving back all the delicious fury she fed to him. She didn't back down—desperate, sharp bites on his lips, along his jaw, down his neck.

He grabbed her ass and lifted, pulling her off the floor. Momentum drove him forward, slamming her back against the wall. Caught up in their kiss, she didn't notice. He tore the tails of her shirt and ripped the lacy bra, tearing the delicate material into two pieces.

Her ankles locked behind his waist as she clawed at his back, trying to get to closer. She raked her teeth across his shoulder—loving the hot masculine flavor of his skin. Her pussy throbbed and ached, creaming as he snarled in fierce response. He snapped his head back and stared at her.

In that moment, she could see the wolf in him. His lips pulled back, growling as he ripped open his shorts. His cock erupted between them—hard and thick. Long.

Mine. She reached for it but he slapped away her hands.

"I'm going to come inside you—" he warned. "Fill that sweet cunt. Mark you so every male knows you belong to me."

The wicked, intoxicating words sank into her pussy and Tate knew she was a breath, a touch away from orgasm. Fallon grabbed the zipper of her shorts and yanked it down, then allowed her only a moment to lower her legs and remove her shorts and panties before pulling her back into his arms, her legs around him, hands gripping his neck.

In one movement he positioned her on his cock and drilled deep into her cunt.

Tate cried out—her pussy clenching and convulsing around his shaft, desperate pleasure flooding her core.

"More," he growled. "You'll give me more. All your climaxes belong to me."

"Yes!" In one heartbeat, she became a creature of pure sensation. She rocked and thrust, driving him deeper as he fucked her. His cock filled her hard and fast, over and over again, until she couldn't take it. Another orgasm shot through her pussy.

Fallon snarled and nipped at her neck—harder than before, sending a different kind of pleasure into her sex. She moaned and pushed against him.

"That's it, baby. This sweet cunt knows it belongs to me. That I'm going to be fucking it, filling it for years to come. That's it. Come again." He rubbed his thumb against the top of her mound, sinking a deep caress into her clit and Tate couldn't stop the long wave of pleasure that rippled through her pussy.

"God, I love the feel of you. Your pussy clamping down on my cock." Even as he spoke he rode her, making her ache and need more.

"Fallon." She moaned his name and it was like a stroke of her tongue across his cock. The delicate little caress so powerful. Too much for him to contain. He reared back, letting his wolf lead, pounding into her, hoping he wasn't hurting her but knowing he needed to be deeper, needed to mark her cunt as his. He shouted as he punched his hips forward one more time, flooding her with his hot seed.

It took long minutes, stretching into forever, for him to recover himself, to find the strength to leave her body. He lifted his head and took stock of his surroundings. They were propped up against the wall. Instinct alone had kept him from letting them fall. His right leg was straight out, keeping his weight pressed forward.

He looked at Tate. She had the same dazed look on her face that he felt.

"You okay?" he asked, remembering the hard, heavy way he'd fucked her. But he couldn't regret it. The wolf inside him was practically licking his lips at the satisfied smile that curled Tate's lips.

"Yeah. You?"

"Yeah. If I could just figure out how to stand up without dropping you." He glanced around to see what she'd hit if they fell.

"I could stand up," she offered, laughter painting her words.

"Naw, I got you."

True to his word, he wrapped one arm around her ass and lifted, keeping her clamped to his side as he powered his way to standing. His cock shifted inside her and she realized he was hard. Again. Still. Hell, she didn't know. But she also didn't expect that she was done for the night.

Keeping her trapped against him, he pulled away from the wall and walked, each step rocking him inside her pussy. Drained, she closed her eyes, dropped her head to his shoulder and let him carry her. The light changed around them and she realized he'd walked into the bathroom.

A nudge of his hands indicated she should release his hips and reluctantly she swung her legs down, hating the loss of his cock inside her. The regret was brief knowing it wouldn't be long before he was inside her again.

Her feet touched cool porcelain and Fallon stepped in front of her, his body blocking hers as the first blasts of water streamed out of the shower. He grunted and she knew that had to be cold.

After a few seconds, the scattered drops of water that made it through his body-shield turned warm and he stepped to the side. Tate smiled her thanks as he moved out of the way, dragging her forward, into the hot spray.

"Too hot?"

"Never." She tried to face him as she flirted but his hands held her steady, face forward, the strong spray striking her nipples. Sensitive from Fallon's loving attention earlier today—God, was it only today?—the sharp droplets made her nipples hard.

Fallon pressed against her back, his cock sliding between her ass cheeks.

"Touch your breasts, Tate. Let me see you stretch those pretty nipples."

As he gave the command, he pumped his hips forward, as if promising a reward if she gave him what he wanted.

She slid her hands up and grabbed her breasts, using the touch she'd only ever used in the dark of night, her vibrator humming between her thighs. She pinched her nipples and pulled, tugging on them, giving them more pressure than any man ever dared.

"That's it, baby. Show me what you like." Soap coated his hands, making their skin slippery as they moved, a slow sensual dance as they washed away the dirt from the hike, blood from the battle and the remaining traces of his cum from between her thighs.

A long time later, Tate tipped her head back letting the water rinse the last of the shampoo from her hair. The heat from the water and the sensual caresses had turned frantic lust into languid desire. She opened her eyes and found Fallon before her—his eyes glowing with the hot, hungry fire she'd grown addicted to.

As if he read her mind, Fallon kissed her, soft and gentle, easing his tongue into her mouth, tasting her with long delicious strokes. Tate leaned into him, savoring the kisses and the freedom to smooth her hands across his body, spreading her fingers wide and rubbing down his back to squeeze that tight ass.

He groaned into her mouth.

"I need to taste you, baby," he whispered, sucking on her lower lip. "Need to put my tongue inside you."

His words were hot caresses on her flesh and she grabbed the shower wall to steady her trembling knees.

With one final kiss, he sank down, whispering kisses across her breasts, delicate bites on her nipples, followed by wicked swipes of his tongue as if comforting the tender flesh. Tate took a shallow breath and tried to fight the raging desire, holding back the pleas that were already forming in her mind.

Fallon knelt down, placing hot kisses on her stomach, a brief caress to the top of her mound as his fingers stroked her pussy lips. "So wet. Always wet for me." He moaned and the sound moved through her skin, tickling her clit.

He lifted her leg over his shoulder, opening her wide to him, giving her a heartbeat to anticipate his touch before he began to lick, laving his tongue across her skin, swirling the hard tip around her clit, teasing and retreating as she squirmed, trying to get closer.

Her pussy tingled and clenched, melting beneath the sweet assault. He thrust two fingers into her as his lips whispered across her clit, soft, fiery caresses, like warm lava flowing through her pussy. With his fingers pumping inside her, his tongue flicked and tasted, making brief forays between her pussy lips, drawing back and focusing attention on her clit.

Tate grabbed the shower curtain to help her stay upright. He lapped at her clit, a delicate teasing stroke before he moved lower, replacing his fingers with his tongue and sliding into her, stretching as far as he could reach.

The shallow, focused penetration sent a sharp ache into her pussy. He rubbed his tongue along the inside wall, thrusting into her like a tiny cock, massaging the sensitive entrance until Tate found herself moving against him, trying to draw him deeper. Make him fuck her.

He drew back, a wicked glint in his eyes promising that he wasn't done.

He put his fingers back inside her as deep as he could reach as his mouth covered her clit and began to suck, delicate, gentle pulls of his lips, perfectly timed to the short pulses of his fingers. The pressure spiked and she cried out as it erupted, spreading to the distant reaches of her body. A crash shattered the silence of the room. Tate opened her eyes and saw she'd pulled down the shower curtain.

Her legs still weak she looked at the man kneeling at her feet. He threw off the plastic curtain and smiled up at her—a wicked animal smile. He licked his lips as if savoring the lingering taste of her cunt.

Abruptly he stood and yanked her close, her body quickly adjusting to his, her legs opening to accept his cock. Her head dropped back, enjoying the aggressive bite of his teeth on her neck.

"I need you."

"Yes," she moaned, squirming to put his cock inside her.

"Not here." He smacked the water off and picked her up, gingerly climbing over the fallen rod and curtain. Some day, Tate would no doubt find it all amusing but now, she needed Fallon, her body tuned to the desire that flowed through his.

He carried her to the huge bed and dropped her in the center, following her down and entering her in one long delicious stroke. They both groaned, the sound reverberating between them as their lips met.

Tate pulled her head away and placed her mouth on his neck, biting down hard, knowing she would leave a mark on him — like the one she knew decorated her skin.

Slow and sensuous disappeared. Fallon's eyes popped open and he grabbed her hips, holding her as he thrust inside. It was a sensual battle for control, each trying to lead, to force the other to come first but in the end, Tate let go, let her orgasm flow. Fallon shouted her name and filled her pussy once again.

Chapter Five

 භ

Her head resting on Fallon's chest, her fingers wandering across his stomach, Tate stared at the slowly darkening sky. A meal had miraculously appeared outside the bedroom door an hour ago. They'd fallen on it ravenously, both of them starving after eating trail mix for the past two days. Now, with sated appetites they lay in silence.

Reluctant to disturb the sensual moment, but knowing she had to, Tate sighed. "I should go. I've got work tomorrow and my neighbors are taking care of my cat."

Fallon raised his head and stared at her with wide eyes. "You have *a cat*?"

"What? You don't like cats?"

Laughter rumbled from his chest. "Probably not the way you do." He pressed her closer, not seeming to understand that she was leaving. "We'll find a way to make it work."

Make it work? What did that mean?

A knock on the door stopped her from asking. With a groan, Fallon nudged her off his chest.

"Come on, honey. We've got to go."

"Go where?"

"Moon's on the rise. It's time for the run."

He climbed out of bed, hating to release her but knowing he needed this run—for himself and for his pack. They needed to see him and they needed to meet Tate, now, before the rumors ran wild.

Tate hesitated for a moment but then dragged herself out of bed. He'd exhausted her, he thought with pride. He gave her enough time to pull on shorts and tie the tails of her shirt beneath her breasts. The bra was toast and her nipples pressed against the material of her shirt. He growled as he looked at her, knowing he had to keep his wolf in control or he'd end up mounting her in front of the pack just to prove his ownership. The pack wouldn't find that outrageous but Tate might have a problem with it.

He grabbed her hand and led her from the room, walking quickly to avoid any questions. He didn't have time to explain — the moon was rising. He could feel it in his blood. He walked out the back door of the compound where many of his pack lived and into the forest, heading for the Gathering Space.

A strange sensation bubbled up in his chest and it took him a moment to recognize it as joy. Pure pleasure at being with Tate and being able to take on his wolf's form. His laughter filled the night and he started to run, pulling Tate with him.

Moments later, they came to the clearing and Fallon slowed his steps. The space was crowded with people, well over a hundred, most of them naked. The few that remained dressed were either stripping or wearing nothing more than blankets for warmth.

A cheer went up as Fallon entered the clearing and walked to the center. Tate had no choice but to follow.

Fallon smiled and raised his hand in greeting. The pack grew silent. "It's been a difficult year — for all of us. But this is the First Moon Rise. A new year. The time when our wolves grow strong and our connection to the land is the greatest.

"It is also a new beginning for me." He pulled Tate in front of him, knowing the other wolves would recognize his scent on her, smell his cum on her thighs. "I have chosen a new mate." She stiffened but didn't move away. A low rumble of discord went through the crowd. Fallon silenced them with a look. "My wolf has chosen her. Though she cannot shift, she will lead at my side. She will raise my cubs." He paused. "She has my heart and I ask you to welcome her as my bride."

There was a long silence then the sound began — the howl. He glanced at Rebecca and knew she'd started it. Luc joined in and slowly all the werewolves tipped back their heads and released the long low sound. Discordant and harmonious at the same time — the sound grew flowing through the trees, reaching out to the packs in the distance.

As it faded away, Fallon nodded his thanks to his pack. He knew it wouldn't be easy but he wasn't letting Tate go.

That battle would come but now it was time to run.

He looked down at her. "Don't be frightened and whatever you do, don't run." He gave her a quick kiss. "The moon rises!" As he shouted the words, he began to change — his bones creaked and stretched, shrinking and shifting. His face elongated and he fell to his hands.

Tate watched, afraid to blink, afraid to look away, stunned by the sudden change in her lover. It was over quickly and she looked at the animal at her feet — the wolf.

She glanced up. She was surrounded by wolves. A few humans remained at the edges of the circle, watching.

A nose nudged her hand and Tate jumped. She looked down. Fallon stood beside her, his tail wagging, his mouth open in a friendly wolf grin.

With a final lick of her hand, Fallon turned and ran, heading into the dark forest. A single line of wolves followed him while others turned and ran down other paths. Within minutes, she was alone.

Shock reverberated through her mind. What the hell had just happened?

"Are you okay?"

She looked up at Caitlin. The woman had been kind to her earlier.

"I think so."

"Are you going to stick around?"

211

She shook her head. "I have to go." She needed time to sort it all out.

"Fallon will want you here when he gets back." Caitlin winked. "Things get very sexual around here near the moon rise. Especially after a run. They'll all come back, horny and looking for someone to mount."

"He knows where to find me." She stalked away. "I've got to go feed my cat."

* * * * *

Tate stared at her desk and the pile of paperwork that cluttered it. It was almost impossible to get anything done. She hadn't heard from Fallon in three days. Not since the night he and a hundred of his friends and relatives had turned into wolves before her eyes.

Caitlin had said things got very "sexual" around the moon rise. No doubt Fallon was working off his urges with one of the pretty female werewolves.

The pencil lead broke against the paper and Tate growled. She was having that kind of day.

Without looking up, she sensed someone in her doorway. Giving her heart a moment to stop pounding, she raised her eyes. The noise from the small station house faded as Fallon looked at her—his eyes glowing with a dark light, a mixture of pain and hunger.

"May I come in?" he asked brusquely. She nodded and he entered, closing the door behind him. He looked a little ragged. His hair seemed longer and she doubted he'd shaved since the morning they'd hiked up the mountain. There was definitely something of the wolf still inside him.

Unwilling to face him sitting, she stood to meet him on equal ground. She placed her hands on her hips and challenged him with her stare.

"I know you're pissed at me and you probably have a right to be," he conceded.

"Damned straight."

"I know it was a shock but I thought you understood. I'm a werewolf." He stepped closer, like he was compelled to be near her. She didn't retreat. Instead she met him at the side of her desk. "I should have allowed you to see me change before that moment and given you a chance to get used to the idea before you saw it that night but there really wasn't time."

She shook her head. "I'm not pissed about you being a werewolf. I knew *that* before I ever climbed that mountain with you."

"What? How?"

She could see she'd surprised him.

"The wolves. They were all killed with silver bullets."

"And from that you decided I was a werewolf?"

The disbelief in his voice made her sigh and she realized she needed to confess. "I knew something was different about this town and after the wolves started to dying, I nagged Rebecca until she told me."

"My sister and I are going to have a chat," he muttered. "But if you're not mad about the wolf thing—what is it?"

All of the anger she'd been carrying for three days poured out. "Fallon—you announced to your entire pack that I was marrying you. Becoming your mate and what was that about being a Luna? What does that mean? Hell, you told *them* you loved me before you mentioned it *to me*." He opened his mouth and she could see an apology on his lips but she wasn't ready to forgive him. Not yet. "And then, you don't come see me for three days. I guess your love doesn't extend past getting your rocks off with one of the hot bitches who lives with you."

Somehow, he didn't think she meant "bitch" the way they did in his world.

"Honey—" He reined in the wolf and slowly approached. "I'm sorry, I didn't think before I spoke. I was so wrapped up

in you, I assumed you knew my feelings and returned them."
He realized now it was an assumption he shouldn't have
made. He'd been so focused on having her, giving the wolf
and his body what it wanted, that he hadn't thought about
how she would feel. He put his hand to her cheek, turning her
head so she looked at him, so he could taste her lips one time
before he said, "I love you.

"And, I stayed away for the past three days because I
wasn't sure I could control the wolf around you. He wanted
you too much. I'd've have pounded myself into you for three
solid days and I knew you weren't ready for that."

She looked up — with defiantly dry eyes.

"You didn't sleep with any of them?"

He shook his head and turned her in his arms, pressing
her back to his chest. Part of his soul eased as she moved with
him, let him touch her.

"Why would I fuck any of them?" Feeling the subtle
compliance in her body, he opened the front of her uniform
trousers and pushed his hand inside her panties. Hot liquid
coated his fingers and he growled. "This is the only pussy I
want." He nipped the nape of her neck, warning her that his
control was close to the end.

When she didn't push him away, he shoved her trousers
and panties down.

"Fallon, someone might—"

"Die if they walk through that door right now." He
rubbed his erection against her ass. "I need you, honey. Now."
He dropped his pants, freeing his cock to press between her
legs. "Open for me."

Knowing what he wanted, she bent forward, pushing her
ass high in the air, spreading her legs to open her wet pussy.
Heat flowed through her sex and her body responded, arching
her back, offering him her cunt to fuck.

Her mind was a tangled mass of thoughts and sensations. He loved her. He wanted her. He hadn't fucked those other women — and he was about to fuck her on her desk.

The professional in her screamed to stop him but the woman in her wanted this. Wanted to be claimed, marked by him.

He growled and she loved the sound, loved the way it made her feel.

He reached around and tested her — checking to see that she could take him. Then there were no preliminaries. He placed his cock to her opening and thrust in.

His cry matched hers and Tate felt the breath leave her body. He stretched her almost to the point of pain but it was too wonderful for her to stop. She could feel him. He was on the edge, barely controlled. She gripped the side of her desk and pressed back, driving him deeper, taking all of him.

Delicious pressure built deep inside her slick pussy as he rode her hard, each thrust pounding against one spot that made her want more, always more.

"That's it. That's where you feel it." He pressed against the same point, creating a new pressure, deep inside that seemed connect to every nerve in her body. Another hard thrust and the sensation built, pouring pleasure into her veins. Fallon growled and held himself inside her, the contractions of her orgasm triggering his own.

Satisfaction filled him as he poured himself into her again.

Breathless moments later, Tate straightened, a little lightheaded as she turned in his arms. He held her close, his cock still semi-hard between their bodies.

"I love you," he whispered against her lips...and he waited.

For a moment she thought about withholding the words. It was too soon. They didn't know each other well enough, but her heart knew the truth.

"I love you."

He smiled and the words seemed to encourage his cock to hardness—though from her experience, he didn't need much encouragement.

"Come home with me."

She was tempted. If she did, she'd spend the afternoon flat on her back—or bent over something, or pressed up against the wall. The position didn't matter. If she left now, she'd spend the day with Fallon's cock inside her. And while that wasn't a bad thing, she didn't want him thinking he could command her into bed or away from work on his whim.

"I have to work." A sharp nip on his lower lip accompanied her words to let him know she still wanted him.

The lines around his eyes deepened and she knew this was a man who wasn't used to being told "no" very often. If ever.

"Until when?" he said with a sigh.

"Six."

She thought he might protest but instead he nodded. "I knew you were going to be a challenge. One of the reasons I tried to stay away from you." He backed away and pulled up his shorts, grabbing a tissue so she could clean up a bit before she redressed.

"What were the *other* reasons?" She lifted her chin—her heart pounding in her ears as she waited to hear why she wasn't suitable.

"You can't change—so it's going to take some of the females time to get used to you being in charge."

Tate blinked, knowing she was going to have to ask about that one.

"And you're too damned distracting." She raised her eyebrows. "It's the way you smell."

"I don't smell good?"

"No, you smell great. You smell like cookies." He gave her a quick kiss. "I'll pick you up at six." He pressed her chin up so she looked him in the eye. "Don't be a minute late and don't expect to leave my bed tonight."

Epilogue

Tate stared at plastic white stick and tried to catch her breath. She looked at Rebecca—who she'd insisted be there since she was a doctor. Rebecca nodded. Tate looked at Fallon, sitting beside her, his hand curled around her hip. She took comfort in his warmth but not in the smug look on his face.

"I'm pregnant."

"I know."

"That's not possible." She looked at Rebecca. "My ex and I tried."

Rebecca shrugged. "Sometimes it's stress. Or something in your body could have changed."

"It's superior werewolf sperm," Fallon announced. He'd been telling her for three months that she was pregnant but she wouldn't believe him. Now, she had no choice.

Tate's head spun with details and questions as Rebecca slipped away. So much had changed in Tate's life in the past six months. She'd married Fallon, become the Luna—and that had been a major transition in itself. As Luna she was leader of the female members of the pack and given that she couldn't turn into a wolf, a few of the women had resisted Tate's presence. But with Rebecca forcefully at her side and a couple of well-placed right hooks at the appropriate moments, they'd learned to accept her.

The biggest challenge had been her cat. The poor beast had been a nervous wreck for the first three months living here. The presence of so many wolves had set her on edge. When Tate was home, the cat was at her side, feeling safe close to her human. When Tate was gone, the cat hid in their rooms, comfortable under the bed where none of the dog-creatures could get to her.

"You okay?" Fallon asked gently.

She nodded. "A little stunned. Happy," she assured him. "But stunned."

"Well, maybe, you and I should slip away." His voice dropped to that low seductive tone that warned he was intent on dragging her to bed. Of course, with Fallon, pretty much any way he spoke meant he wanted to drag her off to bed. "I'll soothe away your nerves and—"

The door burst open and Kaden, Fallon and Merina's son, bounced into the room. Kaden and Mariska had accepted Tate as their mother—particularly once Fallon had explained that his wolf had chosen her. That seemed to hold a lot of weight in this community.

"Hey Kaden, what's up?" she asked, nudging Fallon's hand away from her crotch where it had crept in mere seconds.

"Nothing." He took a big bite of cookie. "Taylor had to go home." He sounded sad.

"You like playing with Taylor?"

He nodded. "She's fun. And she smells like cookies."

With that statement, he turned and ran from the room. Tate watched him, feeling the same surprised tension move through Fallon's body.

"Did our five-year-old son just pick a mate?" Fallon asked.

Also by Tielle St. Clare

ಐ

About the Author

ഔ

Tielle (pronounced "teal") St. Clare has had life-long love of romance novels. She began reading romances in the 7th grade when she discovered Victoria Holt novels and began writing romances at the age of 16 (during Trigonometry, if the truth be told). During her senior year in high school, the class dressed up as what they would be in twenty years—Tielle dressed as a romance writer. When not writing romances, Tielle has worked in public relations and video production for the past 20 years. She moved to Alaska when she was seven years old in 1972 when her father was transferred with the military. Tielle believes romances should be hot and sexy with a great story and fun characters.

Tielle welcomes comments from readers. You can find her website and email address on her author bio page at www.ellorascave.com.

Tell Us What You Think

We appreciate hearing reader opinions about our books. You can email us at Comments@EllorasCave.com.

UNCONTROLLED MAGIC
Ravyn Wilde

છ

Dedication

∞

This book is dedicated to Brandon and Sarah. I'm so proud that you've taken the risk and are living your dream. Enjoy the new places, faces and opportunities that come your way in the next couple of years. I love and miss you both.

Trademarks Acknowledgement

∞

The author acknowledges the trademarked status and trademark owners of the following wordmarks mentioned in this work of fiction:

Hells Angels: Hells Angels, Frisco, Inc.

Chapter One

ဆ

Naked, Marissa sat on the Florida beach under the full moon. She watched her brother Ricardo disappear into the night with her best friend Jane held tight in his arms as he practically ran to their cabana. The coming centuries ought to be a lot of fun while they worked on controlling Jane's newfound magic. Her brother was in for a wild ride.

The tropical air felt warm, yet she shivered in reaction to unseen eyes on her body. Speaking of wild rides, the unmistakable heated gaze of a were-dragon watched her from the dark.

"Come out and play, little dragon," Marissa called softly.

She'd sensed the were-dragon just after Ricardo had completed the ritual that returned Marissa to...well, the dead. The same ritual that had altered Jane's molecular structure into that of a Druid-mage. If Ricardo hadn't been so worried about Jane's conversion, he'd have felt the were-dragon's presence.

Stifling a smile, Marissa took a deep breath, savoring the spicy, rich aroma that made her senses tingle. She *so* loved were-creature blood. The stranger better be willing to share.

"Woman, there is nothing *little* about me." The deep disgruntled voice washed over her, seeming to soothe the aches and pains of her recent ordeal. The fire in her blood ignited, her stomach clenching in hunger. Luckily for the dragon, she'd learned control centuries ago. The steel thread of her will kept her fangs from dropping, her body sitting relaxed on the sand.

What she really wanted to do was jump him. Bury her fangs into the large artery in his neck and wrap her legs around him in blood thrall. Make him beg for more.

When the dark-haired man stepped from the shadows, she had to agree with his statement. Far from little, he stood several inches over six feet, with a massive chest and tree-trunk biceps. He brushed his hair—so black it was almost blue—off his face, long curls skimming the top of his strong shoulders. Meeting his gaze, she fell into the amazing turquoise warmth of his eyes.

Oh baby. This one is hot! Goddess I love my life!

Just not right now. Worn out, her shoulders slumped from the nightmare of being nothing more than dust one minute and pulled back to her blonde, vampy self the next. She was hungry. Hopefully dragon-man wouldn't take a lot of coaxing to volunteer his blood. She didn't feel like attempting sweet talk.

First things first, she needed clothes. She tried to summon the energy to create them with her magic…and got nothing. Not even a thong. "Throw me your shirt."

"Ah, but I like the view," the man grumbled good-naturedly. Grabbing the bottom of his shirt, he pulled it over his head and threw it to her.

Marissa raised her arms to shrug into the extra-large tank top. Not that it covered much. The armholes on the black shirt hung almost to her waist, flashing boobs every time she moved. Ah, well…never let it be said that she was shy. Besides, it was only fair. Ridding him of his shirt gave her a fantastic view. Worthy of poetry, the man's bare chest revealed washboard abs and dancing pecs…beefcake extraordinaire.

"I heard the man call you Jillian." At this he smirked. "My name is Jack, and I would make a trade, vampire."

Jack. His name is Jack? Of course it is.

Jack and Jill went up a hill…and Jillian was about to see if the dragon's claims of "nothing little" had any merit. Slowly she gathered her legs under her, thought about standing on her own two feet. Realized quickly it might not happen. If vampires could sweat, she'd be doing it about now.

The man walked forward, holding out his hand in assistance. "I have a proposition for you."

Cocking an eyebrow at him in question, she hoped it was the kind of proposition a prim and proper girl would slap him for. Marissa would consider bending over to kiss his...toes.

Just to get things moving in the right direction.

Setting her small hand in his much larger one, she allowed him to pull her off the sand. Her legs wobbled and she swayed. It took a few moments before she could release her grip on Jack to stand on her own. She used the time to catalogue his many and varied assets. Strength. Yummy smell. Topping the list—flexible body parts. If she wore panties they'd be wet right now.

She would deal with his use of her hated first name, Jillian, *after* she heard his proposal. "Go on," she purred. "I'm all—ears." She grinned at him, negating this comment by flicking her tongue over her fangs.

"Blood for..."

When he hesitated, she cheerfully filled in the blank. "Sex?" she added hopefully.

"No! For escort." The man sounded appalled at her suggestion.

She narrowed her eyes at him. "You don't want sex, you want an escort?" Then why was he trying to pick up a naked vampire? If she wasn't such a nice girl, that kind of behavior could get him killed.

"It's not that I don't *want* sex. I just can't. But I *do* need a date."

"Don't try to tell me you can't get a date without offering your blood. I won't believe you."

"I haven't been a were-dragon for very long. I'm afraid I can't figure out how to control the dragon when I'm aroused. And if I get tired or angry or wait too long between changes, I shift whether I want to or not. And once I've changed, I don't command the beast, the dragon dictates our actions. A human woman wouldn't understand that a simple touch could get her killed." He shuddered. "I thought maybe a vampire could maintain enough personal space, would understand the things I need to avoid to live through a date."

"How long?" Marissa asked.

He didn't pretend confusion. "About ten months."

"Oh, poor baby, you've gone without sex for ten months?"

"I told you this isn't about sex. It's about a date. I'd really *like* sex, but it isn't worth your death."

She stepped closer, pressing her body against his and breathing in the invigorating cinnamon-clove scent of spicy dragon. Placing a hand on his warm skin, she used his chest as leverage, stood on tiptoe and whispered in a voice ripe with possibilities, "Honey, do I have a deal for you. Blood for sex. I'll throw in the little escort thingy as a bonus. I can teach you to control your dragon."

"As much as I appreciate the offer, sex isn't a good idea. What if I kill you?"

Marissa wasn't afraid of Jack. Or his beast. She only died when she had good reason to, like hooking her brother up with her best friend. The dragon posed no threat to her Druid-mage-turned-vampire self.

"These are fairly simple lessons you should have been taught by your sire. There's a very strict rule in the paranormal community — if you create a creature, you train it. A group that monitors this stuff hands out fairly severe penalties, so why didn't your sire teach you how to control the beast?"

His head dropped. "I killed her right after my first change. I'd dated her for a while, until she went dragon on me and took a chunk out of my arm. She told me she wanted a consort, one who could handle her beast. She fell asleep on the floor beside me in human form, leaving my arms and legs bound to the wall of her lair. I was pissed." He sounded a little sick.

She could imagine how pissed off she'd be if someone forced such a huge lifestyle choice on her without permission.

"Anyway, after I shifted, I didn't know how to manage the dragon body. I stepped on Nadia's head and my back claws decapitated her." He looked mortified.

Nadia? He'd decapitated Nadia! Marissa choked back a shout of laughter. Oh, that was rich. The dragon-bitch from hell deserved her death. She'd been creating *consorts* for centuries. Kept an entire Scottish castle full of them and Nadia didn't like to share. After training, the new men were locked inside, little more than sex slaves for her perversions. Marissa wondered if anyone had told the boys that ding-dong the bitch was dead. Maybe she'd wander over to Scotland after her escort duties were finished. Um, grateful dragon sex slaves. The mind boggled.

One more question, then she was moving this conversation back to his offer of blood. "So what do you need an escort for?"

Jack frowned at her then slowly answered, "My parents' fiftieth anniversary party."

Not much fazed Marissa, but this floored her. She stumbled back a step, separating their bodies. *His parents?*

"Oh shit. Tell me I don't have to dress in pastels and act like a demure lady. If that's what you need, I'm out. Demure has never been my style." She couldn't keep the little tremble of nervous anxiety from her voice.

Hands on his hips, feet spread, Jack focused a confused gaze on her. "I don't understand. You aren't terrified that I killed Nadia, yet pastels scare you?"

"You did the world a favor. CCOM has been trying to roast Nadia's ass for centuries."

"Who is CCOM and why did they want to kill her?"

Marissa sighed. She wasn't feeling perky enough for an extended supernatural hierarchy lesson. She wanted blood, sex and sleep, in that order. "CCOM stands for Controlling Creatures of Myth. It's an organized body that polices the paranormal, magical and mythical communities. Nadia was a bitch. As you already know, she made were-dragons without asking their permission. You would have become one more in a long line of sex slaves. CCOM does *not* go after someone unless the creature has stepped over the line between rotten and evil. Like I said, you did the world a favor, Jack. And yes, the idea of wearing pastels and meeting your parents scares the crap out of me."

His shoulders relaxed a little. "No reason to worry. Mom and Dad are ex-Hells Angels. Black leather and lace will be the uniform for the party."

Well. That was something anyway. "Where is it?"

"In the Rocky Mountains, just west of Denver. They've rented a bunch of cabins for the weekend."

That was convenient. All her worldly possessions were in an apartment in Denver. Marissa had to think about what month it was...September? October? It would be getting cold. Damn, so much for a few nights in the Florida heat. She really hated the cold. In the last few years she'd thought about moving, but she hadn't wanted to leave Jane. "When do we have to be there?"

"The party is in five days, I'll make airline reservations tonight."

"Airline reservations? Why aren't you flying there in dragon form? We could swing by my apartment and pick up some of my clothes. Use my car to drive to the party instead of waiting at the airport or rental counter." There was no way she'd have time to shop or conjure clothes *and* tame his beast. Coming up with enough outfits for...

"Hey, how long do you need an escort for?"

"The party starts Friday afternoon and ends Sunday night."

Three days. That meant at least eight outfits with coordinating shoes and jewelry. Nope. Even with a private supply of dragon blood, she needed her closet.

"Using the dragon isn't a good idea. The longer I stay in dragon form, the harder the beast is to control. This weekend means a lot to me. My parents have no idea what I've become. My family will soon start to question things, like why I haven't aged. After this party, I'll likely never see them again."

The look of sadness in his eyes unnerved her. She contemplated what being the only immortal in your family would be like. Decided it would suck rocks. Every single relative of Marissa's had eternal life spans. Well…Ricardo's wife and one of his children had been mortal. It devastated her brother when they died.

For centuries he'd lived with the pain and isolation, refusing to fall in love, especially with a mortal woman. But Marissa had a vision. She'd seen how perfect Jane was for Ricardo. The vision had prompted her to let her ex-boyfriend Marcus kill her. Marissa knew that Janie, a vampire hunter by trade—yeah, she had odd tastes in friends—would seek revenge by killing *Marcus*, and her death would serve to get Jane and Ricardo together. In the vision, she'd seen Ricardo bringing her back to life with a Druid ritual. Then she'd seen herself pulling Janie into the magic circle, converting her to an immortal Druid-mage so her brother could live happily ever after.

At least, that's what she'd *hoped* would happen. Visions could be tricky.

Well, she couldn't help Jack with his family. Steeling her resolve, she buried her empathy. This was about sex. And blood. "I'll show you how to control your dragon, you provide the blood and we're definitely having sex. We have a deal as long as we fly by dragon and have a room well away from your relatives. I'd prefer we didn't take the chance of being overheard and have someone running to your rescue."

"Done. But don't say I didn't warn you about my lack of control. There's a good chance someone will need to come to *your* rescue."

"Ah, young one...you have so much to learn. And I've only got a couple days to teach you. Come on, take me to your lair so we can get started."

"Don't you need blood first? How can you control my dragon and feed if you're so shaky?" He sounded worried.

"I'm not really going to control your beast. You are. I'll just show you how to do it, it's very simple." But he was right. If she tried to feed, he'd shift. And in her weakened condition she wouldn't live through the experience. So how...? She looked out at the ocean and slapped her palm to her head. "I am *so* stupid. Water!"

"You need a glass of water?"

Marissa shook her head in disgust. "No, water for *you*. Dragons can't swim. They don't like water because the membranes of their wings are easily damaged, and flapping while in water will definitely cause damage. You can't shift if you're at least partially submerged in water. Rain or a shower won't do it. All we have to do is go sit in the ocean or the pool, then I can safely feed and we can have sex."

"You mean to tell me for ten months, if I wanted to have sex, all I had to do was get in a hot tub!?" Each word was louder than the last.

"Well, yeah. Any body of water over a few inches will work as long as you're lying on your back." Marissa studied the ocean, thinking it would be awfully easy to accidentally tear his throat out if a strong wave tossed them around. "Let's go see what the pool in this place looks like."

Jack still couldn't believe it. *Water would control his beast?* Damn! He wished he'd known that little fact months ago.

He hurried after her, happy that his dragon had been compelled to check out the magic on the beach. Finding a female vampire in need of blood had been fortuitous. It hadn't hurt that he'd been immediately attracted to the green-eyed blonde.

All long legs and very generous curves, with skin as light as the palest cream, she looked so soft in the moonlight. If he didn't have to worry about his claws making an unplanned appearance, he'd run his hands over every inch of her body. He imagined her screams of pain and decided it wouldn't be a good idea.

Wet. She'd said he could have sex if he were in water. Jack shook his head in disbelief.

In the ten months he'd been a were-dragon, he'd kept to himself. Having only seen other paranormal creatures from a distance, he didn't have any idea what Jillian might be capable of. Or what rules governed his existence. He sure hoped she knew what she was doing.

He *did* know Jill required blood. He could feel her hunger hammering at him and the beast inside responding to her silent call.

Weird. Would he sense any vampire's hunger and feel the need to provide for them? Or was it just Jillian he wanted to care for? Well, it didn't matter.

When he started picturing his *wet* hands running over her *wet* body, he clenched his fists and took a deep breath, glancing up to follow Jillian with his eyes.

Her honey-blonde hair fell straight to her shoulders as she walked in the same direction her brother had, toward the private beach resort. Right now the long locks were a little disheveled from the ocean breeze and her recent revival. It looked as if she'd just crawled out of bed...

His pulse jumped, his cock twitching as it started to grow hard. Jack struggled to tamp down his growing arousal.

Her eyes were expressive, moss green and big enough for him to get lost in. Her high cheekbones, eyebrows arched in delicate bows and little pointed chin all worked to give her face a cute elfin expression. But there was steel underneath the sexy package, along with just a trace of inner bitch.

Well, he'd always liked his women strong.

The thought shocked him. She wasn't *his* woman. She was convenient and might be able to help him. Nothing more.

His beast could feel the magic in her, wanted to dip its claws in and wallow in her essence. The surge of power within his body was unwelcome. He quickened his pace, wanting to catch up to her. To tell her this wouldn't work. He felt his skin tighten. Pull. The burning in his gut told him the dragon wanted out. He took a deep breath, sucking in the fragrance of honeysuckle that seemed to cling to her skin. She smelled good enough to eat.

Shit.

He'd ended up with more than he'd bargained for and probably a lot more than he could handle. Yet, she thought she could teach him to control his beast. He wanted to take what she offered, but not if it hurt her.

This wasn't going to work. He should leave now, come back tomorrow night. Let her find someone else to provide the blood she needed so desperately. Deep inside, the dragon snarled in anger and he couldn't say the words that would stop this madness from happening.

She looked over her shoulder to make sure he followed and he got a side view of her body. His eyes focused on the sway of her breasts beneath the soft black cotton of his tank top. Turning, she sashayed toward the pool, keeping him spellbound.

He followed her like a lovesick puppy. From behind, the shirt molded to her ass, hiding her sweet softness. Teasing. When she turned slightly again, moving her arm to point at something ahead of her, plump mounds played peek-a-boo through the armholes. Material snagged on large, dark apricot-colored nipples gathered in hard little buds.

He wanted his mouth on her. He could feel blood start to pound in his groin. The shift of muscle played over his back and skin itched where wings began to form, arousal jumpstarting his change.

Catching up with her at the pool's edge, he started to pant. "I've got to go. Now!" he growled between clenched teeth. Fighting the break and snap of bone hurt. Bad.

Looking at him in question, she quickly stepped back, raised her arms — and shoved him into the pool.

Jack's head came out of the water and he gasped for breath. Immediately he felt his beast settle, his muscles unclench and his skin stop burning. The urge to shift receded, allowing other urges to fill the void.

Oh God! For ten months he'd avoided anything more than the first stirrings of lust. Every time he felt the rush of desire, he changed into a were-dragon. Now his erection pressed full and hard against his wet jeans, and he reveled in his body's heated sensations. It had been so fucking long since he'd, well…fucked. And standing above him was a blonde goddess, just waiting to take him in hand.

"We have a deal, dragon. When I take your blood, you're going to scream my name in ecstasy. It's Marissa, by the way. Jillian Marissa De'Angel. I don't care for Jillian. My friends and lovers use Rissa — remember that when you scream." She had enough energy to do a little flirtatious hair flip. But it made her head hurt.

"I like Jillian better. If you can't manage my beast, Jillian, you'll be screaming *my* name as you die. Again. And it's Jack, little Jill."

Wiping the water from his eyes kind of ruined the effort he'd made to sound menacing. After all, she's the one who pushed *him* in the water. She smiled at his reference to her recent ordeal and his insistence on using her first name. It didn't bother her as much as it usually did, maybe because the sound of their names together was cute, in a nursery-school kind of way.

Yeah. She was back from the dead. And man, did she have an appetite. "I heard your name the first time, Jack."

Chapter Two

ഇ

Standing at the side of the pool, Marissa stripped off the tank top.

His eyes narrowed to slits, focusing on the glorious sight of her naked body. Fantastic breasts, slim waist, small triangle of blonde hair at the apex of her thighs. He swallowed hard.

She kept her gaze locked on Jack's as she slowly lowered herself in the water and swam the few strokes needed to reach him. Tracking her as she slid through the water, with the dragon shackled, he could use his enhanced senses to his advantage. Colors became more vibrant, aromas developed nuances that could almost be tasted on his tongue.

"Look, this pool was made for you. There's a sunbather's ledge, so if you lie on your back, you'll still be in several inches of water. Or over there, behind the curtain of waterfall, is a hot tub."

"Will it bother you if someone is watching us?" His voice was hoarse in anticipation.

"Not really. But it might bother *them*." She shrugged and grinned at him. "After the first taste of your blood, I'll have enough energy to ward the area. No one will come near and we can do whatever we like. I'll touch every bared inch of your flesh with my mouth. Did you know there are more veins than the one in your neck that I can feed from? I promise you, Jack. Every one of those bites will bring you pleasure." Her voice was a seductive invitation to heaven.

He wanted her so badly he started to sweat in the water. "Yes! Oh God, Jillian. Hurry. I can't take much more of this." He raised his hands toward her and she took hold of his wrists, turning them and propelling him back to the edge of the pool.

"You'll take everything I give you, Jack—then beg for more." She laughed wickedly at his involuntary shudder.

He really hoped she lived up to her promise.

"Brace your upper body against the pool ledge and lift up your leg," she commanded.

As he watched her long, slender fingers, the simple act of untying his shoes and slipping them off his feet turned into pure erotic torture. When she ran the tip of one finger up his left instep, he had to bite his lip to keep from groaning in frustrated agony.

Releasing his foot, she slowly moved between his legs, sliding her hands up the wet jeans covering his thighs to cup his erection. "Let's make a little more room for this bad boy, shall we?"

The feel of her hands on his groin had his hips shifting in silent supplication. Every sweep of her fingers against his bulge sent another shudder of forgotten pleasure through him. His entire body tingled. Pulsed with life.

He could only manage to nod. His eyes darted between small hands stroking over the fabric and the perfection of her naked breasts gleaming with droplets of water. She massaged him through the cloth, grinning wickedly at his groan. He knew she could hear every pounding pulse of his blood.

Jack wanted to scream. His mouth went dry and he felt as if a vein were about to pop in his head. Both of them.

"Take my pants off!" he demanded.

She laughed huskily, shaking her head in denial. Moving her hand up to push the center of his chest, she sent a clear message that she intended to be in charge. "Say please."

He finally managed a strangled, *"Jillian, please!"*

Hearing him call her Jillian, when no one else dared use the name, gave her a small thrill. Meeting his gaze, she teased his bronze skin with the tips of her fingers, drawing her hand down his stomach toward the waist of his jeans. His body tensed when she traced small circles around his navel.

He watched through the water as her fingers unbuttoned his pants and they both struggled to push the soaked fabric down his thighs and off his legs. Jack tossed them out of the water to land on top of the shirt she'd discarded earlier. He listened as the breath rushed from her lungs and she sighed in delight.

"Ah, looky here—no underwear. I love a man who goes commando. It shows such confidence in his assets."

When Marissa allowed her breath to sigh over his skin, his cock jerked in response. Jack's heavy erection was a thing of beauty. Thick. Long. The dark blue vein throbbed wildly.

Bursting into delighted laughter, she hugged herself in an effort to keep from diving on him.

Jack's eyebrows rose in question. "Care to share your thoughts? It's a blow to a man's ego, getting naked only to have you laugh after the first good look."

"No blow to your ego here. I'm very impressed with your equipment, Jack. I just had a stray thought." She knew her sense of humor often left others puzzled. "I realized I'm going to be your first sexual experience as a supernatural creature. You're a were-virgin."

His bark of laughter brought a contented smile to her face. He got her joke.

Marissa reached to meet Jack's hands. The water level was just above his waist. Perfect. Slowly she skimmed her palms from his wrists, up his arms and to his shoulders. Stepping closer, she pressed her length against his, naked flesh against naked flesh. Enjoying the sensation of all that hyperwarm skin. Were-dragons put off a lot of heat because of the fire in their blood.

Suddenly serious, her eyes turned black. Moonlight highlighted his face. And neck. Neither dragon nor vampire needed light to see in the dark. No, her eyes had gone black in predatory anticipation of tracking his every move.

She leaned over, dragging her breasts over his smooth chest. Bent her mouth to his ear and whispered in a voice deepened to a husky murmur, "As a were-dragon, the sensation of every touch is multiplied. It will seem like a dozen hands—or mouths—are on your body. You'll beg me for release. But your dragon also gives you so much control. It will take a concerted effort on my part to make you come. My hands, my mouth, my body will bring you physical pleasure you've never dreamed of."

Moving to his mouth, she sucked his bottom lip between her teeth. Looking into his eyes, she smiled in slow erotic suggestion. She traced the shape of his lips with her tongue and nibbled with her fangs, demanding entrance. Allowing him to taste the promise of all she would do to him. Jack opened for her and the kiss went on forever.

She knew no one watched from the dark, but the risk of being seen added a thrill to her play.

"Tilt your head to the side." The soft whisper made him shiver in anticipation.

Marissa put her hands on his shoulders and used the leverage to lift her legs, wrapping them around his waist. Leaning forward to reach his neck, she traced the bulging vein there with her tongue, tasted the salty tang of extremely aroused male. Nipping at him, she finally gave in to her own desires. Sucking over the vein, she allowed her fangs to sink deep into his flesh.

White lightning hit Jack and he stretched into Jillian's bite. Ah, *damn* that felt good. Every cell in his body came alive and his blood pulsed in fevered ecstasy. Losing control, he pumped his hips. Seeking more. His bobbing erection found what it wanted, the tight clenching heat of her pussy. He whimpered when she took her mouth away from his neck, moaned in pleasure when she relaxed over him. He rocked his hips and impaled her with his cock at the same time she sank fang in a vein over his heart. With his hands at her hips, he raised and lowered her slowly.

The jolt of energy from his dragon's blood sent Marissa into a spin. Quickly she wove a ward of silence and dread over the pool, keeping mortals away. She reached for him with her mind. Wanting to share the incredible sensations swamping her body.

Jack's body convulsed around Jillian every time she drew on him and took more blood. He could feel the pull from his toes, burning a direct path through his groin and up to her mouth. By the time she'd bitten a half dozen places on his upper body, he decided he'd gladly volunteer to be her personal blood bank.

One of her hands fell from his shoulder to glide down his chest. She pinched his nipple between her finger and thumb, and his blood and body surged.

He jerked and almost sank to his knees. Lifting her off his cock, he positioned her breast in front of his mouth so he could suckle her tempting nipples. "God, you taste good," he mumbled around her flesh. "But this isn't working for me. I need more leverage."

"Just make sure you stay in water up to your thighs," she purred as he carried her underneath the waterfall to the private, man-made cave enclosing the hot tub.

Quickly stepping from the pool into the swirling water, he positioned Jillian over the edge of the hot tub, her ass a sweet temptation. "So good," he murmured as he took his cock in his hand, slowly guiding it to her entrance. The water just brushed the apex of his thighs, teasing his balls. Bumping them. He jerked forward and buried himself balls deep. "Damn, you're tight!"

"Damn, you're huge," she groaned, her tone assuring him that was a good thing.

Bending over her, he raked his teeth on her shoulder. Marking her. He rocked his hips, his cock dragging in and out of her clenching pussy.

She sought and found him with her mind. *"Feel everything. Allow the beast to rise and pour it into your sexual satisfaction. He won't get out. He is well and truly caught. But we can use him for this."*

She felt his amazement at their shared mental path, but it got better. Because communication wasn't the only thing they could use their linked minds for. She sent him the sensations she was feeling, taking everything he felt in return.

Panting, Jack tore his mouth away. The impressions spiraling through his mind were incredible. He received a clear picture of what she felt, the tightness and sensitivity of her flesh as his engorged shaft pumped in and out of her. The energy and complete enjoyment she'd taken from first his blood and now his body. Their souls were merging—the entwining passion growing to wrap them both in an escalating surge of desire.

They merged into a single consciousness, sharing their building orgasms. The connection acting as a conduit for her hunger and his yearning loneliness, causing their bodies to pulse with the tempo set by his shaft.

"Think dragon," she gasped.

In his mind Jack could see a picture of what she wanted. He called to his dragon, but the only part of his body that answered was his cock and skin. He felt his shaft grow thicker. Lengthen. His flesh pebbled in sensitivity. The droplets of water on his body felt like little tongues as they ran in rivulets down his chest. "Oh God," he groaned.

"Yes!" Marissa screamed, overcome with the fantastic feel of him pounding his huge cock into her. The hard and fast thrust of his hips drove his erection deep, balls slapping against her sensitive clit. She moaned when he ran a finger down her spine, sliding one hand into the crevice between her cheeks then lower to coat his fingers with their mixed secretions, using them to prepare her puckered anus. Marissa twitched and thrust against him, her keening cries providing encouragement.

Her muscles clenched in anticipation and she forced herself to relax. His finger slid an inch into her tight second entrance. "Oh, yes! Yesyesyes," she chanted. She clutched at the slick tile of the hot tub, desperately searching for something to hold on to.

Jack's stomach pushed against the hand at her ass, driving his finger inside the firm rosette as he dug his cock into the pulsing spasms of her cunt.

"Jack!" Marissa screamed, bucking hard against him. She felt the bite of sensual pain in her ass, the thrust and drag of his long, thick cock in her vagina. When his testicles slapped against her clit, the collective sensations pushed her over the edge. She struggled against him as unbearable pleasure exploded through her body.

Slumping forward, her forehead pressed against the cool tile as she took huge gulps of air.

Marissa's climax rippled over Jack's cock. Her gripping muscles milked his shaft and he still wanted more. He removed his finger from her ass and slid his cock in a slow, agonizing withdrawal from her hot channel. He gently guided her until she sat on a bench below the hot tub's surface. Going to his knees in front of her, he pulled her thighs apart and slid his still-hard cock back inside her pussy as she stared at him with passion-glazed eyes. That look made ten long months of waiting worth every second. She whimpered as he cupped one breast to play with her nipple. He smiled at her hiss and felt her body tense against him. Pressing forward, he bent to lave her nipples, his tongue teasing her sweet skin. Drawing back, he growled, "Bite me." And bared his neck to her.

The white-hot pain as her fangs slid into him was an inconceivable pleasure. "Damn it, suck me. Suck me hard!" he ordered.

With slow, deliberate pressure she drew on his flesh and swallowed the first drops of blood. He tensed and thrust his hips hard against her, grinding as she suckled. They fell into a sensual rhythm, mimicking each other's movements.

Jack roared in erotic fulfillment as he buried himself deep. The sharp slice of pleasure expanded and burst through him like a lash of fire. His control shattered and he felt his semen explode, filling her hot cunt. His chest heaved and he fought for breath as he felt Jillian pull back and lick the two pinpricks at his neck.

Damn it felt good to be alive. In amazement, he realized it had been a long time since he'd felt that way. Carefully he pulled out of her and sat beside her on the bench.

They rested for several moments, not saying a word. Until Marissa realized how late it was getting. The sun would be up soon.

"Come on, time for a quick dragon-control lesson. Then you can take me to your lair."

"Are you sure you want to do this now? I can come back tomorrow."

"No, it's okay. My magical battery is fully charged thanks to you!" She grinned and gave him a quick kiss as they walked hand in hand back to the beach.

Jillian wiggled her fingers. Suddenly he was wearing his jeans and she was dressed once more in his shirt, the wet clothes now dry. At her demonstration of power, Jack allowed his doubts to drift away, focusing on what Jillian was saying to him.

"The first concept you need to learn is that *you* control the magic. The magic does not control you."

"But I can't do magic," he protested.

"You're a dragon. You breathe fire and you fly. You're immortal. If those aren't forms of magic, what are they?"

When Jack didn't answer, she continued, "You need to choose a focal point. Something you can concentrate on and keep with you when you shift. It will help you keep the human side of your brain locked within the dragon body, giving you control of its actions."

Jack thought for a moment and then smiled wickedly. His focal point would be Jillian—naked, head thrown back in the throes of passion as she screamed his name. If that didn't keep his mind human, nothing would. Silently he reached out to trail a finger down her soft cheek. "I've got my focal point, Jillian," he murmured.

Marissa shivered at his touch and the way he said her name. She had to shake off the urge to step into his arms and snuggle—which *so* wasn't like her. "Okay. Let's try to bring the dragon out a little then force him back. Once you've called him, try to shut it off. Just like a woman in labor, hold your focus point and pant until the impulse to change recedes," she advised.

"Oh wonderful. Like panting won't attract attention when I'm out in public. I might as well turn into a dragon," he grumbled.

"The panting is how you start to train your body. Eventually you'll learn to just *think* the beast away. You have to start at the beginning, working your way up to controlling the change with a simple thought."

Jillian stood before him and the space surrounding them began to flicker and vibrate, shielding them from mortal eyes. He went to his knees in pain and began to transform. His jeans seemed to just dissolve into his body. Dragon's blood rushed through his veins like wildfire, shifting the cells and molecules to turn him into a were-dragon. Jack allowed the beast to rise within, used her suggested panting method and visual focus technique to beat it back down. It hurt. His skin started to pull and stretch. A bone popped and he quickly thought of how Jillian's apricot nipples tasted so sweet in his mouth. Panting heavily, he fought the beast and was amazed to feel it receding.

Taking a deep breath, he called it back, waiting until his jeans disappeared again and his skin started to shift into scales. He thought about Jillian as she sank her fangs into his neck, her plump breasts pressed into his chest. He fought again, and the dragon vanished a second time, a little easier than before.

Calling the beast a third time, he waited until scales covered his arms and his hands turned to claws. He recalled the feel of Jillian's tight pussy clenching around his cock and started panting, slipping back to human form. This last time didn't even hurt. "Wow! It worked!"

"Now comes the real test. Hold your focus while letting the dragon emerge. This should allow you to control the dragon's actions."

Jack nodded.

He felt his muscles swell, stretching to re-form as something else. Bones snapped, molded into new shapes and sizes. His clothes were absorbed into his flesh as multicolored shades of red, gray and black scales slowly materialized in place of his skin. Muted to human ears, the crackle-pop-slurping sound of his transformation was like fingernails on a chalkboard — it set every inhuman nerve on edge.

When the noise ended, the dragon stood up, stretched and shook his wings. For the first time since he'd become a were-dragon, Jack looked out through his dragon eyes and knew he was in control. Clinging to the image of Jillian naked, he managed to maintain the highest level of awareness he'd ever had within his beast form.

Every other time he'd changed, he knew he existed within the dragon. But the human Jack had been shrouded in a deep mental fog. The dragon decided what they saw or did. Tonight Jack felt the difference, knew he controlled his beast.

He had no urge to reach out and use his claws on Jillian or to open his mouth and take a bite with the sharp teeth lining his jaw. Neither did he want to roast the woman standing before him by breathing fire over her skin. He retained focus. Flexing his impressive thirty-foot, coal-black wingspan as he would his biceps in human form, he waited for her reaction.

Marissa smiled in relief. She'd done it! Well, Jack had done it, but she'd shown him how. Piece of cake! She knew it had worked because his eyes remained turquoise. If the dragon ruled, the turquoise would be swallowed by fire. In dragon form, Jack's eyes were bigger and a little slanted, with internal flames shining inside turquoise orbs. Beyond the bonfire she could see intelligence as he processed his success and waited for her to acknowledge his dragon in some way.

She wasn't afraid of his dragon. Energized from tonight's feast of both blood and sex, she had no doubt that she could handle him. "So. You want me to just climb on up or did you plan on bending down and offering a lady your knee?"

The dragon lowered its long neck to the ground, squatting to allow her to climb on its back. How majestic and graceful Jack was in the large beast. He may not have learned how to control the magic, but without his realizing it, he'd learned to control the body.

Marissa tried to get comfortable. She held onto his neck to keep from falling, the sharp red and gray scales covering the body making it a difficult task. The rough edges chafed between her spread thighs and scratched her hands, and she had to sit forward far enough to ensure his wings weren't hindered in flight.

"We need to hurry. The sun is coming up." Leaning over, she pulled on his ear to make sure he heard her.

She smiled when he nodded the huge dragonhead and soared into the air.

Chapter Three

ಐ

Landing in front of Jack's house, Marissa looked at the stark beauty surrounding her. With wide, sweeping porches fronting a wall of windows, the house was fantastic.

She was shocked to see he *didn't* have any protection wards on his lair.

She waited while Jack switched into human form, his jeans reappearing once again. "You don't know how to ward your home, do you?"

Frowning as they climbed the steps to his porch, he said, "I don't really understand what you mean. I know what wards are, but I told you I don't do magic. I get that the dragon is magic, but I can't do spells or anything."

"You can do *this*. Paranormal creatures can ward their place of rest. Or anything they want to protect, for that matter. The ability comes from your dragon. Think of warding as a type of magical trap—or maybe a magical security system." She shrugged. "However you want to describe it, you need to guard yourself."

"Show me."

"Okay, we'll use something simple. The symbol doesn't matter, so you can pick what you want. The trick is to inscribe the air and think about protecting your home or whatever you're trying to keep safe."

Jack loved watching Jillian. It turned him on. He tried to concentrate on her movements. To watch her slim fingers weave a protection spell and infuse it with magic. The warm night air filled with her honeysuckle scent. Her blonde hair shifted in the light wind, the silky tendrils brushing the side of his face in a soft caress.

"You're not paying attention," she accused.

"Sorry. You distract me."

As Jillian laughed, he followed her directions, using his finger to sketch a peace sign in the air near his door while thinking *protection*. He was shocked when he felt the magic permeate his house with an almost electrical charge. "Wow! It worked." Jack remembered saying the same words when he'd controlled the dragon.

Marissa could feel the first fingers of dawn reach toward her with their deadly rays. "Hurry, the sun is coming."

Jack pulled her through the house, down a flight of stairs hidden behind a bookcase and into his true lair. The sun wouldn't reach her here.

"Oh goddess! This is fantastic!" She stepped into a cave big enough for Jack's dragon to turn around in. And since his dragon had a thirty-foot wingspan and was about forty feet from nose to tail-tip, that meant the cave was huge. The limestone ceilings stretched high and a small waterfall on one side fell about fifteen feet into a clear pool. The pool would be convenient for training Jack.

Strolling to the center of the room, she turned in a circle, noticing he had electricity. Carved into the walls were small nooks containing light fixtures. They gave off just the right amount of radiance, making the white walls glow softly without hurting preternatural sight. Because the lighting was recessed, the dragon couldn't accidentally scrape them off the walls. Across from the waterfall was his nest. Piles of velvet and silk blankets covering what looked like a very large mattress.

"I didn't know there were caves like this in Florida."

"Florida has dozens of caverns and caves, most of them underwater. This one is near Florida Caverns State Park, which has a few dry caves. There are untold miles of tunnels and caverns like this one, most carrying billions of gallons of fresh water each day to several hundred springs in the area. This was Nadia's lair. Evidently, about a hundred years ago she built a couple of underground dams to channel the water away from this cavern. I bought the house about a month after I…"

His voice trailed off. Marissa knew killing Nadia bothered him, yet she didn't doubt the bitch had turned whoever built the dam into a dragon once the work was finished.

Jack joined her and she enveloped him in a comforting hug, taking a deep breath. Jack's cinnamon-clove scent filled the large room. The smell did something to her. Made her hot. She could feel the moisture start to trickle between her legs and her nipples harden into tight points.

Jack raised his head from her shoulder and sniffed the air. Jillian's honey-sweet arousal called to him.

But it screamed at the dragon within.

Before he realized what was happening, the shift started and this time he couldn't stop it. Jumping back, his strangled cry of shock turned into a growl as the dragon sprang to life.

Shit! She should have known a couple of lessons wouldn't completely tame his beast. And with the rising sun distracting her, she left Jack's wards on the house. Now she was magically trapped with a hormonally charged beast intent on eating her…or worse.

"Jack. Listen to me, Jack. You can reassert your dominance. All you have to do is mentally grab onto your focus and beat the dragon back from inside. You can do it, Jack."

Marissa could sense Jack struggling with the dragon for supremacy. Carefully she crept behind the beast as he momentarily ignored her. If the house weren't warded, all she'd have to do is snap her fingers and go…where? The sun was up. She couldn't even transport anywhere in Jack's house or magically chain the beast to a wall. Ohhh no. Dumb, blonde Marissa showed Jack how to ward his home. Now *she* couldn't use her magic within the shielded walls.

Stupid, stupid vampire!

"Not working." Jack's jumbled thoughts frantically reached her mind. *"Naked you focus. Dragon wants."*

He'd used a memory of her naked as his focus?

Fuck. Fuckfuckfuck. They were so screwed.

"Okay, keep trying. It will help keep him distracted. I'll think of something." She hoped.

The dragon turned his long neck, flame-colored eyes searching for her.

Oh great. No turquoise.

The sound of rushing water echoed in her ears as she stood immobile. Not breathing. Waiting.

The dragon's eyes narrowed on her and he took a deep breath. Marissa knew he was filling his lungs with her scent, assessing if she was prey or mate. Since her arousal had been doused with spine-tingling fear, she was betting on the former.

Marissa shrieked and jumped straight in the air when the dragon opened its jaws and surged toward her. She threw her hands up to keep from banging her head on the rock ceiling and knocking herself unconscious. She was too newly resurrected to become a dragon snack.

She landed behind him. The dragon's back remained to her as he tried to catch her scent. With a flash of inspiration, she dove into the pool.

Thank goddess for that Olympic diver she'd dated a few years back. She didn't make a splash.

"Jack?"

"Here. You okay?"

Underneath the water, crouched below a rock ledge, she smiled. *"Yeah. As soon as you shift to human, would you take the wards off your lair? Think 'open sesame' or something and wave your hand as if erasing the symbol."*

Marissa settled down for a long wait.

* * * * *

Peering through the water, Ricardo frowned at his sister sitting cross-legged on the bottom of the pool. *"Marissa, what are you doing?"*

Hearing Ricardo's voice in her mind, she looked up. And groaned. Shit, big brother to the rescue. Shooting to the surface, she wrapped her cold body in the large towel her brother conjured for her. "His dragon couldn't smell me in the water." She could feel embarrassment heating her face. "What are you doing here?"

"You're not the only one who has visions," he said smugly. "I was sleeping this morning when I sensed you were in danger. It took me a bit to find you in my scrying crystal and then transport Jane and myself here."

Ricardo pulled Marissa into his arms and kissed her on the forehead. "I took the liberty of bringing a collar for your pet dragon," he added, nodding at Jack.

Wearing a gold chain collar around his neck, Jack stood a few feet away, looking miserable over what had happened.

"It's okay, Jack." Marissa wanted to go to him but Ricardo still had his arm around her.

"I see I worried needlessly about you finding something to eat. I want to thank you, Ris. For Jane. Don't ever gamble with your life again." His voice went gruff with emotion as he stood back to shake her.

Marissa smiled. Her blond, Viking-sized brother had figured out what she'd done. "Thanks for the collar, it'll come in handy. I'm going with Jack to a family party he wants to attend, and he'd prefer not to eat the guests or scare the shit out of them by shifting during the festivities."

Marissa loved her older brother at times like this. He didn't raise an eyebrow or ask if she knew what she was doing. *She* could have made Jack a restraining collar, but Ricardo's magic made hers look like prepackaged spells. His was stronger, more flexible, which meant there would be no margin of error, an important issue when dealing with dragons. Besides, she never would have thought to do so.

Jane bounded into the room. "This place is great! Have you seen the bathroom upstairs, Marissa?" Her big blue eyes widened in confusion and she veered toward Jack, circling him before putting her nose close to his neck to sniff. "What is he?" Obviously Jane's newly awakened Druid-mage senses were working. She just needed reference points to process Jack's scent.

Marissa laughed, walking over to hug her best friend. "Jack is a were-dragon, Janie. He's also my new lover for the next week." A pang of remorse shot through her body. She wasn't sure a week would be enough. Ignoring the thought, she raised her blonde eyebrows at Jane's outburst.

"Are you nuts? You go from macho-bullshit vampire who kills your ass to a dragon!? Damn, girlfriend. Get a vibrator." Jane winced. "Sorry, Jack."

"No problem," he mumbled drolly.

Since it was obvious Jack felt uncomfortable, Marissa explained to Jane and Ricardo where she'd be for the next week, all the while guiding them to the exit.

Jack didn't miss the threat in Ricardo's moss-green eyes. Eyes that looked so much like his sister's, except for the foreshadowing of death if Jack somehow managed to hurt Jillian. He nodded his understanding before Ricardo left the room, Jillian closing the door behind him. Jack didn't have a problem with the brotherly warning, he agreed with Ricardo's unspoken intent. He would deserve to die if he harmed her. He only hoped that by leaving Jillian in his lair, Ricardo believed his sister would now be able to control him with the help of the collar.

The flames started to crackle and dance in the fireplace by his nest. Jillian must have started it. He watched her walk across the cavern, peeling off wet clothes before climbing onto the mattress to burrow under the blankets.

"My wards prevented you from using your magic?" he asked her.

"Yes. Sorry, I didn't think."

Jack shook his head violently. "You have nothing to be sorry for. I couldn't control—"

"Stop it. I'm the one who forgot about the wards. I also knew the beast would think I'd invaded its lair. Did *you* know that? No. So stop blaming yourself and come keep me warm. I've been in the cold water for hours because of my own stupidity."

Jack wasn't happy letting her take the blame, but he really wanted to join her under those blankets. He could definitely keep her warm. And volunteer his blood. Stripping out of his clothes, he climbed in next to her, wearing nothing but the gold chain to keep his dragon corralled.

"You don't have to breathe, do you?"

"Nope. Vampires don't need oxygen. The movement is just for show."

"Umm." Nuzzling her neck, he pulled her into the warmth of his very hot body. "Let *me* show *you* something…"

Jack leaned over and claimed Jillian's lips.

The surge of pleasure as his mouth joined hers tore through her body like smoldering fire bursting into flame. Jack kissed like a man obsessed and Jillian welcomed the blaze.

He moved with a power and sensuality that enthralled her. The plunge and retreat of his tongue seemed to carry an electrical charge that zapped every nerve and brought them shrieking to life. Pulsing, throbbing life.

She could feel her sex engorge and spasm, the first trickles of readiness seeping from deep inside to coat her pussy. Breasts swelled and her nipples peaked, demanding attention. She shifted in his arms, rubbing her body against him. The action increased her frustration and need.

Marissa fought to keep still. Waiting. Craving a harder touch. She felt her incisors lengthen in anticipation. Her skin burned, her heart slamming against her chest at the onslaught of powerful need. She ground her mouth into his, spreading her legs slightly to tease the hard ridge of his cock against the apex of her thighs. She moaned as he trailed his hands down to cup her breasts.

Jack couldn't get enough of Jillian as she came alive in his arms. Her mouth welcomed his invasion and she met his wild desire without flinching. Her honey-sweet taste was addicting. With her body pressed strong and lush against him, he questioned his control over the dragon. He made a sound that was half gasp, half growl as his lips moved against hers and he realized the chain around his neck would hold off the beast.

He kissed her with lips and teeth and tongue. The small sounds she made in the back of her throat wrapped around his soul, holding him bound to her with invisible threads. Her hands moved restlessly up and down his back and over his shoulders before she wrapped her arms around his neck and tangled her fingers in his hair.

"Yes," he growled into her mouth. "Oh God. Yes!"

Reaching down, he slid his hands under her ass and pulled her against him, nestling his aching cock at her entrance. Rotated his hips in a slow circle and added a soft flex to tease against her center.

She cried out against his lips and he swallowed her moans, bringing one hand back up to her breast to rub his palm back and forth, torturing her nipple. He took the pebbled bead between his thumb and fingertip, pulling and twisting. At her gasp, he looked into her wild eyes and smiled. Her lips were drawn tight, her fangs down in anticipation.

"Jack, please. Suck on my breasts!"

When he drew her into his mouth and suckled, she couldn't stop the sob or the roll of her hips as she sought his heat. The midnight shadow of his beard scraped over her quivering flesh as he moved his mouth over her nipples. *God, what a wonderful sensation!* She trembled as he moved one hand down to stroke against her core, the slide of his fingers over her wet slit sending spikes of heat coursing through her blood. "Jack, please."

He pulled back, gently repositioning her lower body on several pillows before pushing her knees up to settle her heels by her ass.

He spread her legs and looked with wrenching hunger into her eyes. "Damn, I want to taste you so bad it's killing me." Leaning over her pussy, he used the tip of his tongue to touch her with a bold stroke.

Marissa gasped and the sound launched Jack into frenzied action. He feasted on her as if to capture every last drop of her essence. He groaned in ecstasy, the vibration of sound adding another layer of sensation. He slid his tongue sensually back and forth over her clit, first with a slow, methodic stroke and then with quick flutters.

Marissa writhed beneath him, keening her pleasure. Jack grabbed her legs, guiding them over his shoulders. He positioned his hands on her ass and held her still for his assault. Nipped the swollen bud of her clit and used his tongue to delve deep, plunging and retreating with a slow cadence that had her screaming in frustration. Finally he used his teeth on her, the pressure hurling her into her first orgasm. Without thought for the consequences, she opened her mind to Jack, sharing the pleasure. And her soul.

He shifted position and the feel of his swollen crown against her vagina made it difficult for her to think. Looking down their bodies, she devoured the shadowed sight of his cock with her eyes. He was big and thick and oh so lovely. He flexed his hips just enough to breach her with his engorged head, spreading her entrance.

Surging forward, he buried his long length deep inside her until his balls brushed her skin. He hissed in reaction to the mind-blowing sensation as her internal muscles gripped his cock in her scalding heat.

Jillian wrapped her legs around his hips. The feel of her thighs clenching him, her breasts pressed against his chest and her pussy spasmodically clutching with each stroke made him insane. Sweat broke out on his forehead and he gritted his teeth, fighting for control.

Every new sensation heightened the arousal of her already primed body. The soft brush of his naked chest against her nipples combined with the rocking thrust of his hips as he pressed his shaft deep within her. His pubic bone nudged her clit with each downward thrust, sending a zing of sharp sensation. She brought her mouth to his neck, teasing her senses further with the musky scent of his skin and the intoxicating foreplay of his pulse against her lips. She shuddered and shared the vibration of her body with Jack. He tensed even further, his cock twitching inside her.

"Harder, damn it!" she demanded as she threw her head back, arching her hips up and into him.

Jack moved to appease her and she gloried in each demanding thrust. For what seemed like endless minutes their bodies slapped together in raw primal lust.

"Not enough...never enough," he growled, and lowered his head without breaking the tempo to bare his neck to her.

Marissa's mouth sought and found the bulging vein at his neck. She felt the area with her tongue, smiling as Jack groaned in encouragement. She broke the skin and slid her incisors deep, moaning her pleasure at the combined taste and feel of him.

Jack tried to think. To move. The moment Jillian bit into his neck, pinpoints of heat exploded throughout his blood and surged through his flesh. He noticed his cock seemed to grow harder, thicker, and his body more desperate for release. He wouldn't have thought it possible. The sensations spurred him to plow his shaft deep into Jillian's cunt, and he found the movement of her mouth nursing at his neck punctuated each forward thrust. The mutual sensations hurled him into insanity. An explosive rapture so intense he didn't want it to end.

As he burst within her, Marissa pulled away from the sweet temptation of dragon blood and screamed. Her body bowed, convulsing in crushing pleasure. Their thoughts linked, sharing souls while they climaxed. A small aftershock went through her and her muscles clenched tight, throwing them both into another, softer, detonation.

Hours later Marissa woke to the sound of Jack's soft breathing. Four days of this would wear her out. Her close call with the dragon proved he needed more training. It would have to be done without their mental connection. Already she felt tied to Jack beyond the physical. She forced herself to remember this was all about blood and sex.

Sighing, she snuggled closer to the warm-blooded man and went back to sleep.

Chapter Four

ை

"Explain to me why I'm chained naked to the wall and you've taken the collar off."

She finished checking the spell-infused chains, making sure they were secured in the soft limestone with her magic. "The collar controls transformation, you won't learn anything with it on. These chains let you shift yet magically bind your beast so I don't have to transport into an upstairs closet every time he makes an appearance." She'd searched the house and had indeed cleared out a closet just in case, but she wasn't telling Jack that. He was nervous enough as it was.

"Now comes the fun part. Control the dragon and I'll give you a blowjob. As long as you stay human, I keep sucking."

Jack couldn't breathe. She had to be kidding. "As fun as that sounds, I still don't understand why—"

"Honey, if you can focus your control enough to keep the dragon from appearing during a blowjob, you can do it anytime."

Marissa looked at Jack, at the gorgeous dark-haired man whose turquoise eyes seemed a little dazed at the thought of what she'd be doing to him. His magnificent body was covered in a fine sheen of sweat, his cock heavily aroused. His mind might be trying to come to terms with this experiment, but his body certainly caught on fast. It was going to be a little tricky getting all that male flesh in her mouth.

Dropping to her knees in front of him, she noticed black and red scales starting to roll out of the skin on his stomach.

"Jack, focus. Push him back." Immediately the scales disappeared. Marissa was pretty sure he could keep the dragon at bay unless she really worked to dislodge it. Well, there was no point starting slow.

When Jillian cupped his balls in her cool hand and moved her fangs to his upper thigh, Jack squeezed his eyes shut at the sharp pleasure-pain of her bite. He started to pant, desperately struggling to use his focal point. He wished now he'd decided on something other than Jillian naked. When she pulled away from his femoral artery and slid her lips up in a wet glide to suck his balls, his body convulsed. Tugging against his bonds, he tossed his head in wild desperation. "Aghhh! Jillian!"

Inside his head he chanted, *dragongoaway, go away!*

Flicking her tongue in a long lick up his shaft, she swirled around the very sensitive head. Breath exploded from his lungs. He looked down at her kneeling before him, anxious to see her taking his straining flesh fully into her mouth. Capturing her gaze, he held it as she drove him out of his mind.

When she stopped and sat back on her heels, Jack started to snarl at her. Until he noticed his hands had turned to claws. *Shit! Go away, go away. Think of Jillian naked and pant!*

When the claws receded, Marissa leaned forward to slip her lips as far down his shaft as possible, creating steady suction while sliding her mouth up and down. His flesh tasted of cinnamon. With every stroke, her tongue caressed the vein running along his length. Her nails grazed his tightening sac. She smiled around his shaft when his moans echoed in the cavern.

Once more she stopped and waited while he angrily beat the dragon into submission. After what seemed like hours of carnal torture, he noticed the dragon only appeared when she did something particularly mind-blowing.

Like now. Oh God. He felt her reach around his thigh and tease her fingers across his sphincter, pressing inside a few inches. His body clenched and his control slipped for just a second. Jillian pulled back and gingerly licked the scales around his navel. "You're getting stronger."

"Not strong enough. The dragon's gone. Please, Jillian. More."

She wrapped her fingers around his shaft. Involuntarily, his hips began to rock. One moment her grip was firm with long, hard strokes and he felt the pressure build to the point of explosion. Then she switched to a lighter hold and shorter strokes, somehow getting him to back off. She lapped and sucked, changing the momentum each time his body was close to orgasm. There was no way he'd let the dragon out to ruin this for him. He kept it tightly locked away inside.

She swirled her hot little tongue around the head of his shaft, paying particular attention to the small slit at the tip. Jesus! He was so fucking close…

As if Jillian could read his thoughts, she encircled the base of his shaft with her fingers and clamped down tight. "You've kept the dragon at bay long enough." The collar appeared around his neck and he found himself lying on his back in his nest. Evidently her patience was at an end.

He watched from heavy-lidded eyes as she straddled him, used her hand to guide the swollen tip of his cock to the entrance of her sweet cunt. He could feel her slick heat, the engorged folds separate as her tight sheath slowly enveloped his shaft, until she'd taken every damn inch of him into her body.

Heaven.

Back bowed in reaction to the fullness, she stilled for a minute as if adjusting to his size. Using her knees, she finally began to move, pushing off him then gliding down. She set a deliberate pace. Steady. Rising up then slowly lowering her sweet ass in excruciatingly sexy movements. He bent his knees, using the leverage to dig upward between her splayed thighs. Faster. Closing her eyes, she slammed up and down on his cock.

He cupped her breasts with his palms before slipping one hand into the pool of liquid heat between her thighs to rub her clit. When Jillian gasped and went still, he rose up and flipped her beneath him so he could pound into her tight pussy as fast and hard as he wanted.

Grabbing a fistful of his hair, she pulled his mouth to her breast, arching her back and murmuring his name in encouragement as he closed his lips over her nipple. The murmur turned to a moan when he flicked the tight bud with his tongue. Pulling her into his mouth, he suckled. Nipped the tip.

Jack heard Jillian's sobs, felt her body clench, her pussy contracting around his cock. And he couldn't endure another second.

Unbidden, their minds linked. The excitement spiraled between them. Progressed to such a cataclysmic force it crashed and exploded over their bodies in a burst of colored fireworks. He felt the tight ache in his lower back. His balls drew up and, throwing his head back, he roared his release.

When it was over, heavy silence filled the room, broken only by the ragged sounds of their breathing. He rolled to the side, pulling her with him, amazed at what they'd just shared. He'd seen her, truly seen beyond the sexy, sarcastic vamp to the woman underneath, a woman who hid her compassion and loneliness behind jokes and blatant sexuality.

Sensing she wouldn't like his assessment of her psyche and the gentle feeling it inspired in him, he settled for feeling pleased when she relaxed in his arms, giving a contented sigh.

He should have been bummed he had to be shackled to a wall, or submerged in water, or wearing a damn collar to keep from killing his partner when they made love. But Jack couldn't help his satisfied smile as he drifted off to sleep with a final whisper of thought.

Damn, that was fantastic!

* * * * *

Just before entering her apartment, Marissa helped settle the collar around Jack's neck. They'd taken it off to enable the dragon to fly them to Colorado. Even though he was doing great at controlling the beast's appearance, he still wanted the boost of magic to keep him in check.

When she reached out to turn the doorknob, Marissa's senses started to tingle.

"Jack, someone is inside," she hissed in his mind and motioned him to drop back. His scent interfered with her ability to figure out who or what lay beyond the door. Putting her ear against the wood, she listened. Nothing. Carefully, she eased the door open and stepped into the dark living room.

That's when the wolf attacked.

She ended up flat on her back with the beast's front paw on her chest, his very sharp teeth clamped around her throat.

The large black wolf raised his head from the potentially killing blow, grinned and licked her face.

Marissa blinked. "Well, brother dear, if you don't get off me fast, the dragon behind us is going to shift, roasting your ass and probably eating me."

"I'd like to eat you all right, Jillian."

Jack's mental voice triggered needs she couldn't afford right now. Before he said something else she hurried to warn him, "Jack, my brother can 'hear' you."

Jack had torn off the chain before entering the apartment, intent on coming to her rescue. The wolf turned to stare at him and Jack fought the change. The roar of dragon blood in his veins made it difficult to understand what Jillian was saying.

"Brother?"

Clamping down on the instinctive urge to protect his mate, Jack snarled mentally at the wolf while calling up his focus—the feel of Jillian's naked body pressed against him.

"Mine!"

The wolf became man in the blink of an eye. "Oh, that's just gross. Stop it! Not only can I hear him, I can see the vision he's using to control his beast. Yuck! There are some things a brother just doesn't need to see."

Marissa stepped between the two men, stooped to retrieve the chain from the floor and fastened it around Jack's neck. "Jack, this is Franco."

Standing before Jack was a man with Jillian's moss-green eyes, definitely a family trait. But while Ricardo and Jillian were fair-haired, Franco's black wavy hair mimicked the color of his wolf. With his olive complexion, Franco looked...well, less Nordic than his siblings.

"Our grandmother's heritage is Dark Romany. Gypsy. I get my hair and skin tone from her. Our father and mother have blonde hair. And yeah...almost everyone in the family has green eyes. And a warning — my strongest power is mind reading. Not just what you project at me, but *everything*. So stop thinking about my sister naked before I have to smash your head in. And by the way, dragon-breath, she doesn't like to be called Jillian. She prefers Marissa."

Franco pulled Marissa close for a tight hug. He explained that he'd come to visit, instead finding nothing but the scent of her death. He'd been grieving heavily and frantically trying to get in touch with her friend Jane to find out what had happened.

She spent the next hour explaining everything to her brother.

When she finished, Franco reached out to ruffle her hair, laughing at her manipulative exploits of late. "Good one, sis."

"Ricardo and Jane plan to stay in Florida for a bit. Then they'll probably come back here and pack her stuff to send to France. Jane can hunt vampires anywhere, while Ricardo needs his lab and access to all those moldy books."

Jack stayed silent during Jillian's explanation to her brother. It answered a lot of his own questions. Except one.

"There's something I don't understand. Why are you and your brothers different species?"

"We're not really. At the core we're all Druid-mage. Our family name, De'Angel, comes from an ancient description of our father Michael. He was known as the angel of life." Marissa looked at Franco, expecting him to jump in.

"You're saying you aren't a vampire but an angel?" Jack had seen Jillian's past when he touched her soul. The woman wasn't evil, but she certainly didn't act like any angel he'd heard about.

Franco snorted and Jillian reached out to slap his arm.

"Nope. No angel blood here," she explained. "DMs or Druid-mages are high-ranking magical beings. We have the magic and resources to become anything we wish. The reason I'm currently in vampire form is because every so often, DMs revitalize their essence as a different paranormal creature."

Franco interjected, "This allows us to hone new skills, to experience different lifestyles. It's also supposed to keep us from becoming bored or disinterested in the world around us, although after untold centuries it still gets a bit repetitive."

Marissa frowned at her brother's tone. Great, something else to worry about. "To some extent, we can use magic in any supernatural body, but our abilities are stronger when we're nothing more than a Druid-mage. Thankfully, Ricardo has been studying the magic and elementals of history in our original form. That's why he was able to bring me back to life."

"You can choose any form?" Jack asked in surprise.

"Yes. The reason I understand so much about were-dragons is because I *was* one for a few hundred years. In fact, it was one of my favorite incarnations."

Jack could imagine Jillian as a were-dragon. Flying beside him, living forever in his cavern. He loved Jillian as a vampire. In fact, he wasn't really sure he wanted to give up acting as her blood bank. Yet the thought of her being a were-dragon called to something deep within.

Later. He'd worry about it later.

Marissa looked at her watch. "Jack and I need to get going. We're driving to the mountains for his parents' party. You want to stay here for awhile?"

"I think I *will* stay here while you're gone. You've had a few visitors in the last couple days."

"What kind of visitors?"

"There've been several rogues sniffing around. Vampire. Were. Since I arrived, they haven't tried to come in, but someone searched the place before I got here."

Marissa frowned. As far as anyone knew, Marcus had killed her. Then Jane killed Marcus. Who the hell was looking for her?

Chapter Five

∞

Sunday night, Marissa stood on the balcony, watching Jack walk toward her through the dwindling crowd of relatives. He'd enjoyed the weekend and obviously loved being with his family. She'd come outside to think, worried about the strong connection between them. She felt as if psychic locks had clicked into place. Seeing the very center of Jack's soul, she'd recognized her mate.

No! Not mate. She was only trying to give him the tools to deal with his uncontrolled magic.

Unaware of her thoughts, Jack reached her side and bent down to kiss her softly. "Want something to drink?"

"Umm. I'd love a Blood Bath."

Jack snapped back, staring at her in shock. He could picture it in his mind. White tub filled with blood, Jillian dipping her pink painted toes into —

"Oh dear goddess! It's a *drink*!" she laughed.

"I've never heard of it before." He looked embarrassed.

"If the bartender doesn't know how to make it, wave me over and I'll supervise."

She could have just gone with him, but she needed a few seconds by herself. From the moment they'd walked into the first party Friday night, she'd been part of the whirlwind of people Jack called relatives. Or she'd been immersed in Jack.

The mountain resort was beautiful. They all had private cabins complete with secluded hot tubs. The main lodge had an indoor swimming pool and housed the room in which the current party was taking place. The open, beamed room was large enough to hold a thousand people or more. From the door of the balcony, she looked up three stories and marveled at the massive oak logs.

Everyone in Jack's family accepted her. Loved her. Believed she and Jack were a real couple. The thought hurt and she shied away from all it implied. She was going to miss him.

The weekend had gone really well. For added security, Jack kept the collar on. Each day he spent time alone with his family, waking her with sex in the afternoon before they rejoined the group after sundown.

But their time together was coming to an end. Preferring not to think about it, Marissa stepped back into the room, intercepting Jack and taking the glass from his hand.

"Blood Bath—red wine, raspberry liquor and cranberry juice, hold the blood." He grinned.

Marissa rolled her eyes as they headed for the table with the last of the revelers, most of the partygoers now returned to their cabins. Ben and Cindy, Jack's brother and sister-in-law, were sitting at the table with Marla and John, his parents. Along with a couple aunts and uncles she couldn't keep straight. She tried ignoring the fact that this would be the last time Jack would see his family. She felt his sorrow through their forged link as if it belonged to her. They'd say their goodbyes tonight and drive back to Denver. His family thought they'd be seeing him again soon, confident their invitation to keep in touch would be honored. Marissa knew different, and it broke her heart

Before they reached the group in the corner, trouble with a capital V walked through the door.

"Shit!" Marissa hissed, grabbing Jack's arm to draw his attention to the men.

Opening their mental path, she shared the danger with Jack.

"The guy in the front is Marcus' brother, Jason. This isn't good." She sniffed the air. *"Including Jason, there are four*

vampires. One werewolf, one were-dragon and something I can't quite place. Definitely never a good thing."

"Ah shit," she continued. *"All seven bad-asses are old. Skilled."* She could handle a couple of them. Jack in mortal form could take out one or two. That still left too many to fight without his beast. She tried to ignore the picture of Jack's family members, their mortal bodies broken and stacked like kindling if she and Jack lost the battle she knew was coming.

"Jack, these are probably the rogues Franco scented at my apartment. Go to your family, I'll try to buy us enough time for you to get them out of here." Marissa strolled across the room toward the newcomers, ignoring Jack's protest in her mind. "Jason. How nice to see you. What are you doing here?"

"Looking for you, bitch. What did you do to my brother?"

Marissa tried to ignore the murmurs coming from the table. Jack's family had heard Jason.

"What am I supposed to say? I let Marcus kill me then Janie dusted his ass?"

"I wouldn't recommend it."

Without Jack's droll advice, she knew that statement would get her into trouble in more ways than one. She didn't want anyone knowing there was a spell to bring back a vampire who'd been turned into dust. Nor did she want Jason or his friends going after Jane.

"I've been in Florida, Jason. I haven't seen him for weeks."

"Nice try, bitch. Johnny here sniffed his place." He pointed at the blond werewolf. "Marcus is dead and that friend of yours killed him. We can't find *her*, so you'll have to do."

Marissa had *let* Marcus kill her. Jason wasn't going to get that chance without a serious fight. "Fine. We can do this if you want. Just let the mortals leave."

Asking Jason for anything galled her, but she'd beg for the lives of Jack's family. Not to mention Jack didn't want them to see him in dragon form. But without his dragon, they didn't have a chance. She knew this was going to get ugly.

"Nah. We'll need a little dessert after we finish with you and dragon-breath." He sneered and Marissa wanted to bitch-slap him.

"Okay, so I guess I am *a bitch."*

"Get away from them, sweetheart. Back up toward me."

"Set a protection ward over your family, Jack. I'll add mine to yours. The spells will only last as long as we're alive. Tell your family to run like hell to the indoor swimming pool if they get the chance. Their scent is all over the lodge, so if they get in the pool, the chlorine and water might keep the vamps and weres in the group from tracking them. I have no idea what the unknown creature's abilities are. Make sure they understand the swimming pool is their only hope."

Jack turned and cast a protection spell over his family. He ignored their heated questions and told them to run for the pool as soon as they could. Facing Jillian once again, he drew a ward over her before bringing a hand to his neck. Bending to kiss his mother, he whispered, "I'm sorry, Mom." Handing her the chain, he walked over to join his mate. *"I love you, Jillian. If we get out of this, I want to talk about our future."*

Marissa frowned at him. *"Now? You tell me this now?"*

Jason snarled, showing fangs, drawing Jack's attention as he dove at Jillian. Jack heard a chorus of gasps from his family before he blocked Jason's assault by throwing his fist into his face. Shit. They'd seen the fangs.

He couldn't worry about coming out of the closet right now. Jack allowed the dragon to take over his body. He thought about Jillian. Held her image clear in his mind, intent on doing damage only to those who threatened his mate or his family.

Within seconds his dragon rose up and growled, swiping his claws at the white wolf trying to go for his neck. He resisted the urge to turn and see his family's reaction.

All hell broke loose. He watched Jillian throw one of the vampires across the room. Quickly she flew after him, jumped on his chest and rammed a stake through his heart. Jack took precious seconds wondering where the wood came from. Later, Jillian would tell him that his dad broke a chair into pieces, tossing the heavy wooden leg to her so she could use it as a stake.

Realizing she could handle herself, he turned his attention to the were-dragon. The green and yellow beast matched him in size, and Jack had spent ten months staying away from anything that might bring out his dragon. He hadn't learned how to use the beast to fight.

Time seemed to slow down. The two beasts circled and flapped, heads darting out as they tried to sink their sharp teeth into the other's hide. The actions reminded Jack of two penned roosters. They couldn't fly in the confined space, but they could hop and dart.

A whisper of air was his only warning as the yellow dragon reached for Jack's throat with serrated teeth. He moved and struck out with hooked claws, connecting with the dragon's face. Jack felt the crunch of bone and the warm spurt of blood. It was a lucky shot, shoving slivers of bone into the beast's brain. As the creature hit the floor, it reverted to human form.

Ignoring the dying man, he saw Ben, his father and his uncles standing guard over a little alcove holding his mother and aunts.

Breathing heavily, he turned in time to see Jillian go down under the werewolf. Jack could do nothing but watch as Ben threw his knife, lodging it in the wolf's neck.

The beast exploded.

Jack blinked. Ben's knife must have been pure silver. Never again would he make fun of his family for stashing knives in their boots.

When Jason jumped on his back and tried to stab him with a dagger, Jack reared up and shook his dragon body, swinging Jason through the air like a rag doll and slamming him to the ground. Jillian was there with another stake.

As Jack advanced on the two remaining vampires, they decided this wasn't their fight after all and scrambled for the door.

The dark-haired man Jillian couldn't identify by species stayed out of the fight until he was the only one left. With a nasty smirk, he changed shape.

"Fuck, what the hell is that?"

Jack could feel Jillian's gulp in his head. *"A were-Tyrannosaurus Rex?! You've gotta be kidding me."*

Before Jack could make a move, a black wolf raced into the room. Snapping his teeth, he backed the T-Rex into the corner.

"Jack! That's Franco. Don't kill my brother!"

Franco snarled a command in Jack's head. *"This one's mine, he's wanted for murders in six countries."* Having Jillian in his mind was one thing, Jack wasn't sure he wanted her brother in there as well. But he nodded his dragonhead in acceptance, stepped back and watched.

Franco shifted to his human form. Waving his hand at the dinosaur, he chanted something in a language Jack didn't recognize. The T-Rex looked shocked, shifted back into human—now wrapped in chains—and puffed out of sight. Franco followed right behind him.

"Well, that was anti-climatic."

"Thank goddess!" Jillian slumped to the floor in relief.

* * * * *

"My parents think you have a very interesting family."

Marissa grinned from the hot tub. Jack's family had accepted his dragon.

"They're looking forward to meeting your parents at the wedding."

Oh hell. Her mom and dad were somewhere in the depths of the Atlantic Ocean, this incarnation of their lives spent as mermen.

Stepping into the bubbling water beside his naked mate, Jack pulled her onto his lap, settling her back to his chest.

"Jack?"

Nibbling at her neck, he murmured into her skin, "What, sweetheart?"

"Remember how I don't have to breathe?"

Confused at where this was going, Jack paused and raised his head.

"Let me show you how useful that can be." She slid off his lap and under the water, taking his cock into her mouth. He stared down at the bobbing blonde head in shock. The blood pounded so hard in his cock that he was sure it would explode. *Wanted* it to explode. Long minutes later he rolled his head back onto the edge of the hot tub and said a heartfelt, "Thank God!"

He looked into the future, thinking of the day his Jillian would fly beside him as a were-dragon. But right now, he liked the benefits of his vampire mate just fine.

As the orgasm slammed through his body, he wondered if every creature Jillian chose for a new incarnation would bring different pleasures. He'd have to remember to ask.

Later.

Blood Bath

2 shots raspberry liqueur

14 oz merlot

1 splash cranberry juice

Shake ingredients thoroughly with ice in a cocktail shaker, then strain into a red wineglass. A favorite of several of Marissa's vampire friends, this drink is sweet, blood-red in color and colder than any self-respecting creature of the night!

About the Author

ဆာ

Ravyn Wilde was born in Oregon and has spent several years in New Guinea and Singapore. She is married, has 3 children and is currently living in Utah. Ravyn is happiest when she has a book in one hand and a drink in the other — preferably sprawled on a beach!

Ravyn welcomes comments from readers. You can find her website and email address on her author bio page at www.ellorascave.com.

Tell Us What You Think

We appreciate hearing reader opinions about our books. You can email us at Comments@EllorasCave.com.

Why an electronic book?

We live in the Information Age—an exciting time in the history of human civilization, in which technology rules supreme and continues to progress in leaps and bounds every minute of every day. For a multitude of reasons, more and more avid literary fans are opting to purchase e-books instead of paper books. The question from those not yet initiated into the world of electronic reading is simply: *Why?*

1. *Price.* An electronic title at Ellora's Cave Publishing and Cerridwen Press runs anywhere from 40% to 75% less than the cover price of the exact same title in paperback format. Why? Basic mathematics and cost. It is less expensive to publish an e-book (no paper and printing, no warehousing and shipping) than it is to publish a paperback, so the savings are passed along to the consumer.

2. *Space.* Running out of room in your house for your books? That is one worry you will never have with electronic books. For a low one-time cost, you can purchase a handheld device specifically designed for e-reading. Many e-readers have large, convenient screens for viewing. Better yet, hundreds of titles can be stored within your new library—on a single microchip. There are a variety of e-readers from different manufacturers. You can also read e-books on your PC or laptop computer. (Please note that Ellora's Cave does not endorse any specific brands. You can check our websites at www.ellorascave.com

or www.cerridwenpress.com for information we make available to new consumers.)

3. *Mobility.* Because your new e-library consists of only a microchip within a small, easily transportable e-reader, your entire cache of books can be taken with you wherever you go.

4. *Personal Viewing Preferences.* Are the words you are currently reading too small? Too large? Too... ANNOYING? Paperback books cannot be modified according to personal preferences, but e-books can.

5. *Instant Gratification.* Is it the middle of the night and all the bookstores near you are closed? Are you tired of waiting days, sometimes weeks, for bookstores to ship the novels you bought? Ellora's Cave Publishing sells instantaneous downloads twenty-four hours a day, seven days a week, every day of the year. Our webstore is never closed. Our e-book delivery system is 100% automated, meaning your order is filled as soon as you pay for it.

Those are a few of the top reasons why electronic books are replacing paperbacks for many avid readers.

As always, Ellora's Cave and Cerridwen Press welcome your questions and comments. We invite you to email us at Comments@ellorascave.com or write to us directly at Ellora's Cave Publishing Inc., 1056 Home Avenue, Akron, OH 44310-3502.

erridwen, the Celtic Goddess of wisdom, was the muse who brought inspiration to storytellers and those in the creative arts. Cerridwen Press encompasses the best and most innovative stories in all genres of today's fiction. Visit our site and discover the newest titles by talented authors who still get inspired - much like the ancient storytellers did, once upon a time.

Cerridwen Press

www.cerridwenpress.com

Discover for yourself why readers can't get enough
of the multiple award-winning publisher
Ellora's Cave.

Whether you prefer e-books or paperbacks,

be sure to visit EC on the web at
www.ellorascave.com

for an erotic reading experience that will leave you
breathless.